"Is his name Mac

"Uh-huh." The boy gave her a shy smile. "My ~~~~ owns the Tall Tale Lodge."

Mack grinned at Erin. "Admittedly, an awkward introduction. But you'll have to overlook it." He put his hand to the side of his head. "I can barely think straight."

Erin frowned. What did that mean?

"I'm awestruck," he explained, his grin widening and his voice somewhere on a continuum of flirtatiousness. "It's not every day I come face-to-face with a woman who's a talented musician and also brings battered and charred antiques back to life."

Without thinking, Erin smiled. "Now you're making me blush." It was true what he said. Erin had built her work life around wood restoration, and making music was her favorite hobby.

But those things weren't making her cheeks heat up.

That had more to do with Mack's deep, smooth voice and how her stomach fluttered looking into those amused blue eyes...

Dear Reader,

It's Valentine's Day in Adelaide Creek, Wyoming, and the town is throwing a party to celebrate the grand reopening of its historic town hall. Woodworker Erin Hunnicutt is enjoying the accolades for her role in restoring the fire-damaged building, and meeting Mack Fisher and his seven-year-old son only adds to the fun.

Mack and Erin share a passion for horses, so when horses begin disappearing, one by one, from local stables, they're alarmed. Even ranchers and law enforcement can't explain what's going on. One misty morning before dawn, Mack spots a horse deep in the woods near his house, prompting him to enlist Erin to join forces and solve the mystery. Typical of Adelaide Creek, a new romance is ready to blossom, along with a Wyoming spring.

Enjoy Erin and Mack's romance and then visit my website, virginiamccullough.com, to sign up for my newsletter. You can also follow me on Goodreads and BookBub and on Facebook at virginiamcculloughauthor.

Virginia

FINDING HIS WYOMING SWEETHEART

VIRGINIA McCULLOUGH

Harlequin

HEARTWARMING

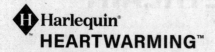

Harlequin®
HEARTWARMING™

ISBN-13: 978-1-335-05138-7

Finding His Wyoming Sweetheart

Copyright © 2025 by Virginia McCullough

Recycling programs for this product may not exist in your area.

 Harlequin Enterprises ULC
22 Adelaide St. West, 41st Floor
Toronto, Ontario M5H 4E3, Canada
www.Harlequin.com

Printed in Lithuania

MIX
Paper | Supporting responsible forestry
FSC® C021394

Virginia McCullough has enjoyed a long career as an author of fiction and nonfiction books, sometimes working behind the scenes as a ghostwriter, editor or coach. A vagabond at heart, she's lived in many places and currently makes her home in Northeast Wisconsin, where she writes multigenerational romance and women's fiction. *Finding His Wyoming Sweetheart* is the fourth book in her Back to Adelaide Creek series and her tenth Harlequin Heartwarming title. Virginia's stories always offer hope, healing and plenty of second chances.

Books by Virginia McCullough

Harlequin Heartwarming

Girl in the Spotlight
Something to Treasure
Love, Unexpected

Back to Bluestone River

A Family for Jason
The Christmas Kiss
A Bridge Home

Back to Adelaide Creek

The Rancher's Wyoming Twins
The Doc's Holiday Homecoming
His Wyoming Surprise

Visit the Author Profile page at Harlequin.com for more titles.

To the Early Birds, a group started by novelist Amy Sue Nathan in 2020, which meets online for a write-in every morning, seven days a week, no exceptions. We've since lost Amy, but we honor her life by showing up for ourselves and each other for this one precious hour of writing. My thanks to Amy and to my Early Bird companions.

CHAPTER ONE

IN ALL HER thirty-three years, Erin Hunnicutt had never shaken so many hands, accepted so many compliments, or said thank-you to so many people. Even more remarkable, those she chatted with and whose attention she enjoyed were now her neighbors and friends. Five months ago, when she'd first arrived in this Wyoming town, Adelaide Creek, she wouldn't have given a thought to the notion that this community, a tiny dot on the map, would become her new hometown. Even more amazing, Erin had been instrumental in the quest to restore one of Adelaide Creek's treasures, its historic town hall. The building had been nearly destroyed in a fire the day before she'd come to town. She recalled the strong scent of the smoke still hanging in the air. Now, here she was, celebrating its grand reopening and restoration on Valentine's Day.

At the moment, Erin aimed her smile at

Quincy Lancaster, who was weaving his way through clusters of people and heading straight for her. Erin's boss, mentor and friend Quincy, a man closer to a father figure than she'd ever had in her life, approached with his face beaming with happiness.

"Congratulations, Erin. This is a huge night for you." He tapped his fingers on the top of the gleaming oak counter that dominated the library, which happened to be housed in the town hall. The building was a point of pride for Adelaide Creek, whose population had recently tipped over the five hundred mark, thanks to Erin and a few other newcomers and newborns. "You've played a big part in preserving our town's history."

Erin accepted his quick congratulatory hug. "Right. And the town owes it all to you." She was proud of her work in bringing the library's historic fixtures back to life after last September's fire. It had been a monthslong project for the mayor and the town council and everyone who'd helped raise funds to rebuild the town hall. Erin had quickly learned it was widely agreed the building was the heart of Adelaide Creek. It was fitting somehow that the grand reopening was scheduled for Valentine's Day.

"You handed me the chance to prove what I can do, Quincy." Her slight bow added a bit of flourish. "And more than anyone else, you know how I relished every minute of the work." She tilted her head and gave him a knowing look. "Plus, I got a new home and a family out of the deal."

"Lucky us, huh? You and I are family now." Quincy pointed across the room at the newlyweds—Willow, his daughter, and Tom, Erin's brother. Her search for her half brother had brought her to this town in the first place. But Tom wasn't the only reason she'd jumped at Quincy's newest job offer. After witnessing her wood restoration skills, the older man had offered her a chance to be part of a team dedicated to restoring a run-down mansion. Saying yes to Quincy meant staying in town rather than packing up her tools in her van, painted in bright sunrise colors on one side and the purples and pinks of sunsets on the other, and moving on to parts unknown with her retriever, Neptune.

Quincy glanced at the library table. "It's pretty special that a newcomer to town helped us salvage these the historic fixtures after the fire. You've brought them back to life, and everyone here tonight can see your expert work."

"Thanks to you, Quincy." Restoring those gems was her first paid project after piling one hundred percent of her belongings and her camping gear into her van and leaving the Indiana town that she'd lived in for several years. Even more significant, when Tom married Willow, Erin gained a sister and a niece, Naomi, Willow's adorable adopted baby.

"Look at them." Quincy's soft voice oozed affection as he watched Willow and Tom. "I've never seen Willow happier, and now my little granddaughter has a daddy. Everybody lucked out." Quincy pointed to himself. "Including me."

Erin kept her gaze on Tom holding Naomi securely on his hip. One of the baby's hands rested on the back of his shoulder, and the other reached for his chin. The baby had always known him as a dad. With the grand opening celebrations winding down, Willow and Tom were saying their goodbyes and heading to the airport. They were trading the snowy deep freeze of Wyoming for a week of sand and surf in Hawaii, a delayed honeymoon after their New Year's Eve wedding.

"And now we're sharing babysitting duty, too, Grandpa Q," Erin said, amused by the nickname she and Tom devised for his father-in-law. Since Quincy was on the town council, he was busier at the evening's celebration and would need to stay later than Erin. It only made sense for her to take the first baby care stint starting that night.

"I'm ready to shift out of party mode and gear up for solo time with Naomi. You should see all the supplies I've hauled into my house," Erin said. "I'm prepared for any contingency, including being snowed in for a day or two. Even if we lose power, I have plenty of wood to keep a fire going in the fireplace."

Quincy had no time to respond to Erin. He turned to the sound of his name coming from the mayor, who got his attention from across the room.

"You're being summoned. Better go handle town business, Mr. Councilman," Erin teased.

"I'll do that, and then when Willow and Tom slip away, I'll bring Naomi to you," Quincy said.

Erin was okay standing at the library counter by herself and soaking up the party-like atmosphere of the grand opening. She guessed that most of Adelaide Creek's residents had stopped in to have a look at the restoration project and share in the happy night. Kids had fun, too, because volunteers supplied a snack buffet and platters of red-and-white cupcakes and sugar cookies in honor of Valentine's Day. Good idea to have the grand opening on the holiday, not that it meant much to Erin. She had yet to meet any special man in her new town, so Naomi would be her Valentine's Day date. If she dwelled on that fact, she'd have to take stock of how many years it had been since she'd had a date on any night of the year.

Over the past months, Erin had been so busy she'd had little time to reflect on how much her life had changed—expanded—in such a short time. When her mom died, over a year ago now, Erin had become a family of one. Two, if she counted Neptune. Her four-legged companion had been with her on her recent cross-country journey, which in itself had been driven by the deep desire for a family. That was what had pushed her to start this adventure with Neptune in tow.

As for her father, her last name was the extent of her link to him. She'd never seen him, not even once, and only a few years ago, she'd learned he'd died. Erin had tucked away the sketchy information her mom had given her about three men who were likely her half brothers.

For better or worse, the Indiana town where she and her mom had lived had absolutely no hold on her heart. Home had been defined by where her mother was, and they'd moved around a lot. Her mom had been on the lookout for hotel housekeeping jobs that promised to be a step up from the previous position. That's why being a vagabond of sorts came easily— even naturally—to Erin. Sometimes her heart lifted when memories of her mom and happy days came to mind, but in quiet moments, the loss still hit hard, and it took time to leave the sadness behind and concentrate on her future.

When she'd left Indiana, though, her new goal was to put down roots. The open question was where she'd plant herself. After she'd pieced together details from her mother's scanty information and confirmed it through internet searches, she'd located her two younger brothers in a town in the Florida Panhandle. Unlike Erin, the two had known their father, but like her, he hadn't raised them. It hadn't taken long for disappointment to set in. As it turned out, neither brother was especially receptive to the news of having an older sister and showed little curiosity about her. Not exactly the welcome she'd hoped for. Even the sandy beaches of the Gulf Coast couldn't tempt her to stick around.

Tom Azar had been a bit harder to locate, mostly because they didn't share a last name. After the lukewarm reception in Florida, Erin had tempered her natural optimism about how this third brother would react to her. She'd known little about Tom, except that he was a pediatrician, presumably in Wyoming. She and

Neptune set out across the country, sightseeing and camping along the way. Finally, she'd plunked herself on Tom's doorstep one September night and waited for him to come home. She'd prepared herself for any outcome, but clung to the hope he'd be pleasantly surprised. Tom was taken aback by her claim of kinship, initially convinced that Erin had made a huge mistake. Later, maybe because she and Tom had the same distinctive dark brown eyes and thick, wavy, almost black hair, his skepticism faded fast.

It was Tom's connection to Willow and Quincy that had led Erin to bid on the contract to restore many of the damaged town hall fixtures. Only a few months later, she found herself a part of the town and celebrating with her new family.

The happy sounds of a baby attempting to talk pulled Erin out of her reverie and back into the noisy party as Quincy approached with Naomi in his arms. Erin looked past him to the other end of the room, where she spotted Tom following Willow out one of the side doors. Secure in Grandpa Quincy's arms, Naomi was happy, at least for the moment.

"Are you sure you're ready to take the baby home?" Quincy asked. "If you'd like, I could take baby duty for the first couple of days."

Erin reached for Naomi. "Not a chance, Grandpa. I've been looking forward to this." She turned one way and then the other as she said, "I'm ready to roll, raring to go." She gave the baby a quick kiss on the forehead. That was the truth. She was thrilled to have an opportunity to take care of Naomi. The baby was part of the whirlwind adventure of Erin's first months in town. She'd watched Tom fall in love with Willow, but even before that, she'd come to know him as the popular and relatively new pediatrician who'd built a reputation for his commitment to the kids and parents of Adelaide Creek. He was a brother to be proud of.

Holding Naomi, Erin did little dance steps in a circle to distract the baby from Grandpa Quincy leaving to return to the party. "We're going to have so much fun at my house. You'll be my Valentine and eat cookies I made especially for you." She touched the tip of Naomi's nose, making the baby laugh, so she twirled again and gave the baby's nose another quick tap.

After making a third full circle, she came face-to-face with a tall man and a small boy standing in front of her. The man looked slightly familiar, but she couldn't quite place him. Whoever he was, she'd recognize him the next time.

He was studying her through his unforgettable bright blue eyes.

"You don't know me," the man said, "but I know a little about you." He looked down and spoke to the boy. "This is Ms. Erin Hunnicutt, the woman with the pretty voice who sang for us at the Halloween party with Dr. Tom."

With a jolt of pleasure in her chest, Erin held out her hand to the boy. "And what's your name?"

"Liam, uh, Liam Louis Fisher." He pointed to the baby. "That's Willow's baby, isn't it?"

"Right you are. Aren't you the smart one? I happen to be Naomi's very proud aunt." Erin couldn't place the name Fisher and why it was familiar. Then she remembered. Still addressing the boy, she pointed to the man. "Is his name Mack? Is he your dad?"

"Uh-huh." The boy gave her a shy smile. "My dad owns the Tall Tale Lodge."

Mack grinned at Erin. "Admittedly, an awkward introduction. But you'll have to overlook it." He put his hand to the side of his head. "I can barely think straight."

Erin frowned. What did that mean?

"I'm awestruck," he explained, his grin widening. "It's not every day I meet a woman who's a talented musician and also brings battered and charred antiques back to life."

Without thinking, Erin returned the smile. "Now you're making me blush." It was true what he said. Erin had built her work life around wood restoration, but making music was her favorite hobby. Although those things weren't causing her cheeks to heat up. That had more to do with Mack's deep, smooth voice and how her stomach fluttered looking into those amused blue eyes. She'd always had a soft spot for a neat—but not too neat—beard. Deflecting attention from herself and back to Mack, she said, "As I recall, you don't live in Adelaide Creek, but here you are, celebrating the return of the town hall with the rest of us. And on Valentine's Day, too."

"We *do* too live here." Liam stood up a little straighter and lifted his chin a notch. "In a *bunkhouse*. Real *cowboys* lived there a long, long time ago."

"That's right, kiddo." Mack spoke to Liam with a laugh in his voice before turning to Erin. "It's a converted bunkhouse on the Hoover sheep ranch. From what I hear, Liam and I are only the latest of many who've had a stint there. For now it's a perfect place for us to call home."

"I've heard all about that bunkhouse. Very cool, Liam," Erin said. "My house is a big cabin. It's pretty cool, too. Ever since Dr. Tom moved in with Willow and Naomi, I've got his place all to myself."

Liam patted his chest. "Dr. Tom is *my* new doctor."

"Lucky you." Erin lowered her voice as if confiding a secret. "But I'm even luckier. Dr. Tom is *my* brother."

A sly smile tugged at the corners of Liam's mouth. "Is the baby going to your house? Do you have Valentine cookies there?"

Obviously not expecting that question, Mack laughed a little nervously. "Uh, I think we've had our share of cookies, Liam."

Erin made a quick decision to keep Mack engaged and maybe surprise him a little. "As a matter of fact, the cookies I made are shaped like hearts. I made some look like Cupid and his arrows. Why don't you and your dad come over to my house and have a treat or two? Or, if your dad really doesn't want you to eat more cookies right now, I'll give you a few to take home."

"Do you mean it?" Liam's eyes widened. A deeper shade of blue than Mack's, the boy's eyes were every bit as distinctive.

Mack shifted his weight from one foot to the other. "I didn't have any idea… I mean, I wasn't fishing for an invitation."

"I know," Erin said. "But I have a ton of cookies, and I was getting ready to take the baby home. She's staying with me while Willow and Tom are honeymooning in sunny Hawaii. You and Liam would be my first guests other than family since living in Tom's house by myself." She shifted her attention to Liam. "Well, I'm not really alone. I share the house with Neptune. He's a golden retriever, and he likes kids."

Liam lifted himself onto the balls of his feet. "Can we go, Dad? Can we?"

Mack looked at Liam and then at Erin. His curious frown made it clear she'd thrown him off-kilter.

Erin flashed Mack a look she intended to be a friendly dare. Her fast invitation flustered him, and her devilish side enjoyed it, perhaps a little too much. She looked away long enough to put Naomi on the counter, snap her into her jacket, and pull on a snug hat that covered her ears.

With his eyes sparkling, Mack lifted his hands in a helpless gesture. "With an invitation like that, how can I say no?"

"Yay, Naomi, did you hear that? We're going to have company." Saying yay to anything was Naomi's signal to do her baby clap. Liam laughed and clapped, too. Erin told Mack how to find her house—not complicated since it was down the road from Tom's office. Erin put her dressy Stetson on her head and slipped into her jacket. "So, we'll be on our way now. See you in a few minutes."

"Okay," Liam said, giving the baby a little wave. "See ya later, Naomi."

Erin turned so the baby could wave at Liam, and chuckled to herself as she went out the side door to the parking lot. "This isn't like me at all," she said to Naomi. "I better watch myself around those big blue eyes, huh?"

FROM THE DAY he was born, Macintyre Nelson Fisher had been called Mack. At the moment, Mack was pondering the source of his name, his maternal great-grandfather, who'd come from the same region of Indiana that Erin Hunnicutt also left behind, or so he'd heard. But unlike Erin, a train had brought the first Macintyre to Casper, Wyoming. Family lore held that Macintyre's first purchase was a horse, which he rode west until he landed a job in a town called Rock Bridge. He was an insurance agent, and from that point on, the Fishers were a town-based family of merchants, insurance reps, bookkeepers, teachers and lawyers—the crowd that formed the support system for the main attraction, ranches. The image of Macintyre boarding a train in the Midwest drifted through Mack's mind when he guided Liam past the brightly painted van parked in front of Erin's small but lit-up and inviting cabin.

Before he had a chance to knock on her door, it opened wide, and he and Liam were greeted by Erin's smiling face. Her Stetson was gone, and she'd piled her long, dark brown, almost black hair in a twist on the top of her head. Or tried to. Her hair resisted attempts to make it stay put, and long, wavy strands had slipped out of the twist to frame her face. With the baby in her arms, she stepped back to let Mack usher Liam inside.

When he'd approached Erin at the town hall party, he'd only intended to introduce himself to this woman of many talents. He'd first spotted her months ago at the Halloween party at the lodge. She played the piano and the fiddle, and her clear singing voice carried through the lobby filled with kids and parents. That would have been enough to captivate him, but her striking good looks had made it hard to stop staring at her while she sang and played her instruments. Or maybe he was drawn to the warmth she exuded as she and Dr. Tom performed. Although he'd not had a chance to meet her that night, he hadn't forgotten her. Now, a few months later, a ten-minute conversation had resulted in an invitation to her home.

Erin's housemate, a peach-hued golden retriever, busied himself sniffing Liam's boots.

"That's Neptune saying hello. He's thrilled to have company," Erin said to Liam. "As it happens, he adores kids—and he never misses a chance to smell your shoes. It's one of his favorite things to do."

Neptune soon turned to Mack, sat back on his haunches, and raised his head to get some attention from the other new person. "What a sweet dog." Mack reached down and rubbed the retriever's raised head.

"Happy Valentine's Day, Liam," Erin said. "And you, too, Mack. I assume you're up for a cookie or two?"

Mack let out a light laugh over the easy way Erin took charge. "I guess so. How can I deny him? Besides, you've charmed my son. He's completely under your spell." Not only Liam, Mack mused, still in awe of this woman with her brown eyes as welcoming as her smile.

Erin glanced at Liam. "Is that so? Under my spell, huh? That's something I don't hear every day. Well then, take off your jackets and prepare to stay a while." Erin pointed to a chair by the door where Mack could unload their outdoor gear. She then lowered the baby into the high chair and put a couple of toys on the tray. "You make yourself comfortable at the table,

Liam, because I'm putting you in charge of entertaining Naomi while I get out the treats. Is that okay with you?"

Liam nodded and turned his attention to the baby, who was watching the boy's every move.

"What can I get you, Mack? Coffee? A beer?" She picked up an open bottle of wine from her counter. "A glass of red wine?"

"Wine sounds good." A few sips of cabernet seemed fitting for the closest he was going to get to a Valentine's Day date. "Thanks for the completely unexpected invitation."

"Yeah, for me, too," Erin said. "Totally spur-of-the-moment. I can be a little like that."

"Apparently." Mack hadn't anticipated having an impromptu visit, but he also realized he'd come on pretty strong when he talked about being awestruck and all that. Not really his style, although he wasn't sure what that meant anymore. Paula, Mack's ex and Liam's mom, had died, and he'd been preoccupied with helping his son adjust. Some parts of regular life like women, dates and romance weren't top of mind.

Mack had something to prove, too, at least to himself. He'd messed up. Big-time. He and Paula had separated shortly after Liam was born, a mutual decision. They didn't fight or present each other with a list of grievances.

As it turned out, their feelings for each other weren't intense enough to spark fights, let alone catch fire as marriage partners. Then again, what had he expected? He and Paula had enjoyed a few too many kisses one evening, and suddenly eloping sounded like such a great idea—so romantic. It made sense. Right? Obviously they were made for each other. No reason to wait.

Maybe because they'd been willing to share the blame for their misguided escapade, Mack hadn't fought Paula when she whisked Liam away and moved closer to her parents in her hometown. She'd been adamant about her ability to raise Liam on her own. Mack had been far too passive in asserting himself, and a long-distance—and emotionally distanced—relationship with Liam had seemed like his only choice. As if the marriage hadn't been mistake enough, Mack had followed it up by taking the path of least resistance with Paula. He told himself the lie that a father-son relationship would be more important when Liam was older. Now, as Liam's only parent, Mack was still paying the price for his infrequent contact with his son. More to the point, Liam paid the price for what Mack lacked in the fatherhood department.

"Wait a minute," Erin said, tapping an index finger against her lips and exaggerating a frown.

"That small plate of cheese and crackers I ate at the town hall party didn't fill me up for long. Now I'm thinking about dinner. Is anyone else hungry?"

Liam's arm shot up. "I am."

Mack groaned. "Liam…there you go again."

"I'd planned to make myself a thick ham and Swiss sandwich with lots of mustard and pickles." Erin nodded at Liam, and then turned to Mack. "What do you think? I've got plenty of everything. Why don't we have sandwiches? The cookies can be our dessert."

Mack didn't know what to say except, "You're going to an awful lot of trouble, Erin."

"I'll take that as a yes, and it's no bother at all." She lifted her hands in the air. "It doesn't tax my limited cooking skills to throw together some sandwiches."

"I like ham sandwiches," Liam said, "a whole lot."

Mack shrugged helplessly. "Who am I to stand between a growing boy and his food?"

"My *mom* used to make us ham sandwiches and chicken noodle soup," Liam said.

"Hmm…yummy," Erin said, her voice low but earnest. She looked like she had more to say, but when she glanced at Mack, it appeared she was reconsidering.

Mack gave his head what he hoped was a

subtle shake, enough to communicate that the subject of the past with his mom wasn't a good idea at the moment. Unless someone else had mentioned it, Erin wouldn't necessarily know Mack and Liam's past.

Liam slouched forward with his arm on the table and rested his cheek in his palm. "She got us cupcakes for Valentine's Day. They were kind of reddish, but sort of like chocolate."

"I bet they were red velvet," Erin said with a rising lilt in her voice.

Liam's eyes widened. "Yep, that's what my mom called 'em...red velvet."

Naomi, who was pushing a little wooden truck across the high chair tray, suddenly squealed and dropped it on the floor.

"Well, aren't you an attention-getter," Erin teased. "I better get her some dinner, too."

"I'll help," Liam said. He got out of his chair, scooped the truck off the floor and gave it back to the baby. Naomi let out a loud laugh. With her eyes fixed on Liam, Naomi tossed the truck to the floor again.

Mack chuckled as Liam dutifully picked it up. "Uh-oh, buddy, Naomi is playing a game with you. I don't think it's a game you can win."

The look Erin gave him was best described as scrutinizing. "Change of plans. Do you think you can handle bouncing the baby around long enough for Liam to help me get our sandwiches on the table?"

Granted, he wasn't nearly as adept with babies as a dad should be, but he was a little insulted that she'd asked such a question. "Oh, I think I can manage to distract her."

Erin lifted Naomi out of the chair, and Mack opened his arms to take her. "Hey, cutie, it's you and me, kid." Did Naomi have to rear back and look at him through such wary eyes? Mack looked down at Neptune, who'd padded over to Mack's side and watched him. "Hey, pal, don't worry, I'll take good care of the baby."

Based on his expression, Liam apparently found it amusing that both the dog and Naomi were skeptical about the strange man in the house. "The baby doesn't know you, Dad. But maybe she'll like you once she gets used to you."

Maybe? "Well, I hope so," Mack said. "No 'maybe' about it. I don't growl or scratch. And I don't spit or bite or anything, do I, Liam?"

This time Erin laughed along with Liam.

"Let's get this show on the road," Erin said, guiding Liam to the counter. She pushed a stool in place and opened the bag holding a loaf of bread that smelled fresh from the bakery. "I bet you're good at putting mustard on bread."

"But…but…it's not brown bread." Liam

spoke in a tentative voice and turned to Mack. "Mom said ham always goes with brown rye bread."

"Okay, true, this isn't rye bread," Erin said in a casual tone, "but it's what I have in the house right now. We'll make do."

Unsure of what was underlying Liam's deep frown, Mack said, "Uh, trust me, buddy, ham and Swiss tastes really good on all kinds of bread."

Liam scratched his cheek and stared at the bread.

Erin switched her gaze from Liam to Mack, as if wondering what might happen next. Then she went to the fridge and took out the mustard jars. "I've got not one, but *two* kinds of mustard to choose from." She twisted off the lids, grabbed the cutting board and put out slices of bread. She handed Liam the butter knife to spread the mustard. Mack exhaled when Liam's shoulders relaxed a little.

Meanwhile, Naomi had a couple of things to say, babbling in a conversational tone, pointing to Erin and waving at Liam. "Aunt Erin is right there, Naomi," Mack said, relieved that Liam's focus was on spreading mustard on the bread. "She'll have your dinner in no time."

Mack might be a fish out of water, but now that Liam was okay, at least for the moment, he was amused by the scene he found himself in. If he'd been paying attention, he might have seen the little fingers that headed toward his nose and latched on to it. "Oh, no, the baby is stealing my nose."

Liam decided this was at least as entertaining as sandwich making, and watched from his perch on the stool at the counter. Naomi tweaked Mack's nose again, and then kept it up, giggling with delight at the attention she was getting.

"I suspect that's a Grandpa Quincy trick," Erin said, taking a photo with her phone. "Preserved for posterity, Mack. Bet you didn't anticipate ending up in Naomi's digital photo album." Erin grinned at Liam. "I'll send one to your dad's phone. You can tease him about Naomi getting the better of him."

While Liam was distracted by Naomi's antics, Erin took a bag of chips out of the cabinet and pointed to it. Mack assumed she wanted to know if it was okay for Liam to have them. He nodded. Why not? He tried to limit that kind of snack food at home, but nothing about this evening had been routine. It was a special occasion, Mack decided. Chips and cookies were allowed.

In record time, Erin loaded the sandwiches onto plates and moved them to the table. She grabbed some paper napkins and put them out, too. "As you can see, Mack, we're being very formal tonight." She opened the bag of chips and dumped them into a bowl she then handed to Liam. "You can take some and then pass them around, but only if you really like potato chips."

"Oh, I do." Liam smiled at Erin and dropped a pile of chips on his plate.

"You're such a friendly boy," Erin observed as she took Naomi from Mack's arms and put her back in the high chair. "Some children can be kind of shy, but not you."

"I have lots of friends back home," Liam said.

Erin's gaze shot to Mack. *She gets it*, Mack thought as he took a seat at the table and rested his hand on the back of Liam's chair. For his son, *back home* was Millerton, a town over four hundred miles across the state, the house where he'd lived with his mother, and the school where he had friends. Home included his grandparents, Eden and Louis, plus the playground down the street and the pool where Paula had taught him to swim last summer. Liam had told Mack all about learning to breathe in rhythm with his arms and legs as he made it across the deep end. Mack sighed. Home also meant ham sandwiches on rye bread.

"Let's see who can take the biggest bite."

Erin made a show of picking up her sandwich and sinking her teeth into it. Liam followed suit.

Grateful for Erin's pivot, Mack turned his attention to the baby, who was taking in everything going on around her. Her gaze followed Erin when she got up to pour Liam a glass of milk and add more bite-size pieces of cheese and ham into her baby dish.

Like the baby's, Liam's gaze also tracked Erin. "Does she like regular food?"

"Oh, yes. She's not too fussy about what she eats. Peaches are her favorite, but she'll eat lots of mashed-up carrots, too. I'll give her some formula in a little cup. She'll watch the way you drink from a glass and practice doing the same grown-up thing. You're her role model. How about that?" In a singsong tone, Erin told Naomi she could learn a lot from Liam.

"You sure make all this kid stuff look easy." A much too familiar sense of inadequacy settled over Mack. "And fun." This scene gave him a great example of the awkward part of being a full-time parent. Awkward for him, anyway. At the same time, Erin's easygoing ways matched his aspirations. As it was, there were times that he sat down to have dinner with his son and sensed something missing. He grappled with what to talk about with the boy that went beyond a short recounting of his day at school.

Even worse, Liam had been *forced* to adjust to these gaps, these empty spaces in his life. Reality could hit hard. Liam missed his mom. And the way Mack sometimes felt, Dad wasn't much of a consolation prize.

"I've been part of Naomi's life for a while now. She knows I like to have fun," Erin said, looking at Liam. "She has lots of cousins, so I happen to know that she loves being around kids."

"Neptune, too?"

"Absolutely. And he likes it when I have company."

"Like us," Liam said, smiling down at the dog.

Erin responded with a firm nod. "Like you."

Mack watched his son across the table, enjoying Liam's easy interactions with Erin and Naomi. Feeling a little out of place, Mack distracted himself by digging into his sandwich. It occurred to him that as welcoming as Erin was, he was the extra person whose place in the group wasn't well-defined. Not a typical position for Mack to find himself in, and he was attuned to these kinds of dynamics. In business he had to be. Erin also treated Liam as if he was one of *her* people, not so different from the baby.

New situations demanded different things

from Mack than what was expected in his work, where his persona as a youngish successful business guy was an easy role to play. He was well established in the tourism business as one-third owner of the Tall Tale Lodge & Spa and half owner with Andy Green of a couple of holiday ranches. For the nearly two years he, Andy and the third owner of Tall Tale, Sydney Berrigan, had run Tall Tale, he and Andy had been based off-site, with Sydney moving to Adelaide Creek to run day-to-day operations.

After Paula's sudden death, brought about by a previously undiagnosed heart condition, Mack took Liam across the state to his home in Arrow Gap, a prosperous town up near Jackson and Yellowstone. That town was home base for Mack and Andy Green, and from there, they ran their businesses and consulting practice. When Adelaide Creek's town hall had almost burned down, Tall Tale became an even more important venture.

He was one of Adelaide Creek's newest residents mostly because Willow Lancaster, who promoted special events at the lodge, had urged Tall Tale's owners to jump in and offer temporary office space to the town leaders. Willow was so persuasive that all three of Tall Tale's owners became deeply involved with the town's activities over the monthslong period of repairs.

"Uh, Erin, why did you name your dog Neptune? It's a planet."

Hearing his name, Neptune raised his head and stared at Liam as if waiting for an answer. "I guess he's curious, too," Mack said.

"Sometimes a dog comes with a name. Like my Neptune. The friends who gave him to me called him that. I'm not sure why," Erin explained. "When they had to move far, far away, they gave him to me, because this handsome golden retriever and I were already acquainted. They knew I liked Neptune very much."

That explanation seemed to satisfy Liam. They ate in silence for a couple of minutes, and then Liam said, "I have a book about planets." He flashed a sly smile at Erin. Mack almost laughed out loud. He knew exactly what was coming.

"Oh, really? I bet you know a lot about them," Erin said.

Liam nodded. "I know that Neptune is a lot bigger than Earth… It's huge. Do you know how many moons it has?"

Erin wrinkled her forehead as if she was trying hard to remember. "I give up. How many?"

"Sixteen."

Mack laughed. Liam had stumped him with that question a while back. "Wow. Imagine

looking up at night and seeing all those moons."
Liam chuckled, clearly pleased with himself.

Mack got a kick out of both Liam and Erin,
and was reminded how quickly his business
partner Sydney had become a fan of Adelaide
Creek. She claimed the spirit of the town was
contagious. Now Mack could say the place also
had worked its magic on him. The lodge's role
in the town hall project triggered his curiosity,
and one of the best decisions he'd ever made
was to bring Liam to the Halloween party at the
lodge. It had been only a few weeks after Paula's death, but Mack was in the midst of evaluating what his son needed most to recapture
a normal life. *Normal*, as Mack now defined
it, was a childhood not completely defined by
grief and loss.

"I remember you from the Halloween party,"
Liam said, as if picking up on Mack's thoughts.
"All the pumpkins had faces and lights."

"Wow, what a party, huh?" Erin said. "Costumes and games and lots of goodies."

"And the big fire," Liam added.

Erin smiled. "Sounds like you had fun." She
nodded to Naomi. "This little one slept through
all the noise."

Mack had so many memories of the night.
The roaring fire had thrown light and warmth
from the lodge's showpiece stone fireplace.

Liam had been entranced by the pyramid of carved jack-o'-lanterns with their flameless but flickering candlelight. The atmosphere and Liam's reaction, especially his smiles, had been signposts for Mack. They pointed the way to a different kind of community, and the experience of that evening shifted something in Mack—permanently.

Once back in Arrow Gap, Mack couldn't quit thinking about Adelaide Creek. Considering what would be best for Liam, Mack looked at the town through different eyes, a dad's eyes. For too long, he'd focused on winning in business, counting his successes, but with a hang loose attitude about everything else, including his relationships with his dad and sister, and even his son.

"How long has it been since you moved to Adelaide Creek?" Erin asked, directing her question to Liam.

"We came after Christmas," Liam said. "I go to a new school now."

"I went to five different schools before I started high school," Erin said. "I became good at making new friends. I bet you're good at that, too."

Mack observed Liam's thoughtful expression as he appeared to consider Erin's words. Then with a little shrug, he said, "I guess so." Maybe

because of the Halloween party, and knowing
that Mack owned the lodge, Liam hadn't protested the move. Mack described their new
bunkhouse digs, and Liam hadn't seemed to
notice that they'd exchanged a large condo, now
up for sale, for a much smaller living space.
Mack shifted his priorities when he'd negotiated a new arrangement with Andy and Sydney
so he could balance working on-site and from
home, along with adjusting his schedule to be
with Liam after school every day.

At the moment, his heart filled when he
looked into Liam's face. His son's eyes, blue
like his own, were open wide and bright with
curiosity. Liam had fixed his attention on Erin
and Naomi. If he was one of Erin's people, she
was one of his. Mack had brought a heartbro-
ken child to Arrow Gap, a boy who seemed
to be adrift. Things had improved some by
the time Mack moved to Adelaide Creek. But
there were still times that Liam would stare
into space and tear up without much warning,
as if memories of his mother would interrupt
him when he least expected them to intrude.
It wasn't the first time something as small as
the way his mother did simple things like making sandwiches with rye bread had triggered a
reaction. Liam would instantly fall back into

the habits of his old life, along with the details
of the house or his school, or a story she told.
Helpless to change Liam's reality, Mack could
only try to make the right decisions to help the
seven-year-old heal.

When Mack saw Liam take a bite of his sandwich and then giggle at something Erin said,
he sent her a silent thank-you. Crisis averted.
Barely.

CHAPTER TWO

ERIN STOPPED OUTSIDE the front door of the reception building of Stanhope's Cabins-in-the-Woods and stomped fresh snow off her boots before going inside. Overnight, a few more inches were added to the white blanket that already covered much of the landscape, including Jeff's corral. Stiff winds had blown the snow into drifts that looked like ocean swells ending at the far end of the corral fence. The conditions worked against Erin riding Raven that day, but nothing prevented her from spending a few minutes with her favorite horse. Besides, she'd made a final decision about Raven, and Jeff Stanhope should be the first to know.

Erin pushed open the heavy door, and on her way to Jeff's office, she passed two older couples at a table, playing cards and sipping coffee. A few other guests were sitting on the couches, staring at phones or tablets. The aroma of fresh coffee mingled with the smell of burning wood in the fireplace. It struck Erin that Jeff had designed a mini version of the same kind of comfy tourist atmosphere as the far more upscale Tall Tale Lodge & Spa. Jeff was meeting the growing demand for the modest one- or two-room rental cabins perfect for relaxing winter weekend getaways or longer visits around the holidays.

Those details didn't matter much to Erin. For her, his stable of horses and the riding school set Jeff apart from the bigger, showier lodges in the county. His old-fashioned sleigh and the pair of brawny Clydesdales who pulled it added to the homey aura of the place and made his Cabins-in-the-Woods well-known among locals.

When she rounded the corner into Jeff's private office, the first things she saw were his long legs stretched out and his crossed feet propped on the desk. The chair was tilted back, and he was holding an open magazine.

"Hey, sorry to interrupt," she said, knocking lightly on the open door. "Wanted to give you a heads-up. I thought I'd pay Raven a visit this afternoon."

Jeff lowered his feet and righted himself as he waved her inside. "Nice to see you. Before you say hello to the horse, tell me how you're doing with Naomi?" He grinned. "Bet you like being Auntie Erin, huh?"

"I enjoy that baby girl more every day. She's in day care at the moment. I have a little time before I need to pick her up. Then Quincy will take over. First thing tomorrow morning, I start my new gig at the O'Connor mansion."

"Busy, busy." Jeff tossed the magazine on his desk. "But, of course, not too busy to show Raven some love. I'm sure she'll be pleased to see you. I'll walk you to the stables. It'll give me a chance to stretch my legs."

Erin nodded at the magazine. "Whatcha reading?"

"Looking at the ads for lodges and cabins in *Western Days Magazine*." He lowered his voice when he added, "Only Olivia knows the details of what I'm considering, but I might add some cabins. I'm also thinking about a second corral and expanding the stable."

Erin rubbed her hands together. "Ooh, a secret?"

"Oh, let's say it's not a fully formed plan yet." Jeff tapped his temple. "My vision is mostly still locked in here. But I know how you feel about horses, so I thought I'd let you in on what's brewing."

Erin nodded. She appreciated Jeff's trust and confidence in her. His words struck a chord, too. It occurred to her that besides the new town hall, other, bigger changes for the region were in the air. Although some large-scale sheep and cattle ranches were thriving, others had trimmed production, reinvented their focus, or gone out of business entirely. Erin had heard about the fallout from the rapid changes from Willow. She and her dad, Quincy, were part of the prominent Lancaster family who had fingers in every economic pie, from her cousins' ranches to Quincy's building and development company.

Jeff Stanhope and his sister had been among the many who'd lost family ranches and had to start over. Eventually, after a stint in Seattle, Jeff had returned to Adelaide Creek and reinvented himself by buying a once abandoned group of cozy vacation cabins. With the uptick in tourism the area enjoyed, his hunch about the demand had been on target. Erin mused about the similarities she saw in Mack Fisher and Jeff, including their decision to make their respective marks in the hospitality business. Jeff had something that Mack didn't, though. He bought and sold horses and distinguished himself with his growing riding school.

Jeff grabbed his jacket. "Let's go out the back door. That way we won't disturb the card games and whatever those folks are doing on their devices."

Erin followed him, her mind shifting to the

aptly named Raven, a nearly all-black Morgan soon to be hers.

The white flakes in the air swirled around in the breeze, barely worthy of being called flurries. "The other night the snow was so heavy for a few minutes that we couldn't see the stables, just the blurry glow in the dark from the outside lights," Jeff remarked as they trudged along the narrow path in the snow.

When they went inside, Jeff's stable hand, Burroughs, was brushing down Dot, a mostly off-white Appaloosa who earned her name because of a few brown speckles spread across both flanks. Erin had taken a couple rides on Dot, a gentle horse, but her heart belonged to Raven, who stood in the stall next door. When Erin called her name, Raven bobbed her head over the gate.

"See that? She's a happy girl now." Jeff grinned. "The first minute I saw her, I knew she was a good horse. And when she sees you, she's raring to go."

Erin had the same reaction. One ride on Raven provided proof enough that she'd found a dream horse. The only downside was her crowded schedule during the weeks before the town hall reopening party. She'd had little time to visit, and in the weeks before Christmas, the snow was too deep and the air too frosty for riding. Erin came by for quick visits whenever she could because she missed her sweet-tempered but lively Raven.

Erin had waited until Quincy had offered her a job on the O'Connor mansion restoration project before she'd declared herself financially secure enough to make the leap and buy Raven and pay Jeff's fee to board her. Today was the day to seal the deal. If restoration work dried up and Erin was forced to relocate, then Erin vowed to take Raven with her. Abandoning the horse wasn't an option.

Erin slipped into the stall and rubbed Raven's long neck. In response, the horse lowered her head and nudged Erin's shoulder. "She's like a dream come true, you know," Erin said to Jeff and Burroughs. A mix of happy and sad feelings washed over her. On the one hand, she finally had a chance to own this beauty of a horse, but her heart hurt a little, too, thinking of her mom. She'd have been so happy that Erin could finally have what her heart had yearned for ever since she was a tiny girl.

"I used to beg my mom to pull off the road so I could climb onto fence railings and watch horses graze in the fields," Erin said, as if it was important that Jeff and Burroughs know that about her. "Mom was so patient with me. She talked the library into buying every new children's book about horses. I'd check them out not just once but many times."

When Erin was learning to restore wood, she'd put aside her yearning for a horse of her own, but the desire had come alive again when she'd landed in Wyoming. She not only saw horses practically everywhere she looked, but she had the chance to ride again for the first time in years. Thanks to Willow, who'd invited her to ride with her cousin Bridget on one of the large Lancaster ranches, Erin was hooked all over again.

"Are you ready now to sign on the dotted line?" Jeff asked.

"If the offer to sell is still on the table…"

"That deal hasn't moved an inch. Knowing how much you want Raven, I'd never have sold her to anyone else without talking to you first." Jeff backed away from the stall. "You take your time here. Enjoy your visit. I'll write up a sales sheet and the terms for boarding. Stop by over the weekend and we'll finalize things."

Jeff started to leave, but stopped and turned back. "Be sure to double-check the latches on the stalls and the building." He had his gaze on Erin, but directed his words to Burroughs, along with a pointed look.

When Jeff had gone, Erin put her arm around Raven's neck and chatted with Burroughs about riding as often as she could come spring. Burroughs, not a young man, for sure, but both physically fit and affable, had a first name, Wayne, but no one ever called him that. In the small world of Adelaide Creek, Burroughs, born and raised there, was like a celebrity. He didn't need two names to be recognized.

"Jeff's a little concerned," Burroughs said. "He got a call from a rancher about a horse that apparently got loose and hasn't found his way home yet."

"You mean like a runaway?"

Burroughs hesitated before answering. "The owner is on the other side of the county," he started, "but there's lots of open land on the trails bordering the ridges that run east of the creek." Burroughs's forehead showed worry creases, and he shook his head. "Horses don't run off that often, especially in the winter. It's a reminder to be extra careful."

"I'll keep an eye out for a lone horse," Erin said. "There's a lot of open land around Tom's house."

"Jeff says he's a brown quarter horse—only three or four years old." Burroughs sighed and turned away. "Like I said, a runaway horse is pretty rare this time of year."

"Do you and Jeff think someone might have stolen the horse?"

"We're not making that leap yet, Erin. We don't see much horse rustling around here." Burroughs looked like he had more to say, but then he moved to a horse a couple of stalls down the row.

Erin let out a sigh of her own. She had to pull herself away from Raven or risk being late to pick up Naomi from day care. Erin was having dinner with Quincy at the diner, and then Grandpa Q would start his babysitting stint. "See you later, Raven, and you, too, Burroughs."

Burroughs gave Raven a friendly pat on the head. "I'll take good care of her, Erin. Don't you worry."

The sun was breaking through the grayish clouds and brightening the afternoon landscape, and Erin's mood matched the shift. Seeing Raven always made Erin extra glad to be alive. She picked up her pace, and when she made the curve around to the front of the main building and the parking area, a cluster of people were deep in conversation. Not just any people. Jeff and Mack Fisher were talking on the porch, while Jeff's stepdaughter, Jillian, and Liam were romping around the yard with the dog.

Erin waved enthusiastically. "Hi, everybody." Liam's face showed his surprise, but he raced to her, and she gave his shoulder a little squeeze.

"Guess what, Erin? Jillian's my math tutor now." Liam bounced on his toes.

Jillian caught up to him and stood alongside him. "*Peer* tutor," Jillian explained.

Erin met Mack's eye. He also appeared pleased by the news. "You don't say. A peer tutor."

"He only needs to catch up." Jillian spoke in a grown-up voice full of reassuring authority. "His old school wasn't as advanced as his class here."

"I see." One more adjustment Liam had to deal with, Erin mused.

Mack came closer, too, and gestured to Jillian and Liam. "I thought it would be a good idea to connect with Jillian and her parents now that she's working with Liam." He smiled at Jillian, who, in the few months Erin had known her, had morphed from a kid in the middle of an awkward stage to a tall and athletic young girl ready to bloom as a teenager. The transition might as well have happened overnight.

Mack shifted his weight from one foot to the other, planted his hands on his hips, and then dropped them to his sides. *Why so uneasy, Mack?* Erin didn't know, but Mack's body language told her he was out of his element but trying hard to adjust, like breaking in uncomfortable shoes.

Remembering Quincy and Naomi, Erin said,

stepping back from the group, "I've got to run. It's time to pick up Naomi and deliver her to Quincy. It's his turn to have fun with her until Willow and Tom come home." She felt Mack's gaze following her as she hurried to the car. There was something about him. She couldn't quite name it, but it was beyond his captivating eyes and charming smile. Erin always paid extra attention to a guy who could look that good with a beard.

In her experience, successful guys like Mack moved through the world with a touch of swagger, usually simultaneously attractive and a little annoying. That wasn't true with Mack. He'd charmed her a bit, ruffled her some, but hadn't thrown in any hotshot swagger, at least not yet.

"HE HAD A good session, Mack." Dr. Kelly Harte's gaze followed Liam to a spot in front of a screen in the corner, where kids could choose from computer games and programs. With a tablet in his hand, Liam was creating a space colony on Mars. Earth families with men, women and kids were living in domes. The game gave Liam choices of what the houses and schools would look like— he'd added tubes that zipped passengers around this city on Mars, kind of like the trains he saw outside of town. Mack had been impressed by

Liam adding rivers and lakes, along with tunnels and bridges.

"Not exactly like my grandfather's package of crayons and a notebook," Mack said, amused—and impressed—by the people lounging in their mini-domes or traveling in their clear tubes. Clever.

"My young clients each have a world they build on their own. Having a few minutes with it at the end is their reward for sticking with me in the session," Dr. Harte said. "Liam's world, another planet, one with homes and families, tells me what's on his mind, too. He's opening up little by little. Telling me stories."

"Stories? You mean about his mom?"

Dr. Harte pursed her lips and cocked her head, as if considering his question. "Sometimes, but not today. He was excited about his new tutor, Jillian, and getting some help with math. Even in second grade, he's used to doing well, especially at math. He was quite vocal about it." Dr. Harte's smile added an extra dose of warmth to her words. "Falling behind is not a place he likes to be."

"As a matter of fact, I knew of Jillian through a family friend who works at the lodge," Mack said. "I'm finding that's the way I meet most everyone around here. I brought Liam to Jeff Stanhope's Cabins-in-the-Woods to say hello

before they started getting together for tutor-
ing at school."

The therapist smiled knowingly. "That's the
way it is in all these towns around Landrum.
I'm from Houston, so all the cross-connections
between people in this area were new to me."
She laced her fingers in front of her. "It's like
mesh, and the more quickly you find your place
in the community, the sooner Liam will think
of Adelaide Creek as his home."

Mack took a deep breath and asked his question on the exhale. "How do you think he's
doing? Really."

"He's walking on much firmer ground than
he was when you first brought him here. It's
only been a few weeks." Dr. Harte spoke without hesitation, and in a tone a little more formal
than Mack expected. "He was a frightened boy,
tentative and uneasy at school, although he tried
to be brave and hide his feelings. As you know,
he was prone to tearfulness, anxious about living in a new house."

"I moved him twice, first from Millerton to
Arrow Gap and then again to settle here, so I
understand why," Mack said. "But now he brags
about his room in the bunkhouse and the cowboys who lived there. He gets that the men who
stayed there were shepherds—sheep guys. But
in his mind they're all cowboys. The Hoovers,

the couple that own it, gave him some photos of the ranch from decades ago to put up in his room. The other day he told me when he's done being an astronaut, he's going to be a sheep shearer. He thinks it's the coolest job ever."

"Don't we all?" Dr. Harte's wide smile lightened the mood. "Matter of fact, I heard all about those photos. Being older, the Hoovers give him a sense of safety, like grandparents. And he really misses his grandma and grandpa."

Aware that was true, Mack took a deep breath and kept his eyes on Liam, still absorbed in his video play. "They're good people, and I understood why they wanted to keep Liam close, but I had to make the break now. He has FaceTime with them every week without fail. And sometimes more than once." Mack gripped the back of his stiff neck, a sign of stress and more or less a constant presence for the last few months. "The other day, his grandparents listened to Liam read them a story during their online visit." He paused to let the bittersweet feelings pass. "I promised to take him to see them over spring break."

"Mack, I get it," Dr. Harte said. "You don't need to defend every decision or step. It's natural for his grandparents to miss him, but that doesn't mean it was a mistake to move him here." She glanced at the clock, sending Mack a message that her next appointment would be starting soon. "Your work is here, and you already have connections to build on. From what you've said, Paula's parents understand."

"As best they can." Mack left unsaid that Eden and Louis Brown had not been shy in expressing their preferences, laid out in bullet points. First, they'd wanted Mack to stay close by, maybe even move into Paula's house and raise Liam there. They'd argued that being in familiar surroundings would be a giant step in getting over his loss. Mack had his doubts about that, but no matter, because he reeled at the suggestion he move into Paula's house. Plus, he couldn't imagine settling down in the isolated town hundreds of miles across the state and almost a day's drive from Arrow Gap, his home base at the time.

The Browns delivered a final gut punch when they came right out and said they wanted to keep Liam and raise him. If Mack had been on the lookout for signs pointing toward trouble, that was it. It hit hard, especially because Eden and Louis were serious about it, and they'd come up with justifiable reasons, at least superficially. Their proposition only deepened Mack's commitment to finally be a real dad. But he wouldn't brush off their heartache over losing their only child, so he promised Paula's parents he'd make sure they'd be a permanent part of Liam's life.

"What about your family, Mack?" Dr. Harte asked. "You rarely say anything about your father and sister."

"They're visiting soon. I took Liam over to see them for Thanksgiving." It had been quite a whirlwind, going to see his family and the Browns. He'd made the trek to see Louis and Eden again at Christmas and had been stuck in a blizzard with Liam halfway home. "But the truth is, I haven't seen much of my family since my mother died. That was almost ten years ago."

Dr. Harte acknowledged Mack's words with a nod and a frown, but then she called out to Liam and asked him to wrap up the project. That gave Mack time to blurt, "These sessions help me, even if I sometimes wonder how much they help Liam."

Without missing a beat, Dr. Harte said, "Mack, listen to me. *It's all helping.* Go easy on yourself. You're new at this dad stuff." Dr. Harte's expression changed, and she lightly touched his forearm. "Oh, and before I forget, Liam is a big fan of the person who made ham sandwiches and offered him cookies. I heard about a dog named Neptune, and he told an entertaining tale about a baby grabbing your nose." Her soft exhale was like a gentle laugh showing how amused she'd been. "I'd say he was bragging a little about what a fun Valentine's Day he had."

Mack instantly stood a little straighter. "No kidding? Well, those are exactly the kind of connections I've wanted to make here in town. It was a fun night, nose tweaking and all."

"Make no mistake, Mack, Liam hasn't fully absorbed his loss," Dr. Harte said. "It ripples under the surface, but I can tell from the way he talks about his days that he feels cared for by you and other people around him."

Mack nodded to acknowledge her words. After Liam said a quick goodbye, they were underway to the pickup window at the Burger Barn. Without planning it, ordering ahead for takeout burgers from this restaurant about half-way between Landrum and Adelaide Creek had become a post-counseling ritual. For Mack it was also part of the transition from all the busy-ness of the day to being alone with Liam, then winding down and getting ready for bed. It often coincided with a time of the day when Mack's confidence in himself as a dad could get wobbly, and he wasn't in the mood to figure out what to have for dinner.

As soon as they were back in the bunkhouse, Liam climbed up on a chair at the table and began taking the containers out of the bag while

Mack set out plates and napkins. Every day, Mack was grateful to Paula for how well she'd been raising Liam. He rarely needed to be prodded to help do the little chores he could handle, like unpacking a carryout bag or setting the table. Even at seven years old, Liam was used to being a helper.

After the first couple of quick bites, Liam said, "Mom used to take me to the Red Basket at home. They had the best burgers. Mom usually brought the food home, but I liked it better when we sat in a big red booth."

"So I've heard from your grandparents," Mack said, recalling that Liam went out to dinner nearly every week with Eden and Louis, with or without Paula. "Maybe when it warms up, we'll eat our burgers at one of the picnic tables." Liam's enthusiasm about Red Basket was what had prompted him to give the Burger Barn a try in the first place. "I think they might even have red checkered tablecloths. What do you think?"

Liam nodded as he dipped a french fry into a cup of ketchup, but before he popped it in his mouth, he let out an impish laugh. "But not under the trees. Grandpa Louis doesn't like it when bugs and leaves fall into his food." He laughed again. "Grandma Eden called him an old crab." He elongated the words in an amusing imitation of Eden.

Since Mack had heard similar stories in his childhood, he could play that conversation in his head. It was no wonder Liam found it so funny. In Mack's memories, it was Dad telling Mom she was too crabby about bugs, and after all, even the snake that slithered across their porch was as harmless as a housefly. He wished someone had had a camera handy to catch the looks his mom shot back when his dad said things like that.

"Bet that was funny," Mack said with a laugh in his voice. "Your grandparents sound a little like my mom and dad."

Without reacting one way or another, Liam asked, "When are Grandpa Patrick and Aunt Gayle coming to see us?"

"Soon, Liam, soon. Only a few weeks. It's already almost March." He pointed to the calendar mounted at Liam's eye level on the wall next to the door. He'd highlighted the days of the visit in yellow. "See? They're staying at the lodge. They can use the swimming pool there like we do sometimes."

Liam stared into space for a few seconds. "Why can't Grandma Eden and Grandpa Louis come, too?"

"Well, for one thing, I'm taking you to see

them in April. They'll have you all to themselves." He wished they'd agreed to a joint visit with his family, which would have saved him another round-trip drive. That idea came and went fast. Eden made it clear that Louis didn't like venturing too far from home anymore. Even before Liam was born, the man had become a non-budging homebody. No doubt about it, they expected Mack to bring Liam to them. Mack had decided not to challenge the assumption.

Liam's eyes were serious, but then he dipped a fry in ketchup. "Okay." After popping it into his mouth, he asked if he could watch episodes of *Dragonfly*, his favorite animated series.

"Sure. Get ready for bed, and then we'll watch *Dragonfly* together." Mack was good with this kind of TV. Even he enjoyed watching the antics of a pair of twins living on a farm with their dog, Dragonfly, and their horse, Bluetail.

Meanwhile, Mack finished his burger and allowed himself to enjoy the small victory. An odd word to describe their time around the table. But a victory is what it felt like when Liam could talk about Red Basket and bugs at picnics without a cloud of sadness hovering over them.

Later, after he'd tucked Liam in, Mack escaped into his own streamed series, one with quirky investigators solving a grisly crime that would take the whole twelve-episode season to solve. The last thing he did before crawling into bed was look in on Liam and listen to his slow, soft breaths. Satisfied his son was sleeping peacefully, Mack was ready to close his eyes, too.

When he awakened with a start, it took a minute to grasp what had jolted him out of a deep sleep. And at two fifteen in the morning. He had no memory of being in the midst of a dream, but he quickly became conscious of faint whimpering sounds. He threw back the covers and got to his feet. Across the hall, the door to Liam's room was half-open, the way Mack had left it. From the doorway, he saw Liam sitting up in bed, rubbing his eyes with one hand. He held Thunder, an older stuffed bear he liked to sleep with, in his other hand.

"Liam? Are you okay, buddy?" Mack padded across the carpeted floor and positioned himself on the bed where he could face Liam. His first impulse was to gather his son in his arms, but he didn't want to startle him, so he put his hands on Liam's shoulders.

Liam shook his head. "My mom died."

"Did you have a dream about her?" Mack whispered.

Liam shrugged. "Maybe. I don't know. Long

time ago, Grandma Eden said I might wake up sometimes because Mom's in my dream."

Although this wasn't the first time Liam had awakened in the night, sometimes crying, this was the first time Liam responded that way when he was asked if he'd had a dream about Paula. Mack's chest and throat tightened and threatened his ability to speak. *It's on you to help him...it's on you to figure this out.* He forced air into his lungs. "Uh-huh, that kind of dream happens sometimes. But did it scare you a little?"

Liam nodded. "I thought I'd heard her."

"I see. No wonder you woke up." Mack took in another deep breath. He didn't know the right words, so he said the first thing that came to mind. "How about if you—and Thunder—spend the rest of the night in my bed? We'll both go back to sleep, and when we wake up, it will be morning again."

Liam yawned. "Okay. I'm tired."

"I'll bet you are, buddy." Mack got to his feet and gently scooped Liam and the bear into his arms. Was he doing the right thing? Should he have put Liam back into his own bed?

Mack ignored the second-guessing voices in his head. *I'm in charge here, and this is my decision. What harm could it possibly do?* He carried Liam across the hall, put him into bed, and arranged the bear at his side. Almost immediately, Liam's barely audible breathing fell into an even rhythm.

On alert himself, Mack got into bed next to Liam and propped himself on his elbow to watch him sleep. Like Mack as a child, Liam was a little tall for his age, but he seemed small in the big bed. No bigger than a minute, Mack thought, recalling an expression his mom had used.

In the months since he'd brought Liam home, an occasional nightmare had disturbed Liam and rattled Mack. They came on without warning, but were thankfully rare, especially considering Liam's loss. He was easily quieted before they had a chance to interrupt his sleep for long. He never recalled any images from those dreams, not of Paula or anyone else. The last one was a few days after moving into the bunkhouse post Christmas.

Mack reassured himself, knowing that Dr. Harte would have an explanation. He'd call Tom, too, and get the pediatrician's opinion. A few minutes passed before Mack lowered his head to the pillow and closed his eyes. At least for now, his son was okay.

CHAPTER THREE

ERIN FLOPPED TO the side to rest on one hip as she reached inside the wooden cabinet and walked her fingers up the sides of the damaged wood. Almost every place she applied even slight pressure, the dry, rotting wood splintered or fell off in dusty flakes. The piece sat a foot off the floor on curved legs that ended with cat's paw feet. Definitely not one of the expertly built cupboards or hutches, Erin determined. It would be one of only a handful of pieces in the O'Connor mansion she'd examined so far that wasn't worth saving.

Erin rearranged herself on the floor so she had her back to the wooden doors and jotted her notes on the forms Quincy had provided along with an old-school clipboard. She'd known her boss for six months now. Long enough to understand that although he was as much of a techie as the next person, Quincy clung to a few areas where he liked to put the devices aside and pick up the old-school tools. This extensive hands-on inspection was one of those areas. He enjoyed leaning back in his office chair and flipping through his own customized paper forms to study her handwritten notes.

In the past, many pairs of eyes had assessed the O'Connor mansion and its gardens, declared it a disaster zone and recommended demolition. Neglect had come with a steep price. Now it was the sole dilapidated building on an otherwise lovely tree-lined street two blocks from Merchant Street and the heart of town. Only hints of its former elegance were visible.

"I can't see razing the place," Quincy had said on Erin's first visit to the mansion. He'd turned to her. "You've got an excellent imagination, so tell me what you see."

An exceptional imagination wasn't required to look beyond the cracked windows and crumbling bricks and stonework. Granted, the interior was dominated by blotchy water stains on several outside walls. No one could miss the peeling varnish, and the weakened blackened wood. It might have looked hopeless to someone without her skills. The freezing air in winter and hot sun streaming through dirty leaded glass in the summer had also created damage. "I see a repaired exterior and gleaming restored woodwork and floors inside. Nothing is wrong with the bones of the place." Erin then stated the obvious. "You knew that's exactly what I'd say. Why tear down a building as elegant as this one?"

Quincy had smiled. "Well, like I said, you see beyond the surface."

In Quincy's vision, the structure could be transformed into a new home for the Merchant's Association, a visitor center, a place to hold arts and craft shows, and meeting rooms to reserve. Erin was partial to the impressive stone walls around the main garden. Easy to picture couples exchanging their vows in that intimate setting. But the work would take time, commitment and investment. Erin wasn't exactly sure why, but Quincy had been prepared to offer all three.

Even more than restoration, Erin liked to think of her contribution as rejuvenation. She couldn't always restore something to its original state, but the energy of tired and damaged wood changed when people with her skill and determination picked up their tools and got to work. Unlike the town hall project, which was all about history, the mansion renovation was about repurposing and breathing new life into something the town could take pride in today.

Erin chuckled to herself. She'd made her work sound sort of noble. But this ugly free-standing cabinet with the cat feet would add nothing to the old house no matter where it sat. The monstrosity didn't match the elegance of the built-ins in the kitchen or in other rooms. It had to go. With any luck, Quincy would agree and have his guys haul it to the curb with a big sign saying, Free! Haul It Away and It's Yours.

As she scribbled her notes and filled in the boxes on Quincy's form, she wound down from one of several days she'd spent both crawling around inside low cabinets and cupboards and climbing ladders to reach the high spots. So far her planes and heat guns, glues and finishes were still idle. Quincy wanted this preliminary assessment completed for every corner of every room before anything was ripped out or stripped down to bare wood. She'd be tramping through the mansion evaluating the rest for at least another week before she repaired or restored a single feature. Absorbed in her thoughts, she vaguely heard the front door close. Then footsteps that made the floorboards squeak grew louder as they came closer. "Erin? Where are you?"

She welcomed the sound of that voice. Erin still got a kick out of thinking of Willow as her sister-in-law. *Family.* "I'm back here in the kitchen, but I'll come to you." She got to her feet, brushed herself off, and got as far as the folding doors of the dining room before Willow appeared. She had to laugh at what a long way it was from the foyer of the house, a space as big as one of the bedrooms upstairs. Then the enormous living room, formal dining room, and finally a kitchen were all situated to the right of the extra-wide central staircase. Those stairs led to the second floor. A narrower curved stairway went to the third level, where a door revealed the hidden steps to an attic. On the first floor, a cozy sitting room attached to the library was tucked in on the other side of the stairs and connected to the dining room with folding doors.

"Dad told me I'd find you here," Willow said, plunking down on the window seat and patting the other end, where she expected Erin to join her.

"You're still a little pink from a week on the beach," Erin teased, giving her own face a pat. "On a raw day in late February like this, I bet you wish you were still there. Spring is still a long way off in this part of the world."

"Hmm…maybe so, but I missed Naomi so much." Willow's smile was on the dreamy side. "I ran into Mack at the lodge earlier. He told me he and his little boy spent some time at your house."

Mack. He'd been weaving in and out of her thoughts these last few days since she'd run into him at Jeff's. So much so that it troubled her how often his face—and those unforgettable blue eyes—happened to wander into her mind uninvited. If Erin wanted to talk it over with someone, Willow would be the right person, but she wasn't ready to let her unsettled feelings show. Besides, emotions were fleeting, right? They'd go away soon enough.

Erin airily flicked her hand. "Such a glamorous night, Willow. I made ham sandwiches, and we had cookies." She paused and then added, "I didn't plan it. It was a spur-of-the-moment thing. Turned out to be fun. Liam is a cute little sweetheart." She sighed, surprised that mentioning the boy came with a hint of sadness.

Not waiting for Willow to ask, Erin explained that listening to Mack's son talk about his mom touched her heart. If anyone would understand the early loss of a mom, it was Willow, whose Mom died when Willow was on the brink of becoming a teenager.

Willow's face took on a quizzical expression. "I wasn't aware Mack even had a son until he showed up with Liam last Halloween. Hardly anyone knew about his boy. He'd taken a few personal days in early October but never said why. Kind of odd." A closedmouth smile changed her expression. "On an entirely superficial note, I do like his new look, especially the beard. He's not so buttoned up now that he's exchanged those business suits for sport coats and jeans, at least some of the time."

"I didn't know him before, but I agree he's a handsome guy." Erin's heart beat a little faster. "Those eyes."

Willow tilted her head and stared at Erin with her own amused blue eyes.

"Don't you think it's strange that you didn't know about Liam?" Erin deliberately pivoted away from talk of Mack's looks, conscious of being much too eager for information about a man whose life was none of her business in the first place.

"It could seem that way," Willow said, "but Mack hadn't spent much time at the lodge. He came on-site only a handful of times until he moved down here. I thought of him as simply one of my two absentee bosses, friendlier than Andy Green, but still someone I had to answer to. We never had a conversation about personal things."

"I suppose." Erin tried to shake her thoughts of Mack out of her mind the only way she knew how, by changing the subject to what she and Willow had in common: Quincy. "Your dad has such a vivid vision of the future of this place." She gestured around the room. "I didn't see the big picture until I started poking around room by room. Talk about time-consuming. But Quincy wants all the bad news up front so he can schedule each phase, set deadlines, and hire the right people to fill out the crew."

"That's my dad," Willow said, grinning. "He likes to say it takes a village to build the best houses, not only to raise kids."

"Well, he's assembling some villagers to work with me to plunge into the massive job of refinishing the woodwork on all the doors and windows and other built-in fixtures in every room, and that includes the staircases," Erin said. "Thanks to your dad, I'm getting a chance to learn how to supervise and train other people to do this work. I'll handle the more elaborate fixtures myself." She pointed to the massive ten-foot-long hutch with all its intricate carving and then nodded to the marble and wood fireplace that also was part of the huge dining room. Both of those pieces required her level of experience.

Willow stood and wandered around the room, studying the chandelier and walking her fingers across the marble fireplace mantel. "My dad tells me he's reached a stage where he doesn't worry so much about the bottom line of every undertaking," Willow explained. "He jump-started this project because it's more fun for him to create something valuable for the town than recoup his costs. His main goal is banishing an eyesore."

Erin's phone buzzed, and so did Willow's. "I see it's from Jeff," Erin said.

"Mine, too. Ooh, a sleigh ride." Willow's face lit up. "That sounds like fun."

Erin read the message, short and sweet, with the date and the time, and a reminder that it would likely be Jeff's last sleigh ride of the winter.

She clicked on the thumbs-up emoji. "Done. I'll come in extra early on Saturday so I can get a lot done before it's time to go to Jeff's."

"We're going to label you 'make-it-gleam Erin,'" Willow said, "because of the amount of time you're already putting in here at the mansion."

"Nice of Jeff to include me," Erin said, still surprised at times by how easily Tom had opened doors for her to be part of his local group of friends. She rarely walked down Merchant Street without running into acquaintances or even new friends that came through her brother, and now Willow and Quincy.

Willow waved her off. "Don't be silly. You're part of my family. And you adore horses, the most important connection that makes you one of Jeff's people." Willow headed to the door.

"Speaking of work, I'll let you get back to it. I need to get home."

Erin walked Willow to the front door, opened it and breathed in the crisp winter air. She reached up to hug Willow, who stood several inches taller, and then watched her get into her car and leave. As Willow's vehicle disappeared around the circular driveway, another one took its place in front of the brick stairs to the double front doors. She couldn't place that SUV, but she recognized the driver when he climbed out and Liam followed. Hmm...what would prompt Mack to stop by? Maybe he was looking for Quincy?

She looked down at herself in work jeans and boots. She'd braided her hair and stuck a baseball cap on her head to limit the amount of dust and grime she'd carry home. *Nice ensemble*, she thought, especially the stained gray hoodie. Liam gave her an enthusiastic wave as she stepped back into the mansion and invited them inside. "This is a surprise. What brings you to my workshop?" She addressed her question to Liam.

Liam shrugged. "I don't know."

Mack laughed. "What kind of an answer is that?"

Liam ignored his dad and said, "I'm seeing Dr. Harte today. I'm putting horses on Mars."

"Oh? Interesting." At no time in her life had Erin put horses and Mars in the same sentence, so a logical response didn't easily come to mind.

Mack smiled. "Uh, long story."

"One I'd like to hear," Erin said.

"We'll be on our way in a minute, Liam." He turned to Erin. "I suppose I should have texted you. I saw you were on the group invitation to the sleigh ride on Saturday."

"Right. I'll try to finish up here in time to go," Erin said, glancing at Liam, who'd wandered to the stairway and looked up. "If your dad says it's okay, I'll give you the grand tour of this old place one day soon."

"Hey, I hope I'm invited, too," Mack said.

Erin narrowed her eyes and tilted her head, pretending that she had to think about that. "Hmm… I suppose. You might find it pretty interesting."

Mack pointed to the enormous antique chandelier high above their heads. "I'm sure I will. This place must be filled with treasures like that one." He patted Liam's shoulder. "But we have to be on our way. I stopped by to offer to pick you up on Saturday, and we'll give you a ride to Jeff's."

What? That came out of the blue. The muscles in her back stiffened. It was a friendly enough suggestion. She guessed it would be okay. But pick her up? Like a date? It made her much too nervous.

Mack's expression was both puzzled and expectant.

She finally found the words she was searching for. "Um, thanks for the offer, but you know I'm working on Saturday. *If* I can go for the sleigh ride, I'll be leaving from here." As if she hadn't been clear enough, she filled in nonexistent blanks. "There's so much to do, you see. We just started the project. I'm still working up a preliminary assessment for Quincy. Sort of an inventory. I told Jeff that I'll *try* to be there. I won't know for sure that I can make it until closer to the time."

That was what she'd tell Jeff in a return text. Then what she'd said in one long, rambling statement wouldn't be a complete fabrication.

"Oh, okay then…well, we hope to see you there." Mack gestured to Liam. "Gotta go, kiddo." With his hand on Liam's shoulder, he hurried across the driveway to his vehicle.

"Most likely you'll see me," Erin called out, worried now that she'd offended him. "But like I said, it's a demanding project." *Stop talking!*

Mack waved again before he got inside the SUV, but his smile seemed to slip.

Erin closed the door and rested her shoulder

against it, thoroughly embarrassed. Not by refusing the ride, but by the flustered, awkward way she did it. What *was* she so afraid of?

LIAM SAW ERIN first and shouted her name to get her attention. She was standing in front of a beautiful horse, the one Mack assumed she'd just bought. He'd learned about that by way of Jillian, who'd told Liam. Of course, Liam couldn't wait to share the news. Erin was patting the white markings on the horse's long face, the only part that wasn't shiny black.

Liam broke into a run toward her, but Mack quickly caught up and put his hands on his shoulders to slow him down. "Whoa, buddy, let's be careful. We don't want to startle Erin's horse or the Clydesdales. See? Jeff is putting on their harnesses and getting them ready to pull the sleigh."

Erin, mostly absorbed in showing her horse some affection, gave Jeff a couple of quick glances. So much for her showing up at the last minute. Apparently, she'd arrived early. When he took a few steps to close the distance between them, Erin greeted him with a warm smile, as if pleased to see him and Liam. Quite a contrast with the last time he'd seen her, jumpy and talking nonstop as she backed away from him.

"So this is your new horse, huh?" Mack said when he approached her.

"Her name is Raven, Dad. I *told* you that." Liam's slight eye roll was a bit much for a seven-year-old.

"Right you are." Erin grinned and patted Raven. "I ended up closing up shop early so I could say hello to my girl before everybody else arrived. Now I wish I could saddle her up."

"But it's so cold outside," Liam said.

"Yep. Too cold for Raven. It's a good thing the Clydesdales are used to clopping through the snow on the old road." Erin diverted Liam's attention to the sleigh and the powerful horses.

"I heard a couple of people talking at the lodge the other day about a runaway horse," Mack said. "Any news?"

Erin called out to Jeff. "Mack's asking about the horse that's gone missing. Do you still think he'll come back on his own?"

"Fortunately, they most always do," Jeff said.

He said the words, but in a halting way, Mack thought. "Some like to break free, but they usually know the way back home, even from pretty long distances. He'll probably show up soon, hungry but safe."

"That's a relief." Mack waved to a neighbor he recognized as Clark. "Odd, though, another guy I know who keeps some horses called me this morning and said one of his disappeared yesterday before dawn," Clark said. "She didn't get far. He'd barely noticed she was gone before he saw her galloping toward home along a dirt road on the edge of his land."

"Does this happen often, horses getting loose?" Mack asked. "Andy and I almost never hear of that happening at our holiday ranches. At least, no one's told us about horses breaking out and taking off."

"Not that I've ever heard about," Clark said. "We're all on lookout duty now for the first horse. Fielder, that's his name. Apparently, he's never at his happiest in the stable, and bolts for the field any chance he gets in any kind of weather. But it's more of a nuisance. He's always come right back."

Erin patted Raven's head and stroked her mane. "You stick with me, kiddo. You want adventure? Well, so do I, and we'll have a bunch of adventures together. But no running off."

"Did she get what you said?" Liam asked.

"I'm pretty sure she did," Erin said, not missing a beat. "Maybe not all the words, but horses get your message in their own special way."

Liam nodded like he understood Erin's meaning, and maybe he did. But Mack was only listening with one ear. He couldn't take his thoughts off Fielder roaming around the area on his own. If that horse could find his way home, then the sooner the better. More snow was predicted for Sunday.

"Fielder has been gone for a few days, so the outlook isn't great." Jeff shook his head and tsked in regretful concern. As if deliberately changing the subject, he blurted a question to Erin about her work at the mansion.

Mack was curious, too, but the rest of the group arrived before she got beyond a superficial answer. Olivia and Jillian came out to greet him and Liam, and were closely followed by the Burton twins and Clark's son racing toward the stable. When Mack had first arrived in Adelaide Creek, he primarily relied on Willow, and later, Tom, to fill in facts and details about local people. Early on, he'd met Jeff's younger sister, Heather Stanhope-Burton, the nurse practitioner in Tom's office.

Heather and Jeff each had a family now, and through their history with other families with deep roots in the area, they had an intricate and sometimes confusing network of cross-connections. Heather was married to Matt Burton, the person who had bought the sheep ranch that had once been worked by several generations of Stanhopes. He'd also adopted his late sister's twins, and so had Heather.

Sometimes, Mack could be a little envious

of the way so many local people's lives intertwined. Erin also admitted similar feelings about the town's close-knit families sharing so much history. Many of these friends had gone to school together, and as adults, now their kids were classmates—or family. They all volunteered at various town events and were guests at each other's weddings and birthday parties and Sunday barbecues. The possibility of building these kinds of relationships was precisely what had attracted him to Adelaide Creek in the first place.

"Aren't you glad you're here for the sleigh ride, Erin?" Liam asked. "Dad remembered that you'd said you might have to work and miss it."

For a couple of seconds, Erin looked a little blank. Mack scoffed. So she'd forgotten she'd used work as an excuse to refuse his offer of a ride. She recovered quickly, though, and nodded at Liam. Seeing her affectionate smile directed to Liam, Mack felt a little foolish analyzing Erin's reasons for doing anything. None of his business, end of story.

"Did I tell you I'm going to learn to ride, Erin?" Liam asked. "My dad asked Jeff to teach me, and then we'll be able to ride around here together. Maybe I'll ride Dot."

Liam gave Dot some attention and then scampered away behind Jillian and the other kids at the other end of the stable, where they watched Jeff check every piece of hardware on the sleigh and the harness.

Standing alone with Erin, Mack observed the scene unfolding as the kids hovered around Jeff. Liam and the twins might as well have been on springs the way they were bouncing up and down. Happy and playful. "It makes me happy to see him with other kids," Mack said. "He was excited about a sleigh ride, but I think the real draw is the chance to be around his new friends—and you."

Erin nodded. "He's a content boy right now, isn't he?"

Mack crossed his arms over his chest and widened his stance. "The psychologist I take him to thinks he'll adjust faster if I keep him busy and give him lots of anchors in his life. But then, this parenting business is still new to me."

Erin didn't react one way or the other. It was as if she was waiting for more information.

"As I'm sure you've heard, Liam lived across the state with his mom before she died, so I… didn't know my son all that well…" He fished around for the right words to explain what he now regretted blundering into. "Let's just say I'm learning as I go."

Erin's expression darkened, but she looked

away and put additional inches between them. "Liam seems pretty well-adjusted, especially considering what he's been through. But I suppose it's going to take a while to get over such an enormous loss." She looked at him with eyes that saw right through him. "As for what I've heard, all I can say is not much. Only that Liam's mom died last fall and you moved here to make a new home with your little boy. I never thought that was gossip."

Then what caused the fire in Erin's deep and dark brown eyes? She fidgeted with the sleeves of her jacket, shifted her posture again. Lifting her chin a notch, she said, "I lost my mom last year. I'm an adult, and I still miss her every day." She raised one shoulder in a quick shrug. "It may take Liam a long time to fully accept what's happened."

How long? That question scared Mack. "Yes, you and Dr. Harte—and everyone else I know—agree on that."

Olivia's voice broke through Mack's thoughts and the noise of kids at the other end of the stable. "All aboard. The Stanhope sleigh is departing in five minutes."

Carson, Jeff's teenager, was making a video as the kids left the horses and scrambled to the sleigh. They hammed it up for Carson, who aimed his handheld video camera at them until all passengers were settled in the sleigh.

Mack had seen Carson's videos of events at the lodge. They were more than good enough to dress up sections of the Tall Tale website. He followed Erin into the sleigh, but she maneuvered to get to the other side of Willow, who had Naomi in her lap. Puzzled, Mack claimed the empty spot next to Heather. All the kids grouped themselves behind Olivia and Jeff, who sat together up front in the driver's seat. Carson closed the back panel and gave it a thump, his signal that Jeff could get the sleigh moving. The teen was staying behind at the reception building to handle check-ins and checkouts. According to Jeff, Carson, who'd spent his first fourteen years in Seattle, had zero interest in horses and sleigh rides. He'd given his heart to his dog Winnie, making his movies and basketball. He was only too happy to stay behind and mind the store.

When the bells on the horses and those attached to the side of the sleigh started tinkling, Nick, one of the twins, started singing "Jingle Bells," and the other kids and most of the adults joined in.

Except for Erin, who sat still with a pasted-on smile.

Mack did a quick recap of the conversation

they'd just had at the stables and the one before
that at the mansion. He was looking for clues
as to what had changed Erin's mood. Her expression was flat. Her only genuine smile was
for the kids, especially Naomi, who reached
over from Willow's lap to nudge Erin to get
her attention.

To distract himself, Mack chatted with
Heather. She filled him in about living on the
same ranch that she and Jeff grew up on, but
then lost in a foreclosure. She glowed when she
described the thrill of becoming the mother of
Nick and Lucy, Matt's adopted twins. Then,
like the icing on the cake, her brother Jeff came
back to town and fell in love with one of her
best friends. "With our parents gone, it was just
the two of us, and now we each have a partner
and two kids apiece." Heather laughed as she
added, "So far."

"I've heard bits and pieces of a lot of stories
about big extended families in town. Like the
Lancasters," Mack said. "I like it here, and lucky
for me, my boy does, too." He glanced at Erin,
whose faraway but troubled expression wasn't
focused on anything in particular.

Heather followed his gaze. "Speaking of family, my boss, Tom, couldn't have been more
shocked last year when Erin showed up in her
painted van with her golden retriever, claiming
to be his sister." Heather chuckled. "Tom and

Erin actually look like they could be fraternal twins, don't they?"

Mack agreed. "I learned that part of Erin and Tom's story because I work with Willow at Tall Tale." Heather pointed out landmarks to Mack, outcroppings and ridges in the distance. She also filled in information about a couple of her mother's paintings that Jen Hoover had hung in the bunkhouse. She pointed to the edge of some deep woods that ultimately led to Addie Creek. "Once you and Liam are ready to ride together, we'll tell you how to find our favorite trails."

Mack enjoyed the little jolt of pleasure that came from thinking about riding again, especially the vision of having Liam grow up around horses and exploring these trails together. "It won't be long before he'll have a horse of his own, and so will I. This is exactly the kind of life I want for him." Underneath that statement of fact, Mack heard the whisper of longing in his voice.

"Well then, lucky Liam." Heather fell silent, but when she spoke again, her voice was low, as if confiding a secret. "I keep wondering about Fielder, and the other horse that came home. When I was a girl, people used to tell stories about horse rustling in the old days."

"Did it happen often?" Mack asked.

"Not really, but the stories about it had become part of the lore of the county," Heather said. "In the old days, it was harder to catch rustlers, and a few became legendary."

"What do you mean?"

"Oh, back when my parents were kids, if a horse ran away, people would claim that it was the work of old Woody Johnson, a real guy."

"An actual horse rustler?" Mack asked.

Heather nodded. "But not at all typical. For one thing, Woody worked alone, unlike the guys you'd call career rustlers. Woody got caught but never admitted he stole the horses."

"No confession?"

She shook her head. "Nope. Woody insisted that all he had to do was look at horses and they'd choose to follow him."

Having grown up hearing a lot of Wyoming lore, Mack could almost fill in the rest.

"When a horse ran away," Heather said, "people would say that the ghost of Woody paid a visit. It was a way to explain why a particular horse would disappear one day and show up the next." Heather's expression darkened. "The thing is, horses don't wander away this time of year."

"Right. And Fielder hasn't come back." It was obvious to Mack that Heather wasn't treating the horse's disappearance as the stuff of old legends.

They were close to the point where the flat road ended just as the sun broke through the cloud cover. Bright rays reflected off the snow that topped the rows of pines lining the side of the road. Jeff maneuvered the sleigh to make a wide circle, and they retraced the route home. Even the kids quieted down as the sleigh returned to the plowed path on Jeff's field. Looking at Liam, Mack saw how the gentle, rhythmic rocking of the sleigh lulled him. Liam might have fallen asleep if they hadn't reached the stable, at which point Olivia announced that there'd be hot chocolate for everyone in the reception building.

Liam ran ahead with the twins and Jillian, and Mack held the door for the rest of the adults to follow. All but Erin. Already in her van, she was headed down the drive to the road.

"Looks like she's in a hurry." Tom flashed a quizzical look. "Maybe she wanted to go back to the O'Connor place and get more work in. Or maybe she needs to take Neptune out."

"I guess," Mack said, but he didn't believe it. Maybe Tom had been too busy with Willow and Naomi to notice, but his sister had kept her distance, not just from Mack, but from everybody except the kids. In the short time Mack had known her, he hadn't seen her fall silent or withdraw from anyone. He couldn't shake the notion that her rapid departure had something to do with him.

CHAPTER FOUR

"COME ON UP, NEPTUNE." Erin patted the couch cushion a couple of times. The lively retriever immediately accepted the invitation to jump up and join her. He made a complete circle on the cushion before he plopped down, curled up and rested his back against her thigh. "That's right, make yourself comfortable, Neptune."

Even before Erin opened the photo album, pressure was building behind her eyes. She both welcomed and dreaded the tears that were not only coming but needed to be shed. Her mother had been gone over a year, but every now and then, something triggered bouts of grief that threatened to overwhelm her. Today was one of those days.

Erin stored numerous photos chronicling her life on her laptop, but sometimes, when the ache over losing her mother felt new and fresh, only holding the album in her hands would do. Turning the pages, Erin stopped on a picture of her mom, a favorite because it had been such a happy day. Wearing snug jeans and a flattering red turtleneck, her mom was perched on top of a picnic table in the park. Erin was about twelve when she'd taken the photo on the day Mom had accepted the job offer as the head of housekeeping at a newly opened hotel.

This particular job offer was a cause for celebration because it was in the Ohio town where they'd lived for two years, so for once they didn't need to move again. Her mom was especially happy because the higher salary meant they could get a nicer apartment—maybe even rent a small house. That job had been great while it lasted, almost two years to the day. Then the hotel had closed, and Indiana was their next destination.

Erin had displayed this photo at her mom's memorial service. Most of the people who showed up to pay their respects were staff from her mom's last position in the Indiana town they'd settled down in. It was the place her mom first got sick, and where Erin had gone to community college and discovered her passion for restoration when she apprenticed with a master woodworker. She'd lived in her own apartment, but when her mom's cancer returned with a vengeance, she moved back home to help her through her last year.

Almost every guest at the memorial service remarked on how much Erin resembled Roberta, her mom. They shared the same wide smile and petite body. But Erin had inherited her dark hair and eyes from the father she'd never known. Still, she smiled at the memory of her mom complaining about her thin hair that couldn't quite decide if it was dark blond or light brown.

Erin scratched the dog's head and slid her hand down his back. "No sense fighting the tears, Neptune." The dog's ears twitched at the sound of his name. Erin swiped her fingertips across her wet cheeks. She touched her mom's image in the photo and whispered, "I still miss you so, so much."

When she closed her eyes and rested her head on the back of the couch, an image of Liam came to mind. It didn't take a professional like Liam's therapist, Dr. Harte, to figure out why the boy triggered tender feelings. She'd been a grown woman with her own career when her mom died. Liam had to accept a big and profound loss, but also get used to being with a dad, who apparently hadn't been much of a dad at all. And this realization was the cause of her restlessness and agitation that was edging close to anger. As usual, the bulk of her negative feelings were reserved for her mystery father, but even more confusing, she found herself impatient with Mack, as if he'd done something to offend her.

Eventually, Erin closed the album and put it aside. When she got to her feet, Neptune stirred and padded behind her to the kitchen. She pulled out flour, sugar, molasses and spices from one cabinet and mixing bowls and cookie sheets from another. Hmm…she had enough eggs and butter to make two batches. Her mom's voice echoed in her head: *When you don't know what to do next, Erin, bake cookies… It's the quickest cure for a troubled mind.*

It had been a while since she'd needed to take her mom's advice, but it was true there was something soothing about measuring the flour and spices, creaming the butter and adding the fragrant molasses. When she'd blended the ingredients and turned them into a ball of dough, she pulled off sections and rolled them out flat on her cutting board. Then she used her cookie cutters to make stars and quarter moons. She'd swing by Willow and Tom's house to drop off some cookies. Naomi in particular liked the sweetness of molasses. Liam was still on her mind. And Mack.

As the scent of the molasses wafted through the cabin, her mood lifted, or maybe, like magic, the simple act of baking cookies had mellowed her heart. Whatever the reason for the internal shift, she took it as a sign and regretted leaving Jeff's sleigh ride party so abruptly. It wasn't like her not to say goodbye, but that was what she'd done. Feeling contrite, she texted Mack that she'd had the urge to bake molasses cookies and had set aside some for him and Liam. He could swing by to pick them up later, or she could drop them off the next day.

Barely a minute passed before he texted back. If she welcomed the company, he'd stop by. He added that Liam always liked seeing her. She smiled at those words. She felt the same way about Liam. Her feelings about Mack were complicated, although he was undeniably fun to be around. She'd observed that the night she met him. And who wouldn't want to look deep into those eyes? But then she'd dip into irrational suspicion of what he was really like, when in fact she knew almost nothing about his past. Except what he'd told her before the sleigh ride.

After texting a thumbs-up, she pulled the last cookie sheet out of the oven and moved the rich brown stars and half moons to the cooling rack. She got out a container to fill and send home with Liam. Her heart clipped along a little faster. She wrote that off as the natural anticipation of expecting company in her home, and not specifically about Mack and Liam showing up at the door.

Relief washed over her, too, when her irritation at Mack gradually dissipated. Her mother never tried to justify her father's abandonment, but neither had she lived from a harsh, judgmental place. Erin herself had picked up the weight of negativity about her dad and carried it for any man who ditched his family. In the last decade or so, the realities of her mother's struggle to give her the best life she could manage had had a lasting effect on Erin, and she knew it. Erin washed her hands and exchanged her flour-smudged pullover for a fresh sweater. A cheerful red one. She ran a brush through her hair and secured it in a French braid to keep it off her face. Almost as an afterthought, she ran some gloss across her lips. She smiled at herself in the mirror and said, "Ready for company," at the same time she heard the knock on the door.

When she opened the front door, the first thing she saw was Liam holding a bunch of daisies. He thrust the bouquet toward her, and she lifted it from his hands. "Why, thank you, Liam. These are beautiful. And it isn't even spring." When she stepped aside so they could come in, Neptune greeted Liam in his own shoe-sniffing way. Then the dog thrust his head under the boy's hand to send a message that he wanted a pat or two. She looked up at Mack, who was already watching her. The softness in his eyes threw her off-center and she shifted her gaze back to Liam.

"The lady at the gas station store said the flowers came from far, far away where it's warmer. Like summer." As he spoke, Liam affectionately stroked Neptune's head. "Right, Dad?"

"Yep, that's what she said," Mack agreed, "and she was down to her last two bunches. We got there just in time, didn't we, buddy?"

"The flowers are a lovely surprise," Erin said. "Come into the kitchen and I'll find a vase." She grinned and raised her eyebrows at Liam. "My vase is really a huge pickle jar Dr. Tom left behind when he moved to Willow's house. And I'll need to ask your dad to reach the top shelf and get it down for me while I get you a glass of milk."

"Whatever you need," Mack said with a widening smile.

Liam sniffed and scrunched his face as he followed her to the kitchen with Neptune at his side. "Your house smells nice."

"Well, dontcha know that's half the reason I make molasses cookies." Erin poured milk for Liam and then started filling the well of the coffeepot. "It's a scientific fact that really good smells can make you feel really good, too." As she talked, she pointed to an open shelf above the counter, where the giant glass jar sat way out of her reach. It had been up there so long it was probably dusty, but that didn't matter.

"What's the other half?" Liam asked, his expression quizzical.

"What was that?" Erin asked, wondering what she'd missed.

"I mean, what's the other half of why you bake cookies?"

Amused by Liam's take on her figure of speech, Erin gave a simple answer. "That's easy. It's because they taste so good. Rich and sweet." She pointed to the stools at the breakfast bar. "Take off your jackets and have a seat." While the coffee brewed, she arranged the daisies in the jar, placed it at one end of the bar, and put out coffee mugs and napkins at the other.

"Thanks for thinking of us," Mack said. "Your text was completely unexpected. You headed out so quickly from Jeff and Olivia's today we didn't get a chance to say goodbye."

She dismissively swatted the air. "I had a couple of things I wanted to get to. I'll tell you about it sometime." She nodded at Liam and then gave Mack a pointed look in hopes he'd pick up on her message that she didn't want to talk about it just then. At least not in front of Liam.

Typically, she didn't mind describing her mom and their life together to other people. To really know Erin, understanding her mother's story was important. It was a way to get a glimpse into what Erin herself valued in a person—and in life—and why. She'd thought of her mom as a heroic person. Not just because of the way she'd raised Erin to stand on her own, but because she'd found a way to be happy despite hardships. Her courage during her final year had inspired Erin. Creating a rewarding life was the best way she could honor Roberta's life—not only her role as a mom, but all of her life.

It took only a couple of minutes to get the treats on the table and pour the steaming coffee into mugs. "I don't think I was conscious of the time." She nodded toward the window and the darkening gray sky with bursts of violet pushing through the clouds. "The day passed so quickly."

Liam sat up a little straighter and puffed out his chest. "Dad cut one of his old T-shirts into pieces and gave one to me. I helped get all the dust off the furniture. The living room was kind of messy."

Mack laughed. "Uh-oh, you're spilling our secrets."

As if he hadn't heard his dad, Liam kept talking. "We had to clean up because my grandpa

Patrick and Aunt Gayle are coming to visit. We have to make sure our house is clean enough."

Mack snorted. "Li…am."

"That should be fun." Erin said, pushing the plate toward Liam while she smiled at Mack. "I think I get what you mean, Liam. We all clean up a little when people are coming for a visit. And help yourself to the cookies. I've got a bunch ready for you to take home, too."

"I don't remember Grandpa Patrick," Liam said with a quick shrug. "I used to see my other grandma and grandpa all the time." As if an afterthought, the boy decided to say out loud, "When my mom died, they wanted me to live with them."

Mack and Erin exchanged a quick look. Then he cleared his throat. "Uh, my dad and my sister will be here in March." He turned to Liam. "The end of next week," he said, rolling right past Liam's statement. "We spent a day up in my hometown, Rock Bridge, at Christmas. This will be a longer visit. Your grandpa and your aunt will have time to get to know you better now."

Liam nodded in a noncommittal way, as if none of this was especially important.

"I reserved a suite at the lodge," Mack said, "so they'll have room to spread out for a few days. They can use the gym and the pool."

"Our bunkhouse is too small to hold more people. Dad and I would have to sleep on the floor," Liam explained. "We're going to a play. I've never been to one before."

"A play? You don't say?" A memory of seeing high school kids do a performance of *Snow White* for the grade school rushed in. She'd been about Liam's age and hadn't stopped talking about it for weeks after. The skillfully crafted forest backdrop impressed Erin so much she volunteered for the scenery and props committee in the drama class in high school.

"The kids' theater at the Children's Adventure Center is hosting it," Mack said. "All the actors and production crew are local junior high and high school kids. They're doing a trio of one-act fairy tales."

"No kidding. Very exciting, Liam. And something fun to do with your guests." Even without knowing the whole of Mack's family story, Erin could see he was carefully managing this getting-to-know-you visit.

Liam nodded, but his attention shifted to Neptune, who'd taken up residence next to Liam's stool and kept a watchful eye on him. "Doesn't Neptune get to eat cookies?"

"No, I'm pretty strict about having him stick to dog food and treats made specially for dogs," Erin said. "He's keeping his eye on you, Liam,

and that's his way of telling you he likes you."
Neptune chose that minute to decide to move
to his favorite spot in the living room.

"I like him, too," Liam mused, swinging his
legs while he chewed a cookie and watched
Neptune wander off. "We're going to get a dog
one day. And a horse…two horses," Liam said,
"one for me and one for Dad. And we're going
to find our own house."

Erin grinned at Mack. "I can hear echoes of
conversations the two of you must regularly
have. It's all in the timing, I suppose. That's
what buying Raven was all about. The time
was finally right."

"Did you know we're going to visit my other
grandparents, Grandma Eden and Grandpa
Louis, when it's warmer?" Liam's question signaled that his mind had wandered away from
horse conversation and onto something entirely
different. Suddenly, he took another cookie
from the plate, slid off the stool and headed
for the living room.

It took a couple of seconds for Erin to react,
but she left no room for doubt. "Uh, Liam, I
have a house rule. We don't take food into the
living room. You can sit over there at the table
if you'd like, or come back to the breakfast bar."

Liam stopped walking, but turned and stared
at Erin. "I want to go where Neptune is."

Erin patted the breakfast bar. "That's fine, honey, but put the rest of the cookie here on the napkin first. You can finish it later."

Seconds ticked by. The boy didn't move.

"Liam? Did you hear what Erin said?" Mack ran his hand down the side of his face and along his jawline. "Her house, her rules."

Erin waited.

"Grandma Eden lets me eat in the living room." A deep frown hardened Liam's expression.

Erin wished she'd never opened her mouth. Tom had been clear about keeping food out of the living room and the bedrooms. His attempt to keep field mice and outdoor creatures away. Erin was fine with that, and it matched the rules she'd grown up with. More important, though, she needed to have Mack's back as he supported her stance without hesitation. "Everybody has different house rules, Liam. This one happens to be mine."

"Liam, come on back to the kitchen, buddy." Mack's voice was light, although Erin wondered how much effort it took to force that easy but firm tone.

"I want to go home." Tears filled Liam's eyes, and his face wrinkled, almost like a warning that this episode could escalate to a serious bout of crying. He turned away, trying to hide his face.

"I'm sorry," Erin whispered to Mack.

"No need to apologize. It's not your fault, Erin." Mack got up and picked up Liam, who at first squirmed to try to get away, but Mack tightened his arms around him. The boy sobbed into his dad's shoulder. Mack gently took the cookie from Liam's fingers, and Erin put out her palm to take it. "I think you're overtired. It's been a big day. Happens to the best of us, son."

Erin handed Mack the boy's jacket. When Mack slid Liam down and out of his arms to the floor, the boy pressed his face against Mack's leg. Mack managed to get Liam into his jacket and then slipped into his own. Erin handed him the container of cookies and held the door open for him.

Mack mouthed *thank you* as he went down the stairs.

"See you soon, Liam." Erin couldn't think of anything else to say. The boy's tears brought pressure behind her own eyes. She didn't trust herself to even glance at Mack. The boy had touched the place where her own heart had cracks.

By the time she cleaned up the counter and took Neptune for a walk to the ridge, she was ready to call it a day with hot soup and a good long soak in the tub. Then she propped herself up in bed and tried to concentrate on the cozy mystery she'd started reading the night before. She got out of bed when she realized she'd read the same page a couple of times but hadn't absorbed any of it. She turned on the TV and was still trying to wind down when Mack's text came in.

L sleeping...not sure what happened

Erin stared at the text and smiled sadly. She felt guilty, as if the meltdown was her fault. Or maybe her melancholy mood came from imagining how confused Liam must be about his life sometimes. Not sure what to text in response to Mack, she thanked him for letting her know and left it at that. In her heart, though, she hoped Liam wouldn't try to avoid her now out of embarrassment. She enjoyed being around that little boy. And his dad.

CHAPTER FIVE

LIAM ADJUSTED HIS new cowboy hat, a present from his aunt Gayle, and ran a little ways down Buffalo Street ahead of Mack and their company. Day two of the visit. So far so good. Not too many cranky moments, but some puzzling ones. Liam's mild whining was sort of new, like balking at bedtime or dragging his feet coming to the table when Mack called him. Not typical behavior for the boy. Expected, though. At least according to Dr. Harte. Mack had described the unexpected meltdown at Erin's house over something as ordinary as a simple rule. She believed Liam was bound to begin testing limits and boundaries, even with someone like Erin, who freely offered her affection. All of it was normal and happening in its own time, the therapist assured Mack. He understood that in his head, but his feelings hadn't caught up. When Liam was upset, so was Mack.

So far on their day in Landrum, they'd done

a little shopping and had lunch and were on their way to the Children's Adventure Center to see the play. And, Liam bragged, play with the legendary trains.

"My grandson seems just fine," Patrick said when Liam had walked ahead with Gayle. He gave Mack an approving nod. "Doesn't seem any the worse for wear."

"Thanks, Dad." *Worse for wear* wasn't an expression Mack would have used, but he understood what his father meant and breathed a little easier. As much as he'd wanted Liam to get to know his grandpa and his aunt, Mack had been on edge. He couldn't shake the feeling he was trapped in a hot, stuffy room taking a test that he hadn't crammed for. He'd either pass or fail. For him the question loomed: Could he prove to his father that he could be a good dad?

That question had rambled around in his mind day in, day out. Even in the absence of outright criticism, he defensively reminded himself he was new at this, but had a list of tests he'd passed so far: good school, a therapist, a comfy home, plus a regular schedule with set mealtimes and bedtime rituals. Instead of making him feel better, defending himself only called attention to the reality that six months ago, he barely knew his son. The reality of that abandonment could get pushed down in the day-to-day details of his life with Liam, but it was never far from Mack's consciousness.

When Liam ran ahead of Gayle to look at the games in the bookstore window, she sidled up to Mack and offered her take. "He's happy one minute and clinging to you the next. Or rebelling a little bit."

"Hey, come on," Patrick said, casting a disapproving look at Gayle. "The boy's world turned upside down. A little rebellion can be a good thing. It means he's feeling sure of you, Mack."

Mack nodded at the affirmation of Dr. Harte's opinion.

Gayle didn't respond in words, but the skeptical lift of her eyebrows made her feelings clear. Liam had moved down the street, called out to Gayle and pointed to the sheep and cattle sculptures in front of the County Gallery. The trio picked up their pace so Gayle could have a look.

As it turned out, Liam had a lot to say to his aunt about all kinds of things. "You know all those sheep on the ranch where our bunkhouse is…" Liam said when Gayle joined him. "Mrs. Hoover sells wool to people who make stuff with it. She has spinning wheels. Three of 'em." He held up three fingers as if to prove the point. "We have lots of friends who live on ranches." Suddenly he pointed down the street with one hand and pulled on Mack's sleeve with the other. "Dad, Dad, look! It's Erin."

"So it is." Mack smiled when Erin's face lit up at the sight of Liam. He hadn't seen her since they'd left her house with a container of cookies and an upset boy who fell asleep in the car. They'd exchanged a few friendly texts, though.

"She's our friend, Aunt Gayle," Liam said. "She bakes cookies and makes ham sandwiches. Right, Dad?"

Mack laughed as Erin joined their group and introduced herself, forgoing handshakes since she had a shopping bag in each hand.

"I'm guessing you're having a good visit with your grandpa and your aunt." Erin switched one shopping bag to her other hand so she could give the brim of Liam's new hat a quick tug. "Cool hat." She patted the top of her signature Stetson. "I like hats, too."

"Thanks. Aunt Gayle got it for me. We had burgers for lunch, and now we're going to see the play." Once again he held up three fingers. "They're going to tell three stories."

"I remember you telling me about that," Erin said, smiling at the adults as she interacted with Liam.

"If you're free, it would be great if you could come with us," Mack said, his spontaneous invitation surprising him as much as it did his dad. Gayle frowned as if puzzled. But for Mack, it was as if the other minor meltdown incident hadn't even happened. Liam hadn't shied away from greeting Erin, a good sign.

Liam's eyes opened wide, and he hopped on one foot and then the other. "Say yes, Erin, *please.*"

Mack thrust both hands out as if presenting Liam. "Now, how can you say no after that?" He'd enjoy having her along, and not only because of Liam. Somehow, his new friendship with Erin proved that his life was working. He had friends—a growing circle of them. He and Erin, both new in town, had mutual connections that provided a community in common. "I'll get you a ticket at the door."

Erin's dark eyes sparkled a little when she met his gaze. "I'd like that a lot." She patted Liam's shoulder. "Thanks so much for inviting me to tag along."

Liam looked at Mack before he said a polite, "You're welcome."

"There's a boy with some fine manners," Patrick said, beaming.

With Liam again running slightly ahead, the four of them walked the half block to the Adventure Center. Mack gave his dad and sister an abbreviated version of how they happened to know Erin through their connection with Willow, and by association, Dr. Tom. He added a tidbit about her performing with Tom at the kids' Halloween party.

Erin opened her arms to the side and lifted her hands. "A year ago, I didn't know I had a brother, and now I'm a part of his new family. Mack and I happen to have lots of mutual friends," Erin said, "but then, that's true for most everyone in Adelaide Creek."

Liam followed Mack when he went to the counter where other parents were buying tickets to the play. "See? Because of you, Liam, Erin is making more new friends."

Liam lowered his gaze and stared at his shoes. "Is she mad at me?" he whispered.

Mack winced against the worry in Liam's voice. He quickly paid for the ticket and then drew Liam aside. He crouched down in front of him and put his hands on his shoulders. "She was never mad at you. But she was right to stick to her rules." He tilted his head to the side and gave Liam a teasing smile. "But that's in the past. Erin was really happy to see you today."

The frown stayed in place. "How do you know that?"

"Because the minute she noticed you, she smiled at you—it was a big, happy smile." Mack squeezed Liam's hand. "She's our good friend. One day, when we're back at her house, you can tell her that, just like at school, you respect her rules. Will you do that?"

Liam nodded and then lifted his head. His frown had vanished.

"Come on, let's go find some seats with a good view of the stage." He nodded toward Gayle and Erin. "I see that my sister and Erin have their heads together and apparently have a lot to say." The two women were talking as if they'd known each other for years. As he approached, his dad was reading the brochure for the play, complete with photos of the cast.

As they entered the auditorium, Gayle touched Mack's arm and let the others go ahead. "Erin seems quite nice and is obviously fond of Liam," she whispered. "Why didn't you say something about having a girlfriend?"

"Because it's not true. We're not dating or anything." Heat traveled from the back of Mack's neck to his face, but he couldn't explain why he'd be that self-conscious.

Gayle frowned. "Really? She seems so at home with Liam." She raised her eyebrows again. "And with you."

"That's just because of the time we've spent together in casual ways," Mack said. "I told you about the reopening of the town hall and the sleigh ride. Last week we picked up some cookies she baked for Liam. That's all."

Gayle gave him a sly smile. "If you say so. It seemed a little…uh, too soon to bring a woman into Liam's life, anyway." Not waiting for Mack's response, Gayle went down the aisle, where his dad was standing and waving at them.

Mack hadn't seen that coming. Too preoccupied to give it much thought, he brushed off the remark. He wasn't sure what he'd say, anyway. The auditorium was filled with the sound of kids shouting to each other and their parents shushing them and telling them to settle down. Mack positioned Liam next to him with Patrick on the other side. Erin was on the end next to Gayle. Like magic, everyone quieted when the lights dimmed and the curtain rose.

From the start, Mack got a kick out of the young performers. They were as good as pros. In the first play, Rapunzel was a convincing girl trapped in the tower against her will. The prince was old enough that his voice had begun to change. When the young actor spoke the classic line, "Rapunzel, Rapunzel, let down your hair," Liam sat up a little straighter as the princess unwound her thick blond braid and let it drop several feet.

Mack smiled to himself, thinking of the way Liam used the video game in Dr. Harte's office to make up stories about families living inside bubbles on Mars. Now this old fairy tale swept up his seven-year-old and carried him off to this well-done make-believe world. From the start, Mack noticed Liam's active imagination, his craving for stories. Thanks to Paula. Eden and Louis had shared memories about Liam's regular treks to the library with them and story hour marked on the weekly calendar.

"*Little Red Riding Hood* is next up," Patrick told Liam when the applause died down at the end of *Rapunzel*. The lights came up, and the curtain closed while the kids changed the set.

"I know that one, too," Liam said. Then he leaned across Patrick and Gayle. "Hey, Erin, Rapunzel has even longer hair than you."

Erin laughed lightly and formed a big circle with her hands. "And her braid is that thick, huh?"

"I think it's a wig," Liam said knowingly.

Erin feigned a deep-in-thought expression that amused Mack as he looked on. "You could be right about that," she said.

"Told ya," Liam said as the lights dimmed.

The deep woods of the set stayed the same, but instead of a tower, a little painted house was visible in the distance. Grandma's house, Mack assumed. *Little Red Riding Hood* was about half the length of *Rapunzel*, and when it was over, it took only a couple of minutes to raise the curtain on *Hansel and Gretel*.

Mack found the perils of *Hansel and Gretel* a little scarier than the other two stories, but Liam didn't seem to notice, at least at first. The combination of hungry kids and a witch that lures them into her house with food brought a couple of gasps from the audience of kids when it was clear the witch didn't intend to let them go. Liam also gasped when the witch pointed to the big oven. Every time Mack checked, Liam's gaze was fixed on the stage. He barely moved until the curtain closed. Mack got to his feet with everyone in the auditorium. They rewarded the young actors and their production crew a standing ovation.

"I didn't *think* the witch would eat the kids this time," Liam confided to Mack when the applause died down. "When Mom read me that story, Hansel and Gretel escaped, so I knew what happened. I liked *Rapunzel* best of all."

"I liked that one best, too," Mack said, reminded that Liam's memories of his mother could pop up under almost any circumstances and at unexpected moments.

Patrick found Liam's enthusiasm for the production contagious, and the two of them were soon chatting about the cool costumes and the scary forest that was part of all three plays.

"I admit it. I didn't expect the acting to be so

good," Gayle said. "Only a couple of glitches with remembering lines."

"It wouldn't have occurred to me to get myself a ticket to see a schoolkids' play. My mistake," Erin said. "This was fun." She beamed at Mack and then Liam. "I'm so glad you and your dad invited me, Liam."

Liam responded with a shy smile.

Mack and Erin followed the other three out to the lobby. Liam grabbed Patrick's hand and pulled him toward the enormous interactive train display spanning the far end of the open area by the wall of glass that was the front window. Dr. Harte's modern video game was for telling stories about the present and the future, but this model train, almost as big as a room, was about yesterday. With the landscape of mountains and pastures, the trains chugged along and blew their whistles as they crossed bridges and disappeared through tunnels. Old-fashioned boxcars were piled high at one end, and passengers were lined up waiting to board the train on the platform at the depot on the other.

"Talk about bells and whistles," Mack said to Erin and Gayle. He stood a few steps behind his dad and Liam and observed his dad's gentle ways with the boy. His dad's expression was both soft and curious as he encouraged Liam to see what the controls could do.

"Hey, Dad," Liam called over his shoulder, "look at the tunnels—you can't see through them. You know, like the ones I put on Mars in the game." Then he pointed to a corral filled with horses. "See? The train passes close to the corral. You can see the people in the windows waving to the horses."

"They're like the real thing, kiddo." Clever, Mack thought, noting realistic colors and sizes of the breeds of horses—and the cattle and sheep on the miniature ranches. The animals were detailed, textured, like everything else in the display. Mack stayed a few steps away while his dad showed Liam the buttons he could press to lower the gates to bring the traveling cars to a stop. Other kids were watching a train cross over a river with boats and barges they could move along.

Mack hadn't been directly involved, but Tall Tale Lodge had been one of the founding sponsors for the Children's Adventure Center. For him, it had been an afterthought, since Sydney stepped up to be their lodge's representative on the board. She'd taken to referring to it as CAC in staff memos and reports, and Willow made sure everything the lodge did to support the CAC made it into press releases and the

CAC's fundraising campaigns. Mack scanned the first floor, impressed. The place opened for the weekends around the first of the year. It was only March, and the staff was already able to draw a crowd to a play. Classroom trips were scheduled to start in April.

Mack's business mind began to come up with new partnering ideas for Tall Tale and the CAC. He made a note to talk with Willow about it.

"Speaking of horses," Erin said, interrupting his line of thought, "did you hear that another horse went missing?" Then she scoffed. "Why am I whispering? It's not like it's a secret. So far, the second runaway horse found his way home, but not the first one, Fielder. Now another one is on the loose."

Erin stared off into the room, as if thinking hard about something. "Apparently, the owner has a ranch that's kind of remote. From what Quincy told me, the guy has had a few runaways before. Maybe his place isn't as secure as Jeff's or the Burtons' ranch."

Mack peered into Erin's face. "You look concerned. What are you saying?"

"Quincy thought it was possible someone tried to steal the second horse, and it got away and found its way back home," Erin said. "Maybe the rustlers will try again nearby. Like at Jeff's place." Still frowning, she added, "This latest missing horse has increased my worries about Raven. I mean, if Quincy is right, then Heather's and Matt's horses would be at risk, and a lot of others, too. Jeff's tried to reassure me, but although he admits he's concerned, he still thinks it's highly unlikely anyone would break into his stable."

Despite Mack and Andy owning holiday ranches, horse rustlers had never been on top of a list of their major concerns. "Unlikely? Why would he say that?"

"Apparently, real horse rustlers don't target one horse here, another there. They devise large-scale schemes, herding horses away, crossing state lines to deliver them for pre-arranged sales," Erin explained. "And there's not that much of it going on these days. With cell phones and the internet, it's too easy to get caught."

Mack had more questions, but Liam's voice interrupted his thoughts. "Hey, Dad, Grandpa Patrick said his grandfather took a train from Indiana to Casper a long, long time ago. That's why we're a Wyoming family."

"You don't say?" Erin said. "Indiana is where I came from, and now I'm part of a Wyoming family, too."

Erin stepped closer to the padded rail that encircled the train. "Show me what you're doing here."

When Gayle moved alongside Mack, he said, "Liam's having a good day, huh?"

Gayle shrugged. "Keeping him busy. No whining."

Mack tried to squelch his rising irritation, but failed. Instead, he bristled. "He's not typically a whiny kid, Gayle, so don't refer to him that way."

"Oh, stop...you're doing a good job, given all the circumstances," Gayle said. "You can't expect him to behave all the time, no matter what you do. He's seven years old, and look at all he's been through."

Mack's defenses snapped into place. Gayle had strongly disapproved of him for essentially surrendering his son to Paula. She warned him he'd regret it and had been angry at Mack for not waging a fight for his rights as a father to coparent his son. Gayle had been vocal and blunt. *And one hundred percent right.*

Gayle was also a little too smug. He and his sister hadn't hashed this out, and although the timing was off, he wasn't inclined to let it go. *All he's been through* encompassed a lot. "Do you need to hear me admit—again—that you were right almost eight years ago?" Mack challenged in a tone meant for her ears only. "Don't you think I know what a huge mistake I made? I'm paying for it, too."

With her eyes widening, Gayle nodded. "Of course you're paying the price. But Liam is paying a bigger one. That's all I'm saying. If he acts up a little now and then, so what?"

Mack scanned the area around him, catching the eye of one of Tall Tale's employees from the food service department. He gave him a casual wave, hoping the employee hadn't noticed the less than friendly exchange with his sister. Meanwhile, his dad, his son, and Erin had moved to another spot, this one with controls that let them use cranes to load freight onto an empty river barge. "Uh, let's not talk about this here." Mack sighed. "I can't change the past. And my child needs a good parent now. That's what I'm trying to be."

Gayle's expression softened. "You *are*. You're all he's got." She offered a conciliatory smile. "Don't forget Dad and I are here to help. And his other grandparents, too."

Standing side by side, he and Gayle observed the threesome at the rail. The sight of Liam in these moments when he was happy and absorbed in whatever he was doing gave Mack a little breathing room.

"Uh, Mack, I have a question for you."

No sense avoiding her. "Okay, Gayle, shoot."

"Are you sure Erin isn't hanging around looking for more than friendship from you?"

Mack didn't answer right away, but he watched Erin chatting with Patrick and Liam. She then shifted her attention to Liam, listening intently while he showed her how he could make a crane dump coal on the barge. The warmth in her exchanges with Liam—and Patrick—touched him. But he shook his head. "I don't think she's interested in me, if that's what you're asking." Aware that he was acknowledging Gayle's criticism of him, he went ahead anyway. "Erin and her half brother have their own stories about a father that didn't stick around." That was putting it mildly. "Neither one of them even met the guy."

"Oh, that's tough," Gayle said. "She seems so… I don't know what to call it exactly, but lively, fun. I was thinking…" She shrugged as her voice trailed off.

Awkwardly shifting his weight from one foot to the other, Mack filled in the blank to ward off Gayle's train of thought. "Try 'easy to be with.' She's ambitious, too, in a good way," Mack pointed out, noticing her long, pretty hair hanging loose down her back. She lifted her head to talk to Patrick, and even from her profile, he noted her wide smile. Without thinking about the implications, he murmured, "And beautiful."

He hadn't meant to garner sympathy from Gayle, but the look she gave him sent that message. He'd let down his guard, and Gayle saw right through him.

ERIN WAS PREPARED for the transition from winter to spring in Wyoming. She'd been warned to expect cold wind and blizzards followed by hints of the new season over the course of a balmy day here and there. *Balmy* being relative. Warm spells or cold ones were usually followed by rain. Brisk, cold storms could last for days. Sunny days, like this one, were a welcome surprise and a whispered promise of more to come. After spending her life in the Midwest, Erin brushed off weather complaints and warnings as nothing she wasn't used to. Despite the thick blanket of recent snow, Erin had decided to take advantage of the mild day and ride Raven along the open stretch of road from the stable toward the ridges. Patches of snow were melting, but the mostly white expanse glistened under the afternoon sun. It was much too early for a trail ride on the ridges, but it was a perfect moment to leave behind the mansion, where the air was stuffy with dust and grime. After giving Raven a little exercise and inhaling some invigorating fresh air, Erin had at least begun to settle her mind. Erin had left work immediately after meeting with Quincy, and the crew he'd assembled, to finalize a schedule. It had become clear to everyone involved that the renovation, including the massive woodworking portion, would be a yearlong project—at least. Stripping away years of old varnish on the woodwork and built-ins in every room was right up her alley. Even knowing she'd lucked into an opportunity not easy to come by, the notion of supervising a crew of workers and delegating their daily jobs loomed as a daunting undertaking. Or, more to the point, it rocked her confidence. After an hour with Raven, though, Erin had her head almost back to rights. She was up to the task, she repeated to herself. If Quincy believed she could train and supervise a growing crew of workers, then it must be true. "Right, Raven?" She dismounted, led the horse into the stable and removed the saddle. "Now I'm going to brush you down," she whispered, patting Raven's head.

"Hey, Erin, want some company?"

Erin turned to the sound of Olivia's voice coming from the side entrance to the stable. She hoped her reluctance didn't come through when she gestured for her to come inside. "Sure. That would be great." *The polite answer,* Erin thought. She'd been enjoying the solitude. On the other hand, in the months since arriving in town, Olivia had become a friend, and right now she was someone Erin believed she could confide in.

"We haven't talked in a while," Olivia said, "but from what I hear, your new job with Quincy is going well."

She nodded, appreciating her friend's interest. "It's a huge undertaking, and complex. But I'm learning so much from Quincy about managing a project of this scope. Or at least one major piece of it." She chuckled. "That's the easy answer. I'm also a little nervous."

Olivia's eyebrows shot up in surprise. "Really? Why is that?"

Erin grinned. "I've never been a supervisor before. But now Quincy put me in charge of organizing the multiple stages and pieces of the project and training the crew. Even thinking about the responsibility makes my insides flutter."

"Delegating, quality control. Lots of growth, Erin."

She ran the brush across Raven's flank and simultaneously stood a little taller. "I've always worked by myself from start to finish. Until I met Quincy. He changed everything." Erin gave

Raven a pat. "I came here to ride Raven today and to get over my fears about all the new stuff this job is sending my way."

"You'll do great. Quincy only hires the best." Olivia chuckled. "And that includes our son. You've probably seen Carson shooting the before videos at the mansion. Quincy wants him to do progress videos and then the big finale when the work is done."

The note of pride in Olivia's tone amused Erin, but also touched her heart. She'd seen Carson around the mansion, and she'd dutifully waved for his camera from time to time. The boy's talent had evidently shown itself early and was becoming almost legendary. What started out as a hobby had turned into a side business filming town events and occasional weddings. Having arrived in town the day after Olivia and Jeff's wedding, attended by both Tom and Willow, Erin had soon become acquainted with the newly created family. On impulse, she blurted, "I know this is none of my business, Olivia, but how did Jillian adjust to suddenly having a dad in her life?"

Olivia gave her a curious sidelong glance. "It was a hard time all around, but especially for Carson. He was already a teenager when his mom died, and he never knew his dad. When Jeff brought him here, he wasn't trying to be a substitute parent. He just wanted to do right by his friend, Carson's mom and Carson himself. Carson and Jillian have that in common—not knowing a father. Jillian's dad left, and that was that. I'm so glad that somehow, given their circumstances, the two kids both accepted the notion of a new family. Welcomed it, in fact."

Erin thought about what Olivia had said as she began grooming Raven's long neck. "Then I guess Mack's situation with Liam is a little like what you and Jeff have dealt with."

Olivia shrugged. "I'm not sure, but no matter how good a dad Mack is, the boy lost his mom. Carson still has a photo of his mom on the chest in this bedroom. I imagine Liam has something similar, too."

"I find myself identifying with Carson and Liam," Erin said, "even though my situation isn't the same, not by a long shot. I was a grown woman when I lost my mom. I feel for them. They're such great kids."

"If we've learned one thing," Olivia said, "it's that Carson can love two moms, and Jillian can love the dad who chose her to be his daughter. Still, lots of growing pains. But that's okay. We know we'll get through those times together."

"I hope it's the same for Mack and Liam. But this dad role is still so new to Mack." Erin's mind drifted to the idea of absent dads, and she winced. "Unfortunate situation with the boy's mom, and how Mack had to step in, or so he's said."

Olivia shrugged. "Sometimes things are so complicated."

"Complicated? *Complicated?* Oh, *please.*" She abruptly stopped brushing Raven. Erin took in a deep breath to ease the tightness in her chest and throat. With effort, she got the words out. "Even Mack admits he should have been a real dad to his son from day one. The way I see it, Mack didn't need to step in when Paula died. He had to step up."

She ran out of breath and quickly inhaled more air deep into her lungs while dark images formed of her father's abandonment. How many times had she conjured a vision of her father taking long strides toward the door and closing it behind him? And only a couple of days after she was born.

"Whoa... I didn't see that coming," Olivia said. "I'd apologize, but I'm not sure for what."

Erin offered a weak smile. "I like Mack, but to be frank about it, by his own admission, the guy hasn't acted like a father. He walked away from his son."

"And that hits a tender spot." A statement from Olivia, not a question.

"Right. The whole idea of a child losing a

parent has rippled just beneath the surface lately." She'd leave it at that. Olivia was smart. She could read between the lines. Fears of falling prey to a man like her dad made Erin distrust the whole idea of lasting love. That was the real reason she'd left the sleigh ride early and then directed all her attention to Liam at the Children's Adventure Center. Why open the door and allow herself to have feelings for the man with the intense blue eyes?

"The past catches up with us eventually, Erin. We all learn that. It's good to talk about it." Olivia began to tidy the stable.

"If he'd abandoned his child once, wouldn't that make him likely to abandon someone else? That's what my father and Tom's had done."

"I get why you might think the way you do about that, but I wouldn't dwell on similarities between your father and Mack. For one thing, the guy made a mistake, admits it, and is working hard to fix it. From where I stand, he's doing a good job with his son. But that's only a little unsolicited advice."

Ready to concede the point, Erin nodded. "I can't argue with that part of the story."

Olivia, her expression thoughtful, turned to leave. "My shift starts online in about ten minutes, so I need to get back to the house."

With Olivia gone, Erin led Raven into the

stall. "So, Raven, how do I feel about Mack, anyway?" she murmured. "My stomach does cartwheels and my heart beats faster around him." He'd look at her with a sweet, warm smile that seemed to take over his whole face, and she'd forget to be wary.

By the time Erin finished up with Raven and started home, the intensity of her mixed-up feelings had melted away like the snow in front of the stables. Once home, she went inside to get Neptune, who took charge of their walk through the woods to his favorite spot on the ridge. It wouldn't be long before the sheep would be grazing on the basin below. For now, though, as the sky darkened, so did her mood. Irrational as it was, despite new friends, a real family with Tom, Willow and Naomi, plus a good job, she couldn't shake the sadness she felt at decisions Mack had made in the past.

Logically, it might be best all around to avoid him, even if that meant not seeing Liam. But they hung out with the same people. It was an impractical solution to a problem she'd created herself. As much as she enjoyed spending time with Mack and Liam, she'd fallen into the trap of judging Mack quickly and often. Olivia's words echoed in her mind. Maybe she couldn't forget her history, or Mack's, but she could at least try to quit dwelling on what was over and done, and instead concentrate on the future.

Back in the cabin with Neptune, she filled Neptune's water and food dishes and put them on the floor. "Here you go, pal," she said, leaning against the counter to watch the dog happily scarf down his dinner. Could be it was her ride on Raven, or maybe soaking up Olivia's positive attitude, but for whatever reason, her spirits were lifted.

CHAPTER SIX

WITH PATRICK AND Gayle at the pool, Liam had his regular online visit with his maternal grandparents, Eden and Louis. This week Liam had a big supply of stories to tell. From his new hat to *Rapunzel* to the robotic astronaut Gayle bought him, he went on nonstop. He also had a lot to say about their new family friend, Erin. There was nothing Mack could do about it, but he had to admit it sounded like they were spending a lot of time with her. Mack had hurried to clarify the information Liam had no trouble recounting. "We ran into Erin in Landrum, and since we were headed to the play, it made sense to invite her to come along. She's relatively new in town, too." Made sense, right? Not that he needed to justify himself. He welcomed any chance to be around Erin, but no reason to share that tidbit.

"She's our new friend," Liam had said happily.

Liam's chatter should have eased the stiff formality and tension floating between Mack and his former in-laws, and yet he sensed something was off. Eden, exuding warmth to Liam, continued giving Mack a decidedly cold shoulder. More passive, Louis contributed very little to the conversation. Mack decided the best word for the older man's expression was *glum*. The door to the lodge suite opened and drew Mack's attention and thoughts from the call. Gayle and his dad marched in, full of praise for Tall Tale's pool and luxurious spa. "Hey, Liam, come with me to the deli," Gayle said. "You can help me pick up those yummy sandwiches and sides we're having for dinner."

Liam put his astronaut down and scrambled to his feet. "They call them *platters* here, Aunt Gayle." He separated his palms by a couple of feet. "They're *really* big."

Mack smiled at the correction, and so did his sister. Whatever crankiness the boy might have shown here and there in previous days had vanished now. At the moment, he acted like a child having a very good day.

Alone with Patrick, Mack was conscious of the needy way he searched for any sign that his dad thought he was doing a good job with Liam. Yes, it was a little late in the game, but he couldn't deny—or shake—his desire for affirmation.

"It was good Liam had his regular call with Louis and Eden. Can't help but feel bad for them." His dad spoke as he stared out the wide window that offered a panoramic view of the valley and ridges and snowcapped mountain peaks beyond. A bank of clouds was hanging low across the middle of the range, making the peaks stand out in the distance. "So tough to lose a child. Their only child. It's not natural. That's not how it's supposed to be. I wrote them a note last fall, you know."

Mack stepped alongside his dad at the window. "I hadn't realized you'd been in touch with them."

"Just because I never met them in person doesn't mean I didn't feel terrible for them when their only child died," Patrick said. "I found their address. I'd written it down a long time ago, back when you and Paula got married. Never had occasion to look for it until I got the news about their daughter. I'm sure it added to the heartbreak when their little grandson moved so far away."

"It was hard." Mack paused to gather his thoughts. "But just to be clear, Dad, you do understand why I had to bring Liam home with me, don't you?"

Patrick nodded. "Sure I do. That doesn't take away from all they had to cope with. But for you, well, it was different. Paula's death didn't hit you all that hard."

His father had stirred up something Mack had tried to avoid. "Look, Dad, I promised they'd always be part of Liam's life. I made a commitment, and I've done everything I said I would. He talks to them every week online—sometimes more than once. I'm taking him up to Millerton to see them in a few weeks for his spring break." He lifted his arms and let them flop at his sides. "We send pictures he draws and test papers. I text photos…" He stopped and sighed.

"I didn't mean to rile you up. The boy seems fine with you, Mack." Patrick lowered his head in a slow nod as if affirming his statement. "Good move to cut your hours here at the lodge, by the way. You know, make the boy your focus. It's…" He shrugged.

"About time… Is that what you were going to say?"

Mack hadn't expected his dad's glare. "Don't make assumptions," Patrick snapped. "Do you need me to point out your mistakes? You're doing a fine job of carrying around that load of guilt all on your own."

"I'm sorry, Dad," Mack said quietly. "When it comes to my son, my feelings are all over the place. Hope for Liam and guilt about Eden and

Louis are mixed up. After making mistakes, all I want is to do right by him."

His dad's expression softened. "Now you can understand why I chose my line of work. I liked setting my own schedule so I could be with you and Gayle. And your mom." A frown, a pause, and then, "You wished I was like other dads. They were accountants and lawyers—a couple of dentists and docs."

Mack successfully fought off the urge to break in and stop his dad from filling in the rest. "I embarrassed you," Patrick said bluntly. "It was sort of unspoken. But you didn't bring your friends home to our house very often. That was hard to miss."

A bout of nostalgia washed over Mack. "But we spent a lot of time together as a family. Lots of picnics and camping trips to state parks, and regular treks to Yellowstone."

His dad turned to face him. "By now, you can look back and see that even if we lived more modestly, your mom and I did okay. You and your sister never wanted for anything."

"Dad...really. You don't have to explain any of this," Mack said. "What did I know? I was a kid." Mack lowered his voice and said, "And I appreciate the childhood you and Mom gave us. I get it now."

His dad tilted his head one way and then the

other. His mouth was twisted to the side. Mack recognized skepticism when he saw it.

"Let me ask you this, son. If you had it to do over again, would you make a different decision when your little Liam was born?"

The queasiness in his gut took Mack by surprise. "Oh, yeah, starting with actually *making* a decision. I was passive. It was Paula's prerogative to move back to her hometown to be closer to her parents. I understand that. But I didn't negotiate or even make a case for myself as a dad. I let her take over. That's where I went wrong." Mack braced his hand on the window. "No wonder Eden and Louis—" Mack didn't need to finish the sentence, but he did "—wanted to keep him."

Patrick frowned. "Right. You could have worked out an arrangement with Paula. That was a choice, Mack, but you didn't make it. No two ways about it."

Another roll of nausea hit him in the stomach. Mack scoffed. His dad had always been a plainspoken guy. Nothing had changed. "I've thought about that a lot over the past six months." He put his arm around his dad's shoulders, as solid and substantial as they were when Mack was Liam's age. "I may not like hearing your honest words, Dad, but thanks for not making excuses for me."

Patrick shrugged. "You can nurse your re-grets without my help. What you do next is all that matters now."

Suddenly the door flew open, and Liam walked in, carrying a small container of the deli's french fries in each hand. He held them up as high as his arms would allow. "See? They put the fries in buckets, Grandpa."

Patrick laughed at the excitement in Liam's voice. "Day by day, Mack," he said dryly. "That's how kids grow up and handle whatever comes their way."

Mack took reassurance from his dad's words. He believed them, too, at least during the day-time hours. But last night, Liam had the same dream again, and Mack had rushed into his room to comfort and reassure him. This time, Liam went back to sleep more quickly, and Mack sat next to him until his breathing was soft and steady. Mack still had lots of days, though, when self-doubt and stabs of guilt all came together.

ERIN INTENDED TO pick up only a few things at the market. Famous last words. Dex, the checker, scanned her many items and helped her load two large paper shopping bags. Her backpack was so full it wouldn't zip all the way closed. Dex held the door as she went back out to Merchant Street to start the walk to the mansion. She'd only meant to replenish some baking supplies. She never knew when a baby or a little boy might turn up on her doorstep, and Erin vowed she'd never have a "treatless" house.

It was because of the surprisingly mild late March weather that Erin had taken her lunch hour to walk the three blocks from the mansion to the food market on Merchant Street. The bright sun warmed her shoulders and made a dent in melting the snowbanks along the curb. She watched where she stepped to avoid splashing in the puddles or slipping on the patches of ice that remained. Even as strong as she was, her arms began to ache from the weight in the bags.

On the other hand, an unexpected development in her life made trudging to the mansion a little easier. Lost in thoughts of bluegrass music, it took a couple of seconds to register Mack's voice calling her name from behind.

Coming to Erin's side, he held out his hands in an offer of help. She gratefully handed over the two bags.

"I could see these weighing you down from across the street," he said, looking back at the market and the empty parking spaces in front. "Where did you park?"

She smiled sheepishly. "I walked over."

"Oh, well," he said with a laugh in his voice. "I'll show off my mighty muscles and carry these bags to the mansion." He fell into step with her, and they navigated the dips in the wet sidewalk.

"What brings you to Merchant Street in the middle of a workday, Mack?"

"Meeting with the lodge's lawyer to go over some policy changes. Nothing huge." He smiled and added, "My dad and Gayle are gone. Good visit, all in all."

"I'm glad I had a chance to meet them. What fun for Liam." And for her, Erin thought, thinking of the afternoon at the Adventure Center.

"It was." Mack studied her through narrowed eyes.

"What? Why are you looking at me in that funny way?"

"I'm trying to figure you out," he teased. "Hmm…you seem to be glowing, but in a mysterious way. Do you have a secret? Are you going to share it?"

So, the good news she'd been mulling over showed on her face? "I've discovered your superpower. You can read minds." She laughed. "Or maybe you have special skill reading faces. And you're right. I'm feeling pretty bouncy inside."

Mack snickered. "Bouncy? O…kay. Are you

going to explain, or are you having fun by making me guess?"

"Short version. I got a call from Grisham, the guy who started Grisham's Strummers. Their fiddler-singer broke her arm, very sad, but they need a substitute. *Right now.* They have a gig at Tall Tale Lodge—their first one."

"Wow. I didn't know that. The bar manager handles the music bookings. I hadn't noticed Grisham's Strummers added to the calendar." Mack's expression brightened. "I'm assuming Grisham asked you to fill in."

Her hands free of the heavy bags, Erin clasped her hands in front of her chest. "Even I'm surprised by how excited I am. It's a chance to do something I enjoy so much." She grinned as she pointed at Mack. "And you're the first to hear my news. So don't tell anyone until I have a chance to."

"I can keep a secret," Mack said as they turned off Merchant Street and the mansion came into view down the block. "When is the big event?"

"This coming weekend. Two sets on Saturday night," Erin said, holding up two fingers. "You should come. And bring Liam, at least for the first set when it's still relatively early. The other musicians have kids, and some will be there. They play lots of small events for businesses and family reunions and anniversary parties, so Grisham makes a point of being a one hundred percent kid-friendly band."

"No kidding." He gave Erin a pointed look. "It's a deal. Liam wouldn't want to pass up an opportunity to see you. You and Neptune got many mentions when Liam was talking with my dad and Gayle. And then he repeated his stories online with Paula's parents."

"I'm flattered," Erin said, taking a giant step over a puddle.

"It was 'cookies' this and 'cookies' that," Mack said in a mocking tone, "along with telling his grandparents about the model train."

"He's not the only one," Erin said. "I've also been telling everyone about that afternoon at the CAC. Cool train."

"I'm looking forward to another trip there myself." Mack nodded ahead. "Almost there."

"Let's put the bags in the back of my van," Erin said. "Thanks for interrupting your day to help me out."

"No problem. I was heading back to the lodge to meet with Andy a little later. I wasn't in a rush."

It was only a few steps to the parking lot, and Mack quickly transferred the bags into the van while Erin freed herself from the backpack. Out of the corner of her eye, though, she saw a man hurrying toward them.

"Hey, Mack, isn't that Andy coming our way?"

Mack spun around. "Yep, that's him." While Erin finished arranging the bags, Mack stood in place and watched his partner approach. "Hey, Andy, I was just telling Erin my next stop is a meeting with you."

Erin couldn't miss the impatience frozen on Mack's partner's face. Whatever the meeting was about, Andy was sour on it. Erin didn't think of Andy as a lot older than Mack, but his expression resembled a dad who was none too pleased with his teenager.

"Did you meet with Scott?"

Mack frowned. "Of course. The documents are online. We can go over all the details. I'm heading back now." He smiled at Erin. "By the way, have you two met? Erin, this is Andrew Green, my partner." He turned to Andy. "This is Erin Hunnicutt, a newcomer like me. Dr. Tom's sister. What brings you down to Merchant Street, Andy?"

"I had a couple of errands," Andy said, thrusting his hands in his coat pockets. "I saw you just now and wondered if you'd forgotten the meeting."

So far, Andy had barely acknowledged Erin,

but she spoke up quickly. "Hey, Mack, thanks for rescuing me. I appreciate it." She flexed her arms. "You saved me from sore muscles." She nodded at Andy.

"It was nothing," Mack said. "See you... soon." He leaned down and kissed her cheek. "And congratulations. Liam and I will see you at the lodge."

As she pivoted and started toward the side entrance, Erin touched the spot where Mack's cool lips had been. He'd thrown her off her center. That had to be why her heart beat so fast. She couldn't resist sneaking a peek behind her at Mack and Andy walking toward Merchant Street in animated conversation. At least, Andy was talking. He stopped every few steps to jab the air with his index finger to make his point. He raised his arms in a jerky motion and then let them fall to his sides.

Watching what looked like a one-way argument, Erin found it hard to believe Andy considered Mack an equal partner. At the moment, Andy looked like an ordinary bully.

CHAPTER SEVEN

ANDY COULD BE a hothead. Mack had known that for years. But his partner had gone off the rails this time. It wasn't like him to argue in public, let alone in the center of town. At least now they were in Mack's office at the lodge.

"We had an agreement, Andy," Mack declared as he sat behind his desk. "I'm keeping up my end."

Andy plunked himself in a chair opposite the desk and lightly bumped his fist on the desktop. "You've taken your eye off the ball, Mack. That's the problem. You've lost focus."

The drive back to Tall Tale had given Mack time to second-guess Andy's irrational outburst. Andy wasn't yelling anymore, but Mack still hadn't figured out what had triggered the eruption that seemed to come out of nowhere.

"I'm not playing around here, Andy. What you just accused me of is ridiculous. You know my story. I've got to make up ground with my son. Liam is my priority." Mack continued in a lower voice. "You were fine with these changes before. What's changed?"

Mack had pulled back from the consulting end of their partnership, but that was temporary. When he moved to Adelaide Creek and made the lodge his new home base, he'd adjusted his work hours to be more available to Liam. And he wasn't about to mess with that schedule now.

Andy shrugged. "You've changed. I didn't think your new schedule would go on this long."

Long? "It's only been since the first of the year, Andy." Mack glanced at the time on his phone. "Matter of fact, I have to leave in a few minutes to pick up Liam from school and take him to his therapy appointment."

"And then tomorrow, what? His math tutor?" Andy got to his feet and walked to the window, a glass wall that looked out on the garden, or what soon would be Tall Tale's distinctive spring garden. He crossed his arms over his chest.

His partner's sarcastic tone threw Mack. Andy could be abrupt and demanding and throw his weight around as the older partner. Sarcasm wasn't his thing. Mack considered Andy a mentor, but now the guy he'd looked up to had crossed a line.

"As it happens, tomorrow *is* math tutor day." Mack scrutinized his partner. He wanted to know the reasons for this sudden dissatisfaction, but Andy wasn't being transparent. "I never expected something for nothing. I cut my compensation and recalculated the profit share for this year." Mack gestured around the room. "This was supposed to be a meeting about our advertising budget for our ranches." Mack didn't want to say it outright, but Andy's snit was wasting their time.

Andy turned his head and seemed to study the line drawing of the lodge hanging on the wall next to Mack's desk. "You're not going to come back to Arrow Gap, are you?" Andy asked. "You've made up your mind that Adelaide Creek is the best place for you and your boy. Right?"

"You've known all along that was my plan. Did you think I'd change my mind?" Mack's move had been part of their negotiation. When he started doing small business consulting again, he'd do it online with Andy. That had already become their practice for almost every client meeting they scheduled. In fact, as Mack started to see glimmers of the life he wanted for himself and Liam, the consulting end fit right into it. On the other hand, the far-flung holiday ranches were fading from his vision. Tussling with Andy was fading from his vision, too.

With his arms still crossed, Andy rested his shoulder against the window. "I thought you'd eventually get tired of this little town." He let out a ragged huff. "You know, come to your senses."

"Apparently, you and I view this place differently," Mack said. "Whatever. All I can say is, don't figure another move into my future plans. I'm here to stay, Andy."

"Yeah, I get that now." Andy came back to the desk and sat opposite Mack. "But don't forget that your son needs to see you as a successful man, too."

"Well, that definition is open to interpretation," Mack shot back. "I have a little experience misjudging my dad when it comes to success. I confided that to you before I left to bring Liam home with me."

"Maybe so, but after working so hard to build these businesses," Andy said, "you don't want to slack off now."

"Slack off? C'mon, man." Mack tilted back in the chair. "Rearranging my life to be there for my son after school is *not* my definition of slacking off."

Andy raised his arms in surrender. "Okay, okay, bad choice of words. Sorry. I don't know what's got me stirred up." Andy smirked and took a deep breath.

Silence. Mack decided against breaking the few seconds of quiet.

"Change of subject," Andy said. "What about the woman? The one with the groceries. Not every day I see you hauling a good-looking lady's heavy bags around." Andy finally smiled. "Any chance she's going to be part of Liam's future? Or were you simply rescuing a damsel in distress?"

"Erin would make you pay for thinking she's a helpless damsel." Mack laughed self-consciously, aware his face was turning red. "I carried her groceries, Andy. Nothing notable about that."

Andy's smile broadened. "You sidestepped my question, but I won't press. At least, not yet." He sighed. "Looks like your mind's made up about sticking around here. I'll adjust." His expression turned serious again when he stood and did a half turn toward the door. "But take care of business. Being a dad should not consume your whole life."

Mack wasn't going to debate Andy's last statement, but be satisfied that the meeting was ending on a conciliatory note. After agreeing to meet online the next day to hash out the advertising budget they'd left undone, they exited together and went to the parking lot through the lodge's back door. Andy followed Mack to the road, but he turned in the direction of the highway and the route north toward home. Mack headed to town and added his SUV to the pickup line of cars and trucks at Liam's school. Half an hour after pulling away from the curb, Mack ushered Liam into Dr. Harte's office.

Mack then settled into one of the chairs in the waiting room. He usually used these free minutes to scan his messages or check the lodge's social media sites to see what Willow's staff was posting. Instead, he closed his eyes and rested his head on the back of the high-backed chair and sorted through the details about a life he envisioned for himself and Liam: a house in the near future, with a stable and horses, eventually, friends and families to hang out with, summers spent riding and camping...

Mack's vision easily included Tall Tale, a place where he enjoyed spending time. Working with Sydney and Willow, he'd found a special kind of satisfaction in the way the three of them collaborated on projects. Resuming the consulting work with Andy was on the list. But the holiday ranches had gone stale. So was measuring success with dollars. His future was about Liam and a sense of belonging.

Mack wasn't sure how long he'd been in a

dreamy space, but he jumped at the sound of the receptionist's voice greeting a family of four coming inside. He sat up straighter, and to stay awake, he checked his texts. A string of them were about the live music at the lodge on Saturday night. Willow's office had sent Tall Tale's press release to a wide media list and posted on a long list of social media sites he followed. He noted that Erin also sent notices to her contacts to announce the family-friendly band's upcoming dates.

Recalling how he'd sidestepped Andy's question about Erin made him second-guess himself. Better to avoid questions like that. With all he had on his plate, he had no business thinking about romantic possibilities with any woman. He wouldn't avoid her, but he wouldn't seek her out. Well, except for Saturday night at the lodge. He owed it to Liam to take him to see her play with the band. Mack smiled to himself. Right. He was only going for Liam's sake. Ha…he'd stick to that tall tale.

WHEN MACK ARRIVED at the bar with Liam, Tom and Willow were pushing a row of tables together for Willow's numerous Lancaster relatives. Not put off by a roomful of mostly strangers, Liam shot in front of him to say hello to Jillian and the Burton twins. Jeff and Olivia waved him over to join them at the tables they'd arranged for their crowd to sit together.

Jeff pointed to the chairs next to him. "We saved a couple of seats for you and Liam. We figured you'd be here soon."

Since Mack hadn't expected that, Jeff's gesture touched him. Then his spirits soared watching Liam, so at ease with the adults and the kids at the table.

"Happy to join you." Mack nodded past Jeff to include Olivia.

Jeff jabbed his thumb over his shoulder. "As you can see, our Carson is a little too old now to sit with us." Jeff snickered. "Take a good look, Mack. Sooner or later it will happen to you."

Olivia nudged Jeff. "Hey, the teenager has better choices these days."

Mack turned to see Carson at the end of a table on a riser in the back of the bar. He was surrounded by other teens and was talking to one girl in particular. He'd braced his elbow on the table, but had his video camera in his hand. "Does the boy ever put down his camera?"

"Only when he needs both hands for basketball." Jeff grinned. "Some families record their birthday parties for posterity, maybe some holiday dinners. But our documentarian also has a 'vast video library,' as he calls it, showing the four of us doing regular stuff."

Mack wasn't exactly sure what Jeff meant, and must have looked blank, because Olivia filled in the details. "He catches us flipping pancakes and making toast. Folding laundry, too. You know, fascinating stuff like that."

Jeff snorted. "And don't get me started on Carson's dog, Winnie. She's got more screen time than any canine movie star."

Mack laughed along with his new friends, but he was struck by the unmistakable note of pride in their voices. "I only hope Liam is as happy with his life here as Carson is." No explanation needed. "Let's just say watching your teenager having fun with his friends gives me a lot of hope."

"Hey, man, we know how lucky we are." Jeff pointed with his chin at Liam and the twins at the end of the table. "You're doing a great job. Look at him. It's like your little boy has known the twins all his life."

Except during the middle of the night, Mack thought. He kept that worry to himself. Instead, he nodded his thanks. His conversation with Andy earlier that week had stirred the stark contrast between his life before and after Liam. A few minutes of watching Liam with the giggling twins filled him up in a much sweeter way than profit and loss statements ever had. Feeling pensive and grateful, Mack ordered a beer from the server. Then he relaxed into the chair, the muscles in his neck and shoulders loosening. The room had filled fast with adults and kids, probably because Willow had spread the word that this was a family event. He smiled to himself. At times like this, he enjoyed knowing he had a big stake in this lodge. Others deserved the credit for booking the band and drawing the large crowd, but Mack liked the sense of ownership.

Out of the corner of his eye, he saw Erin coming to the stage with her fiddle and bow in hand. She'd replaced her signature Stetson with a headband the color of cherries and a matching red top, whose beaded fringe added a touch of…he searched for the right word. *Whimsy.* She was following Grisham himself, who played banjo. He carried himself like a man who was having the time of his life. The bass player and two guitarists followed Erin and took their places with an air of casual confidence.

Only yesterday, Norm had told him Grisham and the other musicians hadn't played this kind of club venue before. Maybe not, but Mack had to admire how they commanded the stage. Only Erin fidgeted with her bow and patted her headband. *Smile, Erin.* She looked a little too serious for the festive occasion. But Mack saw her face change in a flash when she spotted Tom in the audience. Her brother gave her a subtle and fast thumbs-up. At last, Mack thought, she looked around as if it was dawning on her that this was her moment to shine.

Olivia leaned across Jeff and directed her comments at Mack. "Now there's one talented woman. Right?"

"And a lot of fun. Liam is a huge fan."

The words were barely out of Mack's mouth when he heard Liam's voice from the end of the table. "I know the lady who plays the fiddle. She's a friend of ours. I've been to her house."

Listening to Liam, Mack concluded his kid knew how to brag with the best of 'em.

"Bet you didn't know she's Dr. Tom's little sister," Jillian teased.

"Course I knew that." Liam flashed a smug smile. "And she's Naomi's aunt."

"You're such a know-it-all," Jillian said, laughing.

"I rest my case," Mack said dryly.

"Jillian thinks she's the coolest person in town for another reason, namely Raven," Olivia said. "She gives that horse a little extra love on Erin's behalf every day."

Mack smiled at Olivia, but then Grisham started strumming the banjo at a slow tempo, keeping the volume low as the guys on guitar joined him one by one, followed by the steady rhythm of the bass.

Without fanfare, Norm, Tall Tale's bar and entertainment manager, jogged to the stage and swept his arm toward Grisham. "Let's give a Tall Tale Lodge welcome to Grisham's Strummers. It's time to get this party started."

The band picked up its tempo. Erin joined in on fiddle for the opening bars of the first tune. High energy and the typically fast tempo of bluegrass spurred the audience to clap to the rhythm. The set was off and running with an instrumental. Every musician took a turn for a solo. Mack couldn't take his eyes off Erin, who closed her eyes and dipped her upper body forward and then arched back, always in motion and matching the tempo. The arrangement called for a long riff of guitar and banjo only, with Erin dropping her arms and tapping her foot to the rhythm.

Instead of breaking at the end, Grisham immediately raised his arm and they made an easy transition into a slower, almost plaintive, mesmerizing melody. Mack fixated on Erin as her voice hit every high note of her slow rendition of an old folk ballad about waiting for a love to come home. The guitars and bass were subtle and soft in the background.

Mack wasn't the only person caught up in

Erin's performance. The room was silent, pin-drop quiet. No one moved, not even the wait staff. Erin might have started out a little fidgety, but not a hint of nervousness came through in her voice. She didn't hold back either, and held the final note until the audience got to its feet. Grisham didn't wait for the applause to die down, but signaled the band to slide into the intro to the next piece. "Y'all know the old song about that famous train to New Orleans," Grisham shouted. "Sing it with us. I want the sweet sound of kids on this one...ya hear?"

Erin beamed at the little kids in the crowd while she played and sang. Mack switched his gaze to Liam and his friends. Their faces were lit up while they clapped and tried to sing the lyrics, but mostly they didn't take their eyes off the band. Mack snuck a peek at the teen-agers, too. Some knew the lyrics well enough to join in.

Mack took a deep breath and watched Liam. He was determined to imprint this scene in his memory. Liam was still young enough to be completely absorbed in the moment, with his eyes open wide and his mouth curled in a smile even as he tried to sing. No yesterday, no tomorrow, Mack thought.

As the set continued, Erin played her fiddle with even greater abandon. They went through a couple of kids' folk classics with the young voices reverberating through the bar before Grisham slowed things down. He took several minutes to talk about one of his favorite songs of all time. Erin stepped to the side and closer to the bass player while the guys on guitar and Grisham took the lead for "While My Guitar Gently Weeps." The kids may not have known the song or understood it, but they swayed to the gentle rhythm of it. Piece after piece, in a mix of folk, classic country and bluegrass, Erin moved from one side of the stage to the other, fiddling and singing, sweeping forward toward the audience and then spinning to face the band when they took their solo turns. Her voice joined with the rest of the band to close the set with a fast version of the classic "Fare Thee Well." The men dropped off, but she held the last note a cappella.

Stunned, Mack joined his friends—and everyone else in the bar—for a standing ovation lasting a long time. Radiant with joy, Erin took her bows and waved to the audience.

Finally, Grisham raised his hand. "Sit tight, folks. We'll be back." Grisham stepped off the stage first, before the applause had completely died down. Erin and the others followed his lead, and Grisham made a point of patting Erin on the back. All five musicians headed to the table in the corner, where Norm and a server brought mugs and two pitchers, one of water and one of beer. Erin's band partners had clustered around her, and Mack could tell from their expressions they were beyond happy with her performance. As well they should be, Mack thought. Then he had to laugh at himself. Erin didn't need defending.

A half-full mug of beer in hand, Erin left the group and headed to Tom and Willow's table, which also included the Lancaster relatives— aunts, uncles, cousins and their kids. Tom and Erin's relatives now, their found family.

A couple of guys Mack recognized as part of Tall Tale's site management crew approached Erin. Given the looks on their faces, they were vying for some attention from the charming fiddler-vocalist.

"Will ya look at that?" Olivia said with a laugh. "I'm sure they're only two of Erin's admirers. Nobody steals hearts like musicians."

"Guess so," Mack said, forcing himself to be casual in his response. Feeling like a teenager, he really wanted to stride over to Erin and insert himself into the conversation. Like he had first claim to the girl. What a joke. The only guy in the room who had that power was Liam. Mack was embarrassed to admit he was jealous of those lodge employees, who were trying to monopolize Erin's time. Trying, but not succeeding.

Erin took a couple of steps and pointed to their table. A small thing, but it pleased Mack. Being completely objective, Mack conceded that Erin pointed to Liam and his pals. She gave her admirers a quick wave as she backed away.

"She could sing for a living," Olivia said with a sigh. "We better not tell Quincy that just yet."

"That's for sure," Mack said. "He counts on her."

"Lucky for me, I'm not on call tonight, so I won't have to miss anything." Olivia let out another happy sigh. "I bet you're pleased, too. These live music dates are no doubt great for the lodge's bottom line."

Mack snorted. "I suppose, but I was so caught up in the music that never occurred to me." An exception to the rule, he admitted. Another sign of the new Mack? Maybe.

Erin smiled at Mack while she moved closer and stood behind the kids with her hand on the back of Liam's chair. She stayed planted in that spot while waving and nodding to well-wishers calling out to her from other tables.

He stood and took a few steps to be closer to her and Liam. "Congratulations." He was irrationally happy to see her for reasons he wasn't quite ready to analyze. "Prepare yourself, Erin.

News of your incredible voice is going to spread fast."

"Thanks, Mack." She leaned in and spoke in a low voice. "I'll admit this only to you, but I had a bad case of nerves when I had to face the audience for the first time." She held out her hand and shook it. "My hands were this shaky."

"Trust me," Mack said, "you hid it well." The fidgeting he'd noted didn't come close to matching her description of what she called her case of nerves.

"I had a chance to work it off on the instrumental. Then I was fine, caught up in the music."

She was talking to him like they were alone in the room, Mack thought, before he let out a rueful groan. "I need to take Liam home. He's up way past his usual bedtime as it is. I told him we'd be leaving after the first set, but I promised he'd get a chance to say goodbye to you."

Erin nodded, then turned her attention to Liam and the twins at the same time Jillian ran off toward Carson. Unlike Liam, she was old enough to stay for both sets.

As if they'd read Mack's mind, Heather and Matt appeared at his side. Without hesitation, Heather said, "Let's go, you two." In return, she got disgusted looks from the twins, but they exchanged a glance and reluctantly slid off their chairs.

"Okay, then, I'll say goodbye now," Erin said, waving at the twins before squeezing Liam's shoulder. "And to you, too, Liam."

"I liked your singing," Liam said shyly, "a lot."

"Why, thank you," Erin said, cupping his chin. "Aren't you nice to say so?"

Assuming that was a real question, Liam said, "I guess."

Without missing a beat, Erin gestured to the stage. "Oops." She pointed to Grisham, who had his hand up, palm out. "The boss is flashing the five-minute warning. I better say goodbye to you two and drink a big glass of water." She shimmied her shoulders. "Gotta get ready for some bluesy ballads in the second set."

Mack recognized an opening when he saw one and led Liam away from the table. Erin pivoted quickly, wound through the tables and people and joined her bandmates at their make-shift headquarters in the corner.

With his hands on Liam's shoulders, Mack navigated around clusters of people standing by their tables and chatting. He wasn't paying particular attention but overheard a woman talking about what she called the latest missing horse. He recognized her as a neighbor down the road from the Hoovers. He couldn't lose an opportunity to get some information about the horses, so he steered Liam closer to her and the other woman standing with her.

"Excuse me," Mack said, "I wasn't deliberately eavesdropping, but I overhead you mention a runaway horse. I've been following this business pretty closely."

"I'm Barb Owens," she said to Mack before directing her attention to Liam. "I'm going to guess that you're the boy who lives in the bunkhouse. I think I've seen you waiting for the school bus."

Liam nodded and air-jabbed his thumb back at Mack. "I live there with my dad."

Barb smiled at Liam, and Mack quickly introduced himself to Barb and to the other woman, Doris. Barb's expression turned serious when Mack asked, "Do you know how many have run away or otherwise disappeared by now?" He could hear the musicians beginning to warm up, a signal that the show was about to restart. "I thought the second one came back, but two are still missing?"

"I'll be right back," Barb told Doris before turning to Mack. "Looks like you and Liam are leaving, so I'll walk you out."

"I didn't mean to interrupt…" Mack let his voice trail off, unsure what he hoped to learn. But he and Liam followed Barb to the lobby.

Barb's forehead wrinkled in a deep frown.

"The last I heard was that a quarter horse got loose from the Rivers' sheep ranch. They're friends of mine, so I've been paying attention, too. Their horse hasn't come back."

"I'm sorry to hear that," Mack said.

"What have you heard?" Barb asked. "People are talking about the situation, but no one seems to understand it."

"From what I gather, for reasons, like you say, no one can figure out, two horses disappeared and came back, two more went missing, and now there's another one."

"That's all I know." Barb's mouth tightened in a grimace. "The Riverses are in touch with the county sheriff's office, but other than keeping track of the reports, there's not much information."

"It's got everyone on edge," Mack said.

"I have to tell you, things do seem a little too odd. It's not something we see that often," Barb said. "The occasional runaway, yes, but a whole string of them? Not likely."

"Then what's your best guess?" Mack asked.

Barb shrugged. "I'm not sure. I don't know what to make of it, but I'll keep my ears open and let you know if I hear anything." She glanced at Liam, who was getting antsy and pulling on Mack's hands still resting on his shoulders.

"Well, I better be getting my boy home, but thanks for talking with me." He smiled as he pointed to the stage with his chin. "You don't want to miss the next set, I'm sure."

"No, I sure don't. Especially not with Grisham's new singer. What a voice, huh?"

Before Mack could respond, Liam spoke up. "Her name's Erin, and she's a friend of ours."

Barb smiled at the amusing touch of pride in his voice. "Well then, lucky you."

"And she has a horse named Raven."

Barb met Mack's eye. "Oh, I see. I like that name."

Mack said a quick good-night and ushered Liam outside.

"Why can't we stay?" Liam protested as they got into the car.

"It's getting really late," Mack said. He noticed Liam yawning, which explained why he wasn't putting up anything other than a mild protest over being pulled away. Liam's grousing was the price he paid for keeping a seven-year-old out way past his bedtime. He was on the familiar road from the lodge to home for about two minutes before Liam's head dropped to the side. Out like a light.

Mack's mind drifted back to the horses, and how odd it was to find himself in the midst of a puzzle that baffled even his neighbors and friends, people with a lot of experience with horses. Unlike him. Although the ranches he and Andy owned kept horses for the guests to ride, Mack was a novice. He had little knowledge about the hands-on side of having horses. On the other hand, when it came to the business side, Mack understood the expense of keeping horses, and could talk about return on investment with the best of them. Folks in suits could rattle off balance sheet numbers to prove that horses were valuable assets in Wyoming's tourist market. But cold, objective assessments didn't take into account Mack's personal affection for horses, or his longing to ride and own them. That had been impractical up in Arrow Gap, but Liam had a heart for horses and wasn't shy about saying he wanted to be one of the "horse kids," as Olivia called them, like Jillian and the twins. And that was fine with Mack. Mack parked in front of the bunkhouse, but Liam didn't stir. Instead of waking him and putting him in his own bed, Mack carried the sleeping boy to his room and put him down in the big double bed. He slipped off Liam's jacket and shoes and pulled the blanket up.

All night, Liam breathed shallowly next to Mack. A reassuring sound for sure, but Mack was restless. His mind flitted and circled around

Erin's performance, the missing horses and his dilemmas about work. Then his thoughts landed again on Erin. He wasn't troubled by the restlessness. Instead, there was excitement rippling beneath the surface. The anticipatory kind that led to the question, *What will I do next?*

CHAPTER EIGHT

MACK PICKED UP the check from the table. "It's great you could meet me this morning."

Erin drained her coffee mug and then thanked Mack for the invitation. "What better way to start a work week than with one of the diner's breakfast specials?"

Mack's invitation to meet had arrived by text on Sunday night, when she was finally rooted in her body again and not floating around in a dream world singing to an appreciative crowd. Excited—thrilled—after performing at the lodge, she found it impossible to wind down until the wee hours. She'd taken Neptune out for the last time around three in the morning, and he'd nudged her awake at almost eleven o'clock. She basked in the pleasure of being greeted by congratulatory texts from Tom and Willow, Heather and Olivia—and many others. A couple of the window installation guys at the mansion also sent texts. She'd expected a message from Mack and was a little disappointed when no text from him came in.

Erin whiled away the rest of the day puttering around the house and making a thick beef stew for the week ahead, enjoying her heady state and humming or singing every piece from the two sets. She'd performed before, but playing with Grisham's guys was a thousand times more exciting than anything she'd ever done. And the best part was her link to so many people eager to hear Grisham and his band.

She was relaxing in a hot bath when Mack's invitation to join him for breakfast at the Merchant Street Diner came in. That was his first text. His second complained in a cute sort of way about Liam's nonstop chatter about his friend, the star of the show. Seeing no particular reason to say no to breakfast, she immediately texted back, confirming the time.

The next morning, Erin slept through the alarm, but she managed to get Neptune out for a quick walk. Back inside, she filled the dog's food and water bowls, then rushed to pull on jeans and a red sweater and tuck her hair into a bun before rushing out. She texted Mack that she'd likely be a few minutes late, but then tried not to be too obviously harried when she flew inside and joined him in the booth for two he'd claimed.

After greeting him, her stomach growled loud enough that Mack heard it.

"I'll tell the server it's an emergency," Mack teased, raising his hand to get the young man's attention. "You need one of the diner's famous breakfasts this morning."

"I do… I'm in the mood for French toast with the diner's legendary cinnamon butter."

When the server arrived, Mack ordered two French toast plates and coffee, and Erin let out a long exhale and slumped against the back of the padded booth. "I didn't sleep much after I got home from the lodge, so I guess I made up for it last night."

"I can understand why," Mack said. "You must have been wired. The band was great. You were great. And I'll bet the audience left wanting more."

"And I'd add my surprise at the whole thing. I had three quick rehearsals, one right before we drove to the lodge." Erin was still puzzled by what happened. "Grisham thought we were okay, considering we hadn't played together before. And they had to substitute a couple of songs, and I had to drop back on a couple I'd never heard before. But then something happened in the real performance. It was like magic." Her arms and hands buzzed every time she thought about the sequences when the five of them had fallen into a magical space, the zone.

"Not one person in the crowd would have guessed this was your first performance with the band," Mack said. "I think that's why all your new friends and family were so caught up." Mack paused and smiled. "Including me. The kids—of all ages, by the way—were as taken with it as the adults. Bowled over, even."

Erin's bubbly feeling lasted all the way through breakfast. By the time Mack left cash on the table and they headed for the door, she was finally ready to get to the mansion and focus on wood. As she stepped from the diner onto the sidewalk, she looked into the faces of Tom and Quincy, who stepped aside to make room for her and Mack to come out. Tom glanced at her with obvious inquisitive eyes before greeting Mack.

It made no sense, but Erin jolted seeing the two men, almost as if she'd been caught doing something wrong. It annoyed her to admit to being flustered. Maybe it was because Tom kept looking at Mack curiously. Erin couldn't very well announce that they'd had a friendly breakfast, not a date. Besides, why would Tom care?

"Hey, looks like we all had the same idea about starting the week out right," Quincy said in his typical friendly tone. He extended his hand toward Erin. "As for you, I heard you put on quite the show. I was sorry to miss it, but I take grandpa duty with Naomi seriously, you know."

"With any luck, Quincy, you won't have to wait too long," Mack said. "I predict Grisham and his crew—now including Erin—will be in great demand. Willow and Norm are probably looking at dates on Tall Tale's calendar as we speak."

Erin might have reminded him that she wasn't a real member of the band. Sooner or later, the original fiddler would be back. But she had no intention of interjecting a new topic into an already awkward conversation. Awkward for her, anyway.

"Well, I'm getting hungry out here, Tom." Quincy then spoke directly to Erin. "Don't forget we have our Monday staff meeting in the library at noon."

"I'm heading to work now," she said. "I've got my progress report ready to go."

"I'll, uh, walk you to your van," Mack said when Tom and Quincy had gone inside.

They started down the block to the one available parking place Erin had claimed since the diner's lot had been full. Erin took a couple of quick steps, but slid across an icy spot on the sidewalk. Her body angled back and to the side, but Mack cupped her elbow and kept her upright so she could find her footing.

"Gotta be careful out here," Mack said, letting his hand drop. "It's March, and that means cold winds and freezing rain. Like we had yesterday. It's miserable."

"Mack, really, you don't have to walk me to my van," Erin said, still embarrassed, for no good reason, by running into her brother and her boss.

"Yes, I do." Mack's tone was light, almost teasing her. "So Quincy has regular staff meetings, huh?"

The question seemed a little odd, but Erin saw no reason not to answer it.

"Uh-huh. He insists on it. He told me it's how he keeps all his plates spinning." Erin twirled her gloved hands in the air. "Today, the plumbing and electrical contractors will be there. He's going to hire two more people for me, so we'll have a five-person crew to speed up progress on the woodwork. There's that much of it."

"Is everything okay between you and Quincy?" Mack asked. "You seemed a little nervous back there…you know, meeting up with him. And your brother."

Erin's swallowed hard. Now she was annoyed at Mack for putting her on the spot. "I was sur-

prised, that's all." Her tone was deliberately adamant. "I didn't expect to see Tom or Quincy."
When it came to her boss, that didn't make a
lot of sense. Quincy kick-started almost every
day with breakfast at the diner, either alone or
with one of his enormous number of contacts
or friends. From last Thanksgiving, when Tom
asked Willow to marry him, Quincy had started
enjoying frequent and early breakfasts with his
new son-in-law.

Shifting the conversation, Erin said, "Quincy
and Tom have become close friends. It's kinda
sweet, really." She smiled at Mack. "It's like he
hit the family jackpot." Erin lifted her shoulders in a happy shrug. "And so did I. Thanks
to Naomi, who's almost a year old, Tom and I
are part of a three-generation family."

"That's a much nicer story than mine," Mack
admitted. "Until I brought Liam home with me,
I wasn't close to my family—and rarely had
occasion to talk with Paula. I never communi-
cated with her parents. Other than Andy, I was
a loner. Work ate up all my time. But now…"

"But now you have a much different life."
As Erin finished Mack's thought, it occurred
to her she was reminding herself that Mack
had changed.

When they reached her van, Mack said, "What

do you think about the latest news about another missing horse?"

"Some are still calling them runaway horses," Erin said, "but that doesn't make sense to me. Seems like a strange mystery. I could be wrong, but from what Willow told me, Heather and Matt and some others have been in touch with the sheriff. Five runaway horses is too many to be a coincidence. Granted, two came back, but still." Kicking at a patch of snow on the street with the toe of her boot, she added, "I can't help but worry about Raven." She wasn't ready to admit how much.

"Of course you'd worry," Mack said, his voice low. "I'm not knowledgeable enough to come to any conclusions about why this is happening. Andy and I have never had a single horse stolen from one of our holiday ranches. In all these years, we've had exactly one horse disappear— for about three hours. She wandered off, but by the time the stable hand started organizing a search party, she'd meandered back home on her own."

They stood together on the sidewalk next to her van in comfortable silence. Erin knew she should simply thank him and be on her way, but her urge to linger was stronger. "I'll ask Willow if she's heard any more about it. Her cousin Bridget has a lot of horses, and she and her hus-

band probably have some opinions about this."
She opened her driver's door and was about to
climb in when she remembered Naomi's upcoming birthday. "Uh, when is Liam's birthday? Don't want to miss wishing him a happy
birthday."

"It's in May." Mack's expression was mildly
troubled when he answered her question. "His
mother used to have a big shindig every year.
She'd hire a magician or a clown. She even
rented outside space a couple of times to have
his party. Eden has told me all about them, and
I pieced together some information from things
Liam said."

Erin found that kind of party a little showy,
but then, what did she know?

Mack's forehead wrinkled, as if he was trying to solve a problem. "I suppose I should do
what he's used to. In the spirit of keeping up
tradition, like taking him to see Eden and Louis
for Christmas. It wasn't the same for them, or
Liam, but at least it was familiar."

"Do you really want to hire a kids' enter-
tainer—a magician or a clown?"

Mack's piercing blue eyes looked directly
into hers. "Why so incredulous? Do you dis-
approve?"

"Whoa. Sorry. I didn't mean to pry."

"To be honest, I'd rather keep it a little more

low-key." He twisted his mouth to the side as if trying to figure something out. "But Tom and Dr. Harte both say consistency is good. And it was his mom's tradition."

Erin had a hunch about this, and she put aside her fear of treading into areas that weren't any of her business. "I know it's not my place, but Liam's young and adaptable, at least in some ways. Whether he asked for it or not, he has a new life with you, and what happens on holidays and birthdays is up to you two now."

Mack leaned his shoulder against the side of the van. When he turned his gaze back to her, his blue eyes were softer, almost amused. "Point taken. You were reading my mind. I don't like the idea of every birthday being such a huge production. I guess because they weren't like that when I was kid. Until I got into high school, they were more about family."

"I understand." Erin's thoughts drifted to memories of the effort her mother made so birthdays would be special, if modest. A pizza party with a few friends who could fit around the table in their small apartment. There were a couple of years where Erin chose a camping-style sleepover in their tiny living room. The year she turned sixteen, her mother managed to get tickets to a concert for Erin and three girlfriends—the first time her birthday was an *extravaganza*, her mom's word for the event.

Mack's mouth turned up in a faint smile. "I'm sensing that isn't all you have to say. I can almost see the gears in your brain doing their thing."

Erin chuckled. "Oh, don't mind me. I was remembering a couple of childhood birthdays. But really, Mack, why don't you create your own traditions now? Perhaps it's too soon for a big bash. It could trigger memories of his mom, and that could be upsetting. Maybe he'd be happy to invite the twins to the CAC to play with the train. Maybe have lunch downtown."

She'd touched a soft spot, because Mack closed his eyes and put his fingers over his mouth, as if surprised by his emotion. "I've been wondering…or, I should say, I'm relieved. I was thinking I should talk to Dr. Harte and Tom about it, but you know what, I'm going to follow my own instincts about this."

Erin was struck by how these kinds of decisions weighed on Mack. "For what it's worth, Tom and Willow had a fairly small gathering for Naomi last week," Erin said. "Sort of an open house. I dropped by, and Quincy, of course, and her cousin Bridget and her teenagers stopped in for cake."

"Huh? No hoopla?" Mack feigned suspicion. "Are you sure? A quiet affair doesn't seem like Willow's style."

Erin grinned. "I thought so, too, but she and Tom wanted to savor the day. Willow has always said that bringing Naomi home from the adoption agency was the most special day of her life." Erin's eyes quickly teared up, and she brushed them away. "Oops, don't mind me. But I sort of tingle all over every time I think of Tom and Willow's story and how Naomi was part of what brought them together."

Erin held Mack's gaze a second too long, leaving another beat of awkward silence before realizing she'd been standing at her car in the cold, chatting with Mack like she had nowhere else to be. "Uh-oh, it's getting late. I better get to work before Quincy beats me there," she said. "It wouldn't do for the boss to catch me out here socializing." Before she was lured into another conversation, Erin opened the door of the van. "Thanks again for breakfast."

"My pleasure. Anytime." He hesitated, but added, "You *always* give me so much to mull over." He turned and hurried down the street.

"Hey, Mack, if you hear anything else about the horses, let me know," she shouted after him. "I'll do the same."

He spun around and gave her a quick thumbs-up. He was slow to look away, but then, so was she.

FOR THE TIME BEING, Erin's work was conveniently headquartered in the dining room, because she was focused on what she called the fancy hutch. It was destined to demand her attention for a while. Thoughts of lost horses competed for space in her brain, at least until she saw Dakota, the newest and youngest worker on the project. Dakota was engrossed in removing the many doors and drawers from the hutch that dominated the room. Supervising the prep work with Dakota centered Erin, and the hours passed quickly.

When it came time for the staff meeting, Erin was the first to arrive in the library, tablet in hand. Quincy had the report she sent to him projected on the portable screen, but he had one hip perched on the writing table he'd turned into his desk. He was engrossed in reading the hard copy she'd left there.

When Quincy raised his head and saw her, he waved the report in the air. "We're starting with your updates. Nice progress." His eyes twinkled in their typical Quincy way. "I'll moderate my compliments, though. Don't want to be accused of playing favorites. You are *family*, after all."

"I like the sound of that. But don't worry. I don't expect special treatment." Last year, when she worked on the town hall project, bantering with Quincy had quickly become one of her favorite side benefits of the job. Nothing had changed.

Quincy tossed the report on the table. "Good running into you at the diner."

This conversation should not have produced flutters in her stomach, but there they were. And she was powerless to stop them. "The best breakfast in town," she said a little too cheerfully. Except for the exceptional buffet at the lodge, the diner offered the *only* full breakfast menu for miles around Adelaide Creek.

"You know, I think I misjudged Mack," Quincy mused. "From the impression I had based on the town hall project, I wouldn't have guessed he'd be drawn to our little town. But I was wrong. From what Willow tells me, he and his little boy are settling in." He gestured to Erin. "Making some friends, I see."

"I know the way to a little boy's heart. Cookies will do it every time," Erin said with a breezy laugh. "On the serious side, Mack wants for Liam exactly what Adelaide Creek offers."

Quincy cleared his throat. "In any case, I'm glad you two newcomers are friends."

Erin smiled, but shifted the conversation in

another direction. "By the way, I like Dakota. She's eager to learn. Kinda reminds me of how I was when I started."

"Excellent. And look how you turned out." Quincy raised his eyebrows and flashed a quick smile.

"I'm putting her to work with the others on the second-floor window frames and trim this afternoon."

Without warning, Quincy's expression turned flat, and he responded with an unenthusiastic nod.

Her boss's mood change wasn't typical, especially when he'd soon preside over a meeting with his plumbers, tuck pointers, carpenters and landscapers, and Erin. "Is something wrong?"

Quincy gestured around the room at nothing in particular. "When I opened the front door today, I couldn't deny reality." He tapped his temple. "My heart is in building, but up here in my brain, I'm a numbers guy, too. I've put in decades poring over hundreds of estimates and cost-benefit analyses, and I know something about financial finagling." His scoff was a little on the cynical side. "Somehow I've miscalculated this one."

That gave Erin a jolt. Quincy's drive to transform the mansion into a one-of-a-kind gem in the community had prompted him to push extra hard to get the work underway. There was still a window of time to save the dilapidated building. To that end, he'd invested several thousand dollars in extensive foundation work before the first stroke of interior restoration began. Quincy had also assured Erin that when this project was done, she'd still have a place in his company. With her on his staff, more projects would come their way. Aging farmhouses were being brought back to their former glory, along with antique fixtures salvaged before crumbling structures were finally demolished.

"Uh, what do you mean, Quincy?"

"I've spent decades building new structures, not restoring old things," he said, "but after the town hall project, I got a little cocky, I guess. I didn't face up to the slow pace of restoration. I mean, the woodwork alone…"

No need for Quincy to elaborate. More than anyone working on the project, Erin understood the magnitude of that single element on a long list. "Are regrets setting in?"

Quincy scrunched up his face as if considering how to answer. "Nah…not really. More like momentary frustration. I'm a master at creating visions in my head, but I come up short on patience." He paused and rolled his shoulders back to straighten his spine. "That's why I'm adding crew. And we'll soon tackle the rest." He waved away his words. "Don't mind me. I'll get my griping out of my system before the meeting."

"No question about it, Quincy, wood restoration eats up time," Erin said. "And money. But adding Dakota will speed things up." *If she proves herself as a quick study*, Erin thought.

Quincy didn't have time to respond because the supervisors of the exterior work and the plumbers came through the open door, followed by the landscape architect, whose work would start in earnest when warmer weather set in.

Quincy's mood instantly changed, Erin was in awe of the switch in his demeanor. All traces of concern were replaced with Quincy's signature good-natured greetings. A couple of minutes of small talk transitioned to business conversation, interrupted only by a text that came into Quincy's phone.

Quincy read the text and frowned, but when he looked up, he spoke directly to Erin. "Crosby's going to be late," he said, referring to the electrician by his last name. "Seems one of his horses ran away last night, and there's no sign of him yet."

Quincy addressed her because he knew she'd been following the story. So the tally had gone up by one. Now four horses were missing. Once again, the claim that they were runaways didn't ring true.

MACK HAD ONE more meeting to go before he left for home to meet Liam when the bus dropped him off. He'd been dreading it all day. It didn't help his mood when Erin's text showed up on his phone and delivered bad news. He didn't know Crosby, the electrician whose horse was on the loose, but her second text clarified that although Crosby wasn't a rancher, he had a bunch of kids and lots of animals, including four horses. One had disappeared right under their noses. Mack was about to reply, but Sydney arrived in his office, and Andy would appear on the screen any minute.

"Andy's going to be in a foul mood," Sydney said with a smirk. "He's not one to hide how he feels. He'll blame Willow."

"As usual," Mack said. "But enough is enough. Not every lead pans out, at least not according to Andy's schedule. That's not Willow's fault." In this latest episode, Andy blamed Willow because they weren't included in a Montana newspaper's last-minute feature on luxury lodges. Ridiculous, and unfair, especially considering all the great PR Willow had drummed up for Tall Tale.

Right on time, Andy's scowling face appeared on the screen, and without the usual pleasantries, he started in on what he called a lost opportunity.

This time, though, Mack wasn't having any of it. For years Andy had been his mentor, and Mack had learned a lot in their collaboration. But they were equals now, and Mack was tired of Andy's lack of recognition for Willow and other staff. "I'd think twice about blaming Willow because we didn't get the placement you wanted," he said. "She's landed us spots in roundup articles in two other magazines."

Still scowling, Andy scoffed.

Even Sydney, who almost always took a conciliatory tone, nodded vigorously. "I'm with Mack on this. Besides, we don't have time to quibble. I have an online meeting with a couple who booked a summer wedding this morning." She smiled brightly. "And that means a hefty block of rooms set aside for the guests."

"I've got nothing to add to what's already in my report," Mack said. "The numbers speak for themselves. We're doing okay. And we're attracting local members to the health club and increasing traffic to the restaurant and deli."

"And don't forget the music," Sydney added. "Willow encouraged us to deepen our roots in the community, and it's paid off."

"You two have always elevated Willow's importance to the lodge." Andy's tone was seriously derisive. "She's one of the senior staff, but that's all. She's not aggressive enough in her approach to these outlets."

Sydney and Mack simultaneously groaned. Mack was glad Sydney was no longer intimidated by Andy's gruff ways. *And getting gruffer*, Mack thought. "C'mon, Andy, you've never given Willow her due, so let's not rehash that. Time to move on." Andy backed off, and they quickly checked items off their agenda. When Sydney left for her next meeting, Andy asked Mack to stick around for a few minutes.

Checking the time on his computer screen, Mack got to his feet. "I have to be home to meet Liam when he gets off the bus."

"We're not done here, Mack."

Mack planted his palms on the desk. "Actually, we are. Besides, we've had this conversation before, Andy. I thought we'd settled things between us for now." Mack didn't wait for Andy to protest, and instead picked up his phone. "I'll call you later." With one click he ended the meeting.

When later came and Mack got back to Andy as promised, his call went directly to voicemail. A few minutes later, Andy sent a text putting off their conversation. Fine by Mack. He tried to shake off his troubled feelings about this turn in Andy. His partner had always been aloof, not an especially gregarious guy, and far too ready to find fault with the staff. In their consulting work, Andy played the more silent bad cop, while Mack leaned toward the engaged good cop role. That worked in some settings, but not at the lodge.

Worse, Andy had once again refused to see that he was wrong about Willow, and he'd been that way about other employees, too. If he'd been an on-site partner like Sydney, and now Mack, he'd surely undermine staff morale. Mack couldn't keep giving Andy a pass on the negative attitude he brought to the table. Apparently, he and Andy needed another face-to-face conversation. Mack also acknowledged the nagging sense that something major had shifted, and attempts at conciliatory conversations would only delay important decisions. He should make his decisions known. Mack grumbled to himself about all this as he heated up spaghetti and meatballs, a favorite of Liam's. He put a lid on his thoughts about Andy when he sat on the couch with Liam and watched an episode of a new anime series. Later, in bed with his stuffed animals around him, Liam drifted into a sound sleep in the middle of a story. Mack lingered, though, after he'd tucked the blanket around Liam's shoulders, to enjoy the sight of his son's face, peaceful in sleep.

He was about ready to crawl into bed himself, but his phone signaled a text. Could be Andy setting up a time for a meeting, he thought. Quickly, he hoped for a more pleasant option, maybe Erin texting with good news about the horses. Instead, it was Matt Burton, and it wasn't good news. Harris, a horse they'd owned for years, was gone. He'd been in the corral all afternoon, but when it came time to put the horses back in their stalls, Harris was nowhere to be found. He'd barely finished absorbing the news from the text when Erin called.

"You heard the news about Harris, I assume," she said.

"Just now. Wow. I imagine the Burtons called the sheriff," Mack said. He didn't know either Matt or Heather well, but after their conversation on the sleigh ride, he understood what horses had always meant to Heather. And this sure wasn't the work of some ghost of Woody, the local legend. "I'm sure they did," Erin said, "but for some strange reason, Crosby said he thought his horse was a runaway and would come back on his own. He claims he's not that worried."

"Unlike the Burtons," Mack said. "Even in a text, you can tell they're frantic."

"I'm frustrated, but I guess there's nothing we can do tonight…"

"I understand. And I know you're thinking about Raven."

"Jeff sent a message before I called you. Every horse in his stable is accounted for." She sighed into the phone. "I better go, Mack. I need to try to sleep."

"Me, too," Mack said. "Let's check in tomorrow, though."

After they said good-night, Mack lay down on the bed, weary, but prepared for a restless night. All the tossing and turning was new to him. He fluffed the pillows and threw aside the heavy blanket, but then was too cold and pulled it back up. The later it got, the more his ruminations went from Erin and the horses to his challenges with Andy and then back to Erin. Finally, after several hours, he drifted into a light sleep that lasted until just before dawn. He got out of bed, went to the kitchen, flipped the switch on the coffeepot and focused on the aroma he looked forward to every morning. Keeping the lights off, he took his mug of coffee to the window and stared at the woods behind the house.

The wooden bunkhouse, built in the 1920s, sat on a plateau. On one side, the view showed a long slope down to the basin that extended many miles before some craggy hills appeared. Behind them, the horizon was dominated by the distant mountains. From the front and the other side of the building, he and Liam could watch Jen Hoover's hardy Shetland and Icelandic sheep, whose heavy coats kept them warm as they wandered in and out of the covered shelter. Jen promised Liam he'd soon see them grazing in the pasture all day. The woods extended back to a hiking and riding trail that were part of a long ridge connecting several ranches and ultimately taking a turn toward Addie Creek.

Mack savored the quiet despite his fitful night. He supposed Harris was on Erin's mind when she took Neptune out for his early morning walk. She'd told him it wasn't unusual for her to be the first to arrive at the mansion—and often the last to leave. Tired and with his defenses down, Mack would have liked nothing more than to confide in Erin about his growing conflict with Andy, and his urge for even bigger shifts in his life. Foolish, really. He didn't know Erin well enough to spill his confusion about his business—or life—dilemmas.

As he stared into the still woods, out of the corner of his eye he caught what looked like fast movement in the trees. When he turned his head, a ghostly form ran by, then stopped at the edge of his line of vision. Probably a deer. A common sight. When he spotted deer around the bunkhouse, though, they were usually in groups of four or five, sometimes more. From what little he could see, the still form in the distance was bigger and shaped more like a horse than a typical deer.

Mack grabbed his phone from the kitchen counter and took a quick picture. But in the dark and cloaked in mist, the woods revealed little detail. He zoomed in, but he saw only that the form was likely a brown or black horse. That described a lot of horses.

He studied the view through the lens and clicked a couple of times to get shots he'd save to look at later. That opening didn't last long. Suddenly, the horse shot to the left and disappeared. He attached the best of the photos to a text for Heather and Matt, but he hesitated before hitting the send button. Would they be up this early? But what difference did it make? They'd want to know where he'd spotted the horse that could be Harris. Whether that was Harris or not, a sighting of any of the horses would start a search. But since the Hoovers' place was more or less next door to the Burton ranch, chances were good it was their horse. Most likely they'd want to immediately search the woods or the ridge trails on horseback.

He sent the text describing exactly what he saw. Minutes later, Heather's text came in:

thanks...on it...will let you know

One more time, Mack scanned the woods, thankful that it was March and the vast acres of trees were still bare. Unfortunately, the woods revealed nothing in the early daylight. Only mist and more mist. Fully awake and now oddly energized by the sighting, Mack took out mixing bowls and the ingredients he needed for a pancake breakfast. It wasn't long after he'd dropped the first dollop of batter in the pan that Liam wandered into the kitchen still in his pajamas. With a big smile lighting up his face, he climbed up in the chair. "I smelled the pancakes in my sleep."

"That's a super way to wake up," Mack said. "How about we eat first this morning? And when you've had all the pancakes you want, you can get dressed and ready for school." Mack spontaneously showed off a high and theatrical pancake flip. Luckily, it landed back in the pan and not on the floor.

From Liam's happy expression, Mack decided that flipping their routine upside down once in a while was a good thing. Turning his attention to getting Liam ready for school before the bus showed up at the end of the road, Mack didn't have time to focus on his stray thoughts about the horse. But a few minutes after settling behind his desk at the lodge, Mack got a call from Matt to thank him for contacting him and Heather. No good news to report, though. They'd taken the trail from the ranch to the bunkhouse and explored the woods, but saw no sign of Harris, or any horse on the loose.

"I've texted Jeff and Tom," Matt said, "so they'll keep their eyes open."

"I'll alert Erin," Mack said, "just in case." In case of what? True, she might get a glimpse of the horse around her cabin, but mostly he took the horse spotting as an excuse to reach out.

Later, when Mack had a couple of free minutes to reflect, he had a good laugh at his own expense. When he sent a text to Erin about the horse, he also invited her to dinner that night, adding that she could be on horse watch with him. He liked the idea of pulling chairs up to the window when it got dark and talking while they kept an eye out for the horse. Maybe some wouldn't find that particularly appealing, but Mack's gut told him Erin wasn't one of them.

When Erin didn't reply immediately, Mack found himself antsy about what was taking her so long. She could have other plans. He should have given her more choices. If she couldn't make it that night, there was always tomorrow night, or any evening that worked for her. Two hours after he hit the send button, he still hadn't heard from her, but there was no time to dwell on it. He and Sydney were absorbed in interviewing applicants, some in person, some online, to fill a handful of open staff jobs. They worked through lunch and into the afternoon. Before he left, he went through a long list of messages sent through the lodge's internal communications system. He was nearing the end when Erin called.

She bypassed a greeting altogether. "Is the invitation still open? I missed the text. Too much renovation racket going on around me, and I didn't hear it."

"You bet it is." He hesitated. "Liam will be so pleased that you can come."

"The feeling is mutual. Want me to bring anything?"

"Nope...we don't need a thing." He'd come up with something for dinner. "Well, maybe binoculars if you want to join me at the window to keep an eye on the woods out back. But that horse must be out there."

They settled on a time, and Mack closed up his office and waved to Sydney on his way out. He met Liam at the bus drop-off spot at the end of the road and settled him in the car. "Guess who I invited to come over for dinner? It's one of your favorite people."

"Does she have a horse?" Liam posed the question in a sly tone of voice and smiled.

Mack laughed. "I guess I didn't fool you. That's why we're going shopping."

After a serious consultation with his seven-year-old inside the downtown market, they settled on having pizza for a main dish. He got salad fixings and a giant-size package of breadsticks. He already had two flavors of ice cream at home. "We're all set, buddy," he said to Liam, who'd already told Tina, the checker, they were having company for dinner.

"Did you know that we have the best pizza in the county?" Tina pointed to the wall where the poster announced their number one status. "See? I'm not exaggerating. We got most of the votes."

Mack chuckled. Primarily a grocery store, the market also was a reliable source of prepared meals, including their homemade pizza. Mack and Liam knew their menu like the frequent customers they were.

"My mom said the Pied Piper made the best pizza place in Millerton. That's where we lived," Liam said. "Then she died."

Mack snapped to attention. He hadn't seen that coming. From her expression, Mack saw

Liam had caught Tina off guard. Why not? She couldn't have anticipated the shift from their light banter into serious territory. Her expression changed, but only for a second or two.

"Well, I'm very sorry to hear about your mom, but I'm glad you live here now."

"Thanks, Tina." Mack admired her seamless response.

On the drive home, Mack listened attentively to Liam tell him a couple of stories about him and his mom. Was buying a pizza the single trigger for the string of memories and stories about what used to be? The market's already prepared food wasn't a novelty. The market also supplied pizza to the deli at the lodge, so now and again, Liam's after-school snack was a hot slice Mack brought home.

Mack finally surrendered. He couldn't put his finger on what in that exchange with Tina brought on Liam's recollections. More puzzling to Mack was the boy's willingness to talk about Paula with a relative stranger. A silver lining existed, though. During his earliest days with Liam, the boy had little to say about anything and was visibly upset when he asked his grandparents or Mack about his mom. Today at the market, Liam wasn't emotional as he spoke. Maybe he'd reached a stage of grief when he could have simple exchanges about his mom;

and Tina's friendly demeanor had brought out Liam's talkative side.

A couple hours later, when Erin and Neptune arrived, the cheese topping the pizza was melting nicely in the oven, and mixed aromas of sausage, tomatoes and onions filled the bunkhouse. Mack's green salad sat in the middle of the table.

Liam proudly pointed to himself. "*I* helped tear the lettuce into little pieces."

"I'm sure it's going to be the best salad I ever ate," Erin said, squeezing his shoulder.

"Is it your birthday?" Liam asked.

"Uh, no." Erin met Mack's eye. "My birthday isn't until late June."

"Oh, okay. Dad said we were having a special dinner for a special guest."

"I meant because she's our good friend," Mack said, conscious of his face warming. Impossible. Blushing wasn't his thing. Later, he'd tell her he was only referring to being on runaway horse watch. That should clear things up.

CHAPTER NINE

ERIN FELT RIGHT at home. Maybe too much so. She'd taken over bedtime story duty while Mack cleaned up. Instead of her reading to Liam, he read two chapters of a kids' mystery tale to her. She left Liam's room when Mack came to tuck him in while she took Neptune out for a quick turn around the bunkhouse. She knew her dog was completely at ease in Mack's house because his tail wagged wildly when she brought him inside. Even without a fire going, Neptune wasted no time curling up on the rug in front of the fireplace.

"Shall we?" Mack said, flipping off the bright kitchen lights. He pulled two dining table chairs up to the side window. Erin joined him. To keep ambient light from filtering in, he closed the blinds of the windows on the front and the other side of the house. It wasn't a perfect solution, but it blocked out much of the light from the road and the Hoovers' house.

Then, like Mack, Erin settled in the chair and propped her feet on the windowsill, binoculars in hand.

With the lights off and her night vision taking over, the woods became sharper and the trees differentiated. The town in Indiana where Erin was from was situated in flat farm country, one of the vast parts of the state where woods were scarce. Until she moved to Adelaide Creek, she hadn't lived among stands of trees and rocky ledges, in basins surrounded by mountains. Every day her eyes scanned a landscape that was never the same twice. Now Erin couldn't imagine her life without these sights. The woods still held an air of mystery, like a world apart that thrived without the need for humans to even notice or interfere.

In the silence, Erin picked up her binoculars and zeroed in on the ground between the clusters of trees where they had a better chance of sighting the horse's movements if he wandered near Mack's place. Erin wasn't sure how much time had passed, but at one point, Mack left to check on Liam. Lost in her own thoughts and observations, Erin didn't hear him return to the main room.

"Can I get you anything?" he asked in a voice just above a whisper.

She held up the bottle of local Jadestone beer.

"I've barely touched this, so I'm good. I think the woods hypnotized me. For real."

"Uh-oh. Are you going to cluck like a chicken?" Mack asked as he took his place next to her. "Or do a jig in the middle of the room?"

"Ha! Maybe *mesmerized* is a better word for the state I'm in. Same difference, though." She lowered her voice and added, "Your bunkhouse views are different in every direction, but put 'em together and they're like a built-in stress management kit. Really."

"I agree. When we first moved in, I had a hard time concentrating on anything other than Liam and a long to-do list. But if I sat here and watched the snow come down in the woods, I could relax a little." He nodded toward the row of windows that looked out at the distant mountain peaks. "I almost never close those blinds. On clear nights, the view goes on and on, one row of mountains after another."

Mack returned his gaze to the woods in front of them. "I don't know why, but I can't shake the idea that the horse is Harris, and he will come back this way."

"Everyone is on alert now," Erin said. "Willow mentioned it in a text, and she and Tom will keep their eyes open. They're close to the creek, a source of water. If the horse you saw belongs to the Burtons, he's very close to home. Heather says the horses typically won't travel far, but they can be skittish and hide from people— avoiding encounters with strangers."

"Natural instinct, I suppose. Makes sense." Mack picked up his binoculars again. "Horses that ride the same trails day after day, like at our holiday ranches, can always be trusted to know the way home."

Erin agreed, but with a caveat. "Horses will avoid places where they've been frightened. That's why they'll balk sometimes, and even the owner doesn't always know what's riling them up." Another theory occurred to her. "Maybe somebody frightened the horse you spotted. And maybe did the same with the other ones."

"You mean, like a prank?"

"I can't say that for sure. But it's a possibility." Erin shrugged. "Seems no one wants to come out and say the horses were stolen. Folks have been quick to rule out theft."

Mack nodded. "Most everybody around here talks about horse theft like it's practically a thing of the past." Mack scrunched his face in disgust. "I would like to think that, too, but…"

Erin settled back in the chair and attempted to purge the images of horses being taken away, scared and alone. "I hope Raven's okay. I mean, I know she is. I just talked to Jeff this afternoon."

"I had thought it wouldn't be long before I got a horse for Liam and one for myself, but I'll have to hold off on that. Meanwhile, I wish the one we're waiting to see wander out of these woods would show up. It was like a ghost appearing and disappearing in a veil of fog." He lifted the binoculars to his eyes. "What we're doing is probably futile."

But fun, Erin almost uttered. She managed to swallow the words in time. Mack might see it as flirtatious. That wouldn't do. In the time she'd known him, she'd reminded herself more than once to keep him at arm's length. Since here she was, sitting in his darkened living room, she was failing miserably at that. A casual friendship between two relative newcomers to town. That was the single attitude toward Mack that made any sense at all. A couple of pals, that was what they were.

"But it's sure an enjoyable way to spend an evening," Mack said in a low, dry tone.

Erin squelched a laugh this time. Mack's flirtatiousness was exactly what she'd intended to avoid. Yet, matching his tone, she added, "After a really good dinner." She smiled, but didn't look at him. "Ex...cellent breadsticks." In an ordinary tone that wouldn't have come off as coy, but she'd made it so.

"Right. That's why I invited you here. To show

off my ability to buy good food, already pre-pared." He scoffed. "I was referring to the company, ya know."

Erin laughed this time. "You and Liam are great hosts."

"Kidding aside, it's good for Liam to have people over," Mack said, his voice low, even sober. "But…"

Erin's curiosity won out. "Um, but what? You didn't finish the sentence."

"If I tell you what I was thinking," Mack said, sounding like his regular self again, "I already know how you'll respond. And I don't want to make too much of it."

Wondering what he meant, she pushed the conversation forward. "Be brave. Tell me, what-ever it is. You can trust me, Mack. What you tell me stays with me."

In the dark, Mack reached for her hand and gave it a quick squeeze. "Thanks. It's about Liam…of course. And the way his mom comes up."

In a tone showing mild concern, Mack told Erin about Liam's spontaneous story about his mom that he shared with the checker at the market. To Erin's ears, it didn't sound like anything to be worried about. On the other hand, who was she to tell him what to be, or not be, concerned about? Yet in a roundabout way, he was asking for her opinion.

She took a deep breath. "Okay, here's my take, but remember, I'm no expert on kids. Is it possible it's a positive sign when his mom comes up in casual conversations? Isn't it a confirmation that he knows she's really gone? Kids do adapt to change, and maybe he accepts that his old life isn't coming back. Or accepts it as much as such a young child can."

Mack stretched his arms over his head and then rolled his shoulders forward and back. Erin recognized his movements as a way Mack handled stress.

"I'm not sure. Most of the time I think he's acting like a typical kid, but then he has one of his middle-of-the-night moments. Or, like earlier, he's suddenly recounting a memory of his old life."

"But Mack, Liam's confident behavior out in the world is not your imagination. Ask anyone who sees you and Liam, and they'll tell you he's exactly like a regular, untroubled kid. And you've been smart enough to bring in Dr. Harte to help." Erin sighed. "What I'm saying is that you have allies. Like me. I'm one of many new people in your son's life—adults and kids." She paused and then chuckled. "I suppose I'm bragging, but not every kid is lucky enough to have my brother as his pediatrician."

"Or a personal cookie baker." Mack grinned. "I'd never forget to add you to the mix. And the pooch who's snuffling at your side. Must be dreaming of good smells." He reached out to squeeze her hand again, this time letting his fingers rest over hers for a couple of seconds.

Erin let out the breath she'd been holding. "Does Liam ever feel like his mom is with him or looking out for him?"

"Sometimes he believes she's there with him, but he seems uncertain whether that's a good feeling or not."

Erin put her hand on his arm, missing their contact from a moment ago. "I can tell you this, Mack. I miss my mother every day, but what comforts me is the idea that she knows I'm okay."

"You think she's watching over you?" Mack asked in a soft voice.

"I sometimes sense that, but I don't know how things work—" she made circles with her hand above her head "—on the other side. But it's the idea that love doesn't die that's important to me. Liam is old enough, and smart enough too, to understand that, if you talked to him about it."

Mack nodded. "I like that. You're right. I

haven't been that clear because I'm not sure what I believe."

"It's possible he'd be less worried if you assure him that even if he can't see her, his mom always knows where he is. Could be it's enough for a seven-year-old to have a sense of her closeness and that she's not just…gone." Erin took a gulp of her beer, got to her feet and walked closer to the window. "Soon enough, I suppose, Liam will accept her death as one of life's mysteries. Like these woods."

"Right. So far, the trees aren't giving up their secrets about the horse."

"At least not tonight." Erin looked around her, as if she'd forgotten how long she'd been sitting with Mack. "I wonder what time it is."

Mack looked at his phone. "I can't believe it. It's almost midnight."

"Whoa, I better go." She nodded at Neptune, who shifted his position, ears twitching.

Before she could gather her backpack, Mack froze. "Liam is up." He gestured for her to follow him. Was that a good idea? It seemed intimate, an invasion of his privacy. Mack gestured again, so she quit analyzing her question and tiptoed behind him to the door of Liam's room. Neptune followed, but didn't make any noise. Liam looked so small sitting up in bed and rubbing his eyes. "Hey, buddy," Mack said. "You're awake, but it's not morning. Let's get you back to sleep."

"My mom died," Liam whispered, his head slumped forward, his chin touching his chest. "I wish she was here." Mack turned to glance at Erin over his shoulder.

"It's okay, Liam, because your mom knows exactly where you are. She can always find you, buddy."

Liam was silent.

"She'll always love you, and you will always love her. Don't ever doubt that."

"Are you sure? Can my mom really see me?" Liam asked.

Mack gazed at Erin again before bringing Liam closer to his chest. "I'm sure she knows you're safe here with me."

Erin brushed tears from her cheeks. This was so, so different from being an adult when she lost her mom, especially because she'd been with her and had taken care of her mom during the last year. She'd known the essence of her mother. No question, no problem there. She'd wanted a full, happy life for Erin and lived to see Erin find work she was passionate about. She'd been proud that Erin taught herself to play the piano and violin in high school. Erin had memories to cling to. But Liam had much more to cope with.

"C'mon," Erin whispered to the dog, leading him back to the main room and leaving Mack to settle Liam under the covers. "Time to go home, Neptune," she whispered. "Let's get in the van."

Instead of following her, Neptune sat on his haunches and stared down the hall. Erin tried to coax him to follow her, but not this time. She was still by the door when Mack came down the short hallway. Only then did the dog agree it was time to leave and wander to the door. "Thanks so much for the chance to watch for the horse. I hope Liam's okay now."

"I carried him to my bed, and he's already asleep." Mack wrapped his arms around her in a goodbye hug. "We didn't spot the horse, but it was fun trying."

"Yes." A dangerous kind of fun. Risky to her heart.

She started to ease from his arms, but before she did, he pressed his lips to her cheek and then took a couple of small steps back. Surprised, her fingertips touched the spot where his soft beard had caressed her skin. When she raised her head, he lowered his mouth and kissed her again, this time on the lips. A kiss that enveloped her in his warmth. When it was over, she rested her cheek against his chest. His heart was beating hard.

Saying a soft good-night, she avoided his gaze and gave Neptune all her attention. "Come on, Neptune, let's go."

She didn't look directly at Mack until she was at the door of her van, where she turned to wave goodbye. She was both exhilarated and confused, happy despite her underlying sense this was a fleeting moment. And that was what it should be.

HE HADN'T PLANNED the kiss. But he'd followed his desire—and his sense that she'd respond—and took the risk. He'd have liked to hold her in his arms longer, but the moment came to an end. Then Erin avoided looking him in the eye. From shyness? Surprised by the intensity, the pure pleasure, like he'd been? Maybe. He could hope that was true.

After her van disappeared down the driveway, Mack returned to Liam. Even in the dim light, he could see his tousled hair on the pillow and one arm stretched across his body. Mack climbed into bed and stared at his son's hand with its long fingers so like his own.

At times like these, Mack wondered how he could've ever thrown away his chance to experience this kind of love. It was hard to explain this change that had come over him. He doubted Erin was aware that he'd picked up on her skepticism of him. Mack could read faces if not minds, and hers was an open book. Erin knew the facts of Paula's death and how he came to have Liam, but knowing wasn't the same as understanding what had transformed Mack. Her quizzical expressions revealed that.

Erin also didn't realize how much Mack was haunted by the contrast between him and so many of the men he'd met, guys he admired. Matt, Jeff and Tom were dads to kids that weren't theirs, at least until the family court made fatherhood a legal reality. They'd already become dads in their hearts long before lawyers and judges had their say.

Jeff had taken charge of an orphaned teen and now Jillian. Matt Burton was raising his late sister's twins, and when Tom married Willow, he immediately filed adoption papers. Before her first birthday, Naomi had two parents. According to Erin, they'd soon work with the agency again and adopt a brother or sister for Naomi. Mack already knew more about these men and their families than he'd ever known about Andy's wife and children. With rare exception, Andy didn't like talking about much of anything except business.

With images of Erin flitting around in his

head, he almost gave up hope of sleeping, but Liam's peaceful breathing eventually persuaded him to sleep. He stirred early, though, before six o'clock. He hurried to the window as if an invisible arm led him there to get a glimpse of the horse standing quietly, not so deep in the woods this time. But then, as if an internal signal had gone off, the horse turned and vanished.

Mack's view of the horse had been at least good enough to see that he was brown and had some white markings on his face and chest. Without a second to waste, Mack contacted Matt first, and then Erin. When he turned to start the coffee and get the morning underway, his eye caught something red hanging on the back of one of the kitchen chairs. Erin's scarf. He plucked it up, and without thinking, he recognized the soft wool's scent. Of course it smelled like cinnamon and freshly cut wood. A combination of sweet and outdoorsy, like her.

He hadn't expected to react like this, not to this scent, not to her. He had no business pondering the way Erin smelled. Or how hearing her laugh only egged him on to make it happen again. Mack was no fool. He recognized the signals that his world was tilting. Those telltale signs hadn't flashed in front of him for a good long time, but they were obvious now.

Forcing his attention back to Liam and getting ready to take off for the day, Mack scrambled some eggs and piled strawberry jam on a toasted English muffin. Then he checked Liam's backpack for the library book and his lunch card for the school cafeteria. He waited until after Liam was on the school bus to send a text: scarf not lost...i have it...will get it 2 u. Feeling buoyant inside, like a teenager, he detoured to the bakery on his route to work. He got two coffees, extra cream for her and a box of doughnuts. Then he headed to the mansion.

Before going inside, he left a message for Sydney that he'd be a few minutes late.

After hearing Erin's descriptions of the hutch she was working on, Mack rounded the corner into the dining room, expecting that was where she'd be. He was right. He found her.

She wasn't alone.

Quincy was with her, along with three other people he didn't recognize. They were looking at architectural drawings spread out on the table. Five heads went up when he stopped at the threshold into the room.

Erin's eyes, wide-open in what fell short of happy surprise, fixated on the cardboard tray with two coffees and the container of doughnuts balanced in his other hand. Worse, he'd left her scarf on the front seat of his SUV. *Smooth, Mack, smooth.* For a guy who'd always considered himself confident, he felt pretty foolish.

"Doughnuts, anyone?" he asked with a laugh in his voice. "I've got a big box of them fresh from the bakery."

"Well, good morning, Mack," Quincy boomed. The smile he sported was obviously as much amused as friendly. "So nice of you to visit us."

"Uh, Mack, thanks for the coffee," Erin said, her gaze shifting to the carton holding the cups. "We're…having a meeting right now. Can I get back to you later?"

Quincy flashed a puzzled look at Erin and opened his mouth as if to speak, but apparently changed his mind, because he lowered his head and focused on the drawings.

"Of course, sure. I'm sorry to barge in like this." He spotted a worktable off to the side and put the tray and the doughnuts down. "Call me when you get a chance."

Erin nodded. "I will. Uh, soon."

Feeling even more like a red-faced teenager, Mack retraced his steps and headed for Tall Tale. He detoured to Sidney's office, but then was surprised, and not in a good way, to see Andy's image on her screen.

"We didn't have a meeting," he said, "or did we? Did I forget?"

Sydney stared at him, clearly puzzled. Mack didn't forget meetings. "Matter of fact, we did."

"What happened?" Andy demanded.

"Nothing big. I had to drop off something

downtown. A personal thing." Wasn't exactly a lie. Mack settled in the chair opposite Sydney, surreptitiously peeking at his watch, reassured that he couldn't possibly have missed more than a few minutes of the conversation. "What's on this morning's agenda?"

Sydney tilted her screen so Mack could see it, too. "Willow's art show," Andy said with a smirk.

Andy could smirk all he wanted, but the exhibit of local arts and crafts had been the Tall Tale Lodge & Spa's first major event that brought people from the community to the lodge. They didn't trickle in, either, but showed up in notable numbers, a fact not lost on the reporter who wrote about the art show's opening reception.

"Good," Mack said. "I assume we'll hold it in mid-June again. Willow and her team will want to get the press releases out. Start building anticipation. Is the list of exhibitors complete? Maybe we'll get some new artists…you know, emerging…" He willed himself to stop rambling on.

"Willow has it covered, Mack." Sydney shot a pointed look at him. She might as well have told him to shut up. "She wants to expand—put up a couple of tents in the green space outside and hold the reception on the veranda."

Mack glanced at Andy, who hadn't said a word. "Willow knows how to throw a party."

Sydney smiled in agreement, but Andy's pinched face brought to mind what happened when Liam bit into a lemon before Mack could warn him.

Andy shrugged. That was that.

But it wasn't. Not for Mack. Things had been tense between the two of them before, during, and after their big talk, which Mack mistakenly had thought cleared the air. This tension didn't get past Sydney. It would soon complicate her life—if it hadn't already. Somebody had to end this hostility, and it looked like it was going to be him. His mind started writing the script of his arguments, the ones he'd use later.

Mack didn't get far, because Sydney broke in and caught him off guard. "Okay, you two, what's going on? You act like you barely know each other, and what you do know, you don't like much."

"Hey, Sydney," Andy barked, "this is for Mack and me to work out."

"Maybe so," she said, "but something's changed in your partnership, and I'm not refer-ring to Mack's hours." She paused. "And what-ever it is, I don't like it. I own this place, too, you know. The place runs very smoothly, thank you. I think you both forget what I do here."

"It's about Liam, Sydney," Mack said.

"Not the boy himself. I'm not heartless." Andy directed his words to Sydney. "Mack and I had a conversation about the changes in his life. It's like he's someone he never was before."

In a wry tone, Sydney said, "It's called being a dad, Andy. You should know."

"C'mon, Syd, he can be a dad and still take care of business," Andy insisted.

Like a game of ping-pong, Sydney shot back, "Give the man time. Right now he's dad and mom, too. As far as I can see, Mack is holding up his end of the agreement. You're looking for something to gripe about."

Andy immediately lobbed another comment. "His head's not in the consulting game anymore, plus the holiday ranches are opening soon for the season."

"So what? It's not like those are a brand-new thing—you've had them up and running like well-oiled machines for years," Sydney argued.

Mack had had enough. "Stop…stop. You're talking about me like I'm not in the room." Mack had a powerful—but irrational—urge to tell Andy he wanted out of the ranches, but had the good sense to hold himself back. It was way too soon to make that kind of decision, let alone blurt it out. Instead, he apologized for coming in a few minutes late. "It's not a habit and won't become one. Andy, you and I can talk about the ranches on our time, not Sydney's.

Nothing new to do this season. It's my job to track our numbers, and I'll do that as always."

And for as long as their increasing profits year over year had remained their joint priority, the system they created worked. But Mack's center had shifted, and it would never go back. When it came to figuring out his future as a business guy, he looked less Andy's way and more in the direction of his new friends. And his own father.

When a phone call came in for Sydney, Mack left. Although troubled by Andy's attitude, his thoughts drifted. Erin. A horse lost in the woods. And Liam and his grief. He didn't have much room for Andy's complaints.

MACK HAD LEFT the treats on the table, but the scarf was nowhere to be seen. A confusing guy, Mack. He walked in on the meeting with no warning. Like the way he'd surprised her with that kiss. Erin thought she'd created a little cubbyhole in her mind and named it Mack. Her friend had a charming son she enjoyed spending time with. But then, after a fun evening, when she was supposed to remind herself he was only a friend, he'd kissed her. A romantic kiss. With his arms wrapped around her. An embrace, not a friendly hug. Sweet enough that it interfered with her sleep. But then she'd started her day dreamy and unfocused. That wouldn't do. Not at all. It wasn't even like her.

It had been a long time since she'd enjoyed the feel of a man's lips on hers. She'd just as soon forget some of those memories when pleasant kisses hadn't led to anything but a bunch of hurt feelings later. A particular guy had walked away when Erin gave up her apartment and moved in with her mother to take care of her. That didn't sit well with her boyfriend, who complained—whined—that she didn't have as much time for him. True. But she'd learned an important lesson. That man had been selfish and unreliable. Family held no importance for him. At least she'd had a glimpse of the real person before she'd done something drastic like marry him.

It only made sense that thoughts of Mack would lead to a restless night, where disturbing memories intruded. Hadn't she spent a lifetime resenting a man who'd abandoned her? She'd had enough of that theme in her life already.

She worked on the intricately carved piece, removing what was old and prepping the spots that needed special attention and repairs. Another little voice intervened and insisted on arguing the other side. This voice challenged her. Hadn't Mack changed his ways? He was even a little tortured by his mistake. She'd seen

the love in *his* eyes when he was with Liam.
Maybe he'd seemed kind of awkward with Liam
on Valentine's Day, but now everything had
changed. Who would guess that Mack hadn't
been part of his son's life from the day he was
born? No one.

Erin focused on brushing away the sanding
debris from the section of the hutch. In her spe-
cialized piece of the restoration, she measured
progress in inches and the number of curves
stripped clean. The drone of sanders filtered
down from the upstairs rooms. Her crew had
used heat guns to strip away the old varnish,
and now they were using sanders to smooth
window trim and wainscoting and the long pan-
els of built-in armoires. Their daily accomplish-
ment was obvious—measured in large swaths
of exposed raw oak. But as slow as her work
was, day by day, she could see her progress.
Maybe Mack thought about his bond with Liam
the same way. Slow and steady.

The direction of Erin's thoughts changed
again. She drifted back to the bunkhouse window, sitting in silence. Watching, waiting. No
pressure to talk, but no lack of things to talk
about, while they watched the woods for signs
of life.

Thinking about the lost horse triggered an
idea. She grabbed her phone and texted Mack.

CHAPTER TEN

EARLY ON SATURDAY MORNING, Erin led Raven out of her stall, while Jillian and Olivia came inside the stable with Liam in tow. She and Raven were going to join Mack on an Appaloosa named Sherwood, one of Jeff's horses, for a ride. They had all watched earlier as Mack had led Liam on Dot around the corral for the first time.

"It's so sunny today, perfect to play outside with Winnie," Olivia said, patting Liam's shoulder. "Neptune's here, too."

"Okay." Liam spoke politely, but he was more interested in saying goodbye to Dot, who was standing with Burroughs. Erin would swear that spotted beauty had deliberately bobbed his head and nickered to get Liam's attention. Meanwhile, the two dogs wanted to be noticed.

Other than school, Erin knew that Mack hadn't left Liam with anyone. But when he accepted her invitation, he acknowledged it was time to trust the people he considered his friends to watch over his son. Then he'd scheduled the Saturday morning corral ride with Liam before the ride with Erin, a plan Jillian liked a lot. She'd pick up a few dollars babysitting for the boy she already knew pretty well.

Erin agreed it was a fine day for not only a ride, but maybe a chance to again spot the horse Mack presumed to be Harris, or one of the other missing horses. As the forecast promised, the morning mist was already evaporating in the fields and woods, replaced by sunlight breaking through the cloud cover that had been with them most of the week. Sporadic warm days were scattered among the typical cold, windy stretches of April. Slushy rain could turn to ice, making its unique kind of racket as it hit windows and windshields. But not today, Erin thought.

Erin watched as Mack handled Sherwood, a responsive horse, relatively young like Raven, as he eagerly picked up speed on the wide path they'd chosen.

Erin and Mack had been warned about a few potential obstacles or tricky spots on the trail near the top of the hill behind the cabins. Armed with information, Erin was eager to get to the trail, where the views were spectacular.

"I have been looking forward to this since I

drove into Adelaide Creek on the first of January," Mack said, puffing out his cheeks, followed by a loud, satisfied exhale.

He'd spoken slowly and with such conviction that Erin laughed. "You sound like a desperate man."

"Desperate for this kind of change," he said, patting Sherwood. "Those couple of times I saw the lost horse in the mist, I really wished I could put a saddle on him and ride him home."

Erin brought Raven to a stop at the end of the path, and Mack followed her lead. She gestured across the acres of pasture that bumped up to the hills and slabs of rock that formed ledges in the distance. "The trails circle around to the other side of town, where the Hoovers and the Burtons are. That's where the horse you've seen could be roaming."

Erin saw the concern in Mack's expression. "Some folks think the horse may be stuck on the trail, but getting enough water because of the spring melt, which exposes shrubs that provide food. He might stay in the same place because he's surviving," Erin said. "Or maybe he's scared, and he won't go back."

They rode toward the ridge, gradually picking up the pace until Erin spotted one of the hazards, a configuration of slabs, flat as kitchen tables, but crisscrossing each other at the corners, effectively blocking access to the trail above. "This is where we have to slow down and let the horses pick their way through the dips and holes," Erin said. She leaned forward and patted Raven's neck. "You can do it, girl. You're not going to let a pile of rocks stop you."

Mack chuckled. "Sounds like you're talking to yourself. A pile of rocks wouldn't stop you either, any more than charred wood keeps you from seeing the beauty underneath it."

Erin tilted her head and said a quick thank-you, but she kept her eyes on Sherwood expertly navigating the slabs and bypassing Raven to make it to the trail. "Wow, Sherwood looks like he's done that before, huh?"

"He probably has," Mack said. "Jeff bought him last summer and uses him as a trail horse with adults and older kids."

They stopped talking while Mack and the trail expert, Sherwood, led the way through the rocky terrain to the flatter ground. "Good job, Sherwood," Erin said, amused, and pleased Raven followed the other horse without balking.

Mack gave the horse a friendly pat on his mane. "I like a guy who knows his way around."

Maybe he'd found his horse, Erin thought. Or Liam's. "Will Liam be one of Jeff's new students this summer?"

"That's the plan right now. He'll be eight, a

good age to start. Today was a practice run. He had a chance to get used to the saddle and stirrups and holding the reins. Heather and Matt's twins already ride now, too, on their ranch, but they're still learning," Mack said. "They'll be a good influence on Liam."

"I'm sure you're right," Erin said. "I was thinking the other day that when I drove out here from Florida to find Tom, I had ideas, maybe some fantasies about a new life. Hard to believe it was less than a year ago. But as much as I envisioned my new life, I'd never pictured it falling into place so fast." The image of the kids in the stable prompted her to add, "I never thought kids would be such an important part of my new home."

"Thinking about little Naomi, are you?" Mack teased.

"Well, of course. But don't forget not-so-little Liam," Erin added with no hesitation. "I mean, he's my pal, too. And I enjoy the twins and the older kids."

"Uh, do you want to have kids yourself?"

Erin made herself not look at Mack. She might blush if she did. So ridiculous. It was a simple enough question. "I do. One day." She injected more conviction into her voice than she'd intended.

"You'll be a wonderful mom," Mack said, "whenever that happens."

The heady, intimate tone sent a pleasant buzz traveling through Erin's arms and down to her fingertips. Deflecting her attention away, she said an enthusiastic thank-you so loud it surprised her. Then she gestured toward the grassy slope that went down to the vast basin, still not fully green, yet dotted with a few sheep and their lambs. "Speaking of mothers, what a sight, huh?" She gestured to the curve of the ridge behind them.

Mack pointed across to the long rocky swath of land marked with outcroppings, but edging against the woods. "And if I'm not mistaken, the Burton and Hoover ranches have acres that back into that ridge. The view of the basin from every part of this town makes me doubly glad I moved here."

Erin sighed. "I got my first view of the basin the morning after I arrived on Tom's doorstep, and I couldn't help but feel it welcomed me. I got little shivers and goose bumps." She glanced at Mack, but quickly looked away. "That probably sounds lame to a Wyoming native."

"Not at all," Mack said quietly. "I get it."

If Erin could read Raven's mind, she'd claim the horse was happy to be on the brink of what would be the best part of the year. As fickle as a Wyoming spring could be, Raven still would spend many more hours outside. Watching Sherwood navigate the trail from memory reminded Erin how attuned horses were to their environment. Sherwood knew the road and trails by heart, and the winter hadn't faded his memory.

"Penny for your thoughts, and all that," Mack said, breaking their silence.

"Just thinking about our two horses. I'm impressed with Sherwood. If we ever get lost, we have a horse to show us the way home."

"Speaking of horses, all this makes me think of ours out here somewhere." Mack frowned. "I hope it's surviving okay and hasn't been injured somehow."

"Crosby, the guy on the mansion's crew, is worried about Sundown, and from the description, he could be the horse you saw," Erin said. "Crosby told Quincy he'd been thinking about selling Sundown." Before Mack had a chance to respond, Erin's phone chimed and yanked her back to reality. "Oops. That's my reminder. We have to turn back. I'm meeting Quincy and a couple of my crew." She caught Mack's eye and confessed. "Tell you the truth, I was so absorbed out here, I forgot my afternoon plans." She waved her phone. "But there's no ignoring them now."

Mack smiled. "I understand. The way I feel out here riding with you, I could forget appointments, too. No worries. We'll pick up speed on the road. The horses will like that."

With Sherwood again leading the way, they picked their way back through the slabs and onto the farm road. Neither horse needed coaxing to break into a gallop on the home stretch. "That reminder about the meeting put me in work mode," Erin said when they slowed down on the path to the stable and corral. As soon as they dismounted and walked the horses to the barn, Erin hurried to remove the saddle from Raven and started brushing her down.

Mack put his hand on her shoulder. "You go. I'll finish up with Raven. Liam and Jillian are probably around, and they'll want to help with the horses."

"You sure? We really did ride too far for the time we had." She smiled as if sharing a secret. "But it was fun. Let's do it again. When you get back from Millerton."

"Count on it. As much as I want Liam to have his visit with his grandparents, I don't want to miss what's going on here."

"I'll keep you posted," Erin said. "Believe me, if anything happens with these horses, you'll be my first text." Mack put his hand against her cheek and began to lower his head, but he dropped his hand when Burroughs came inside. "You better get going. Don't be late. I'll see you in a week or so."

Erin nodded and broke into a jog. She called out to Neptune, who left the kids and Winnie and jumped into the van when Erin opened the back. Climbing into the driver's side, she put her fingertips on her cheek where Mack's hand had been. Why did she do that when he touched her? The answer was so obvious. She didn't want the memory of his touch to fade.

MACK STEPPED INSIDE Eden and Louis's house, pointed at Liam, and lifted his voice as if introducing a star. "Here he is. Prepare to be entertained. Everything my son seems to do lately becomes another rollicking chapter in a young boy's adventure story."

"I can't wait to hear it all," Louis said. "He's like his mom. She was a fun storyteller, too."

Louis's words gave Mack a start. They'd barely arrived and taken their jackets off before Louis brought up Paula. Mack kept his eye on Liam during the initial exchange, and sure enough, a little frown appeared. The boy's blue eyes, so like Mack's, darkened almost imperceptibly. Eden must have noticed, because she hurried them into the kitchen and put out an early dinner of hot dogs and chips.

As they sat around the table, Eden asked Liam about Jillian. Liam took the bait, quickly making a detour, first to describe Winnie, Carson's dog, and then to tell them about his new friends, the Burton twins, Lucy and Nick. "It's fun at Jillian's house. Yesterday, I had my first ride on Dot. We were in the corral, and then we rode on the path. Right, Dad?"

"That's right." He turned to Louis and Eden. "I've got some pictures I'll send to your phones."

"Dad and I are going to get horses, and they can live in the stable with lots of other horses," Liam said, adding more details to the picture he was painting for his grandparents about his life. "Our friend Erin has a horse named Raven. She lives there. When Dad and Erin rode along the trail way, way far away on the ridge, he took Sherwood." Liam swept his arm forward and over his head to show how far away the ridge was.

Now it was Eden's turn to frown. Feigning curiosity, she said, "Isn't that the person you call the cookie lady?"

As if she didn't know, Mack thought. Liam had talked a lot about all these friends during his FaceTimes with his grandparents. He'd brought up Raven and the stables numerous times. Mack could almost feel his guardrails rising. He'd hoped that Eden was going to ask Liam a lot of questions to elicit a few of his colorful stories. But was it also a way to grill her grandson about how he and Mack spent their time, and with whom?

"Yep, Erin's job is fixing old wood." Liam spoke in the bragging tone he often used when talking about Erin. "One night, we heard her sing and play her fiddle."

"Yes, Liam, I remember you telling us about that night at that *bar*."

"Well, not just any bar, Eden. It's a restaurant with a bar at Tall Tale," Mack said defensively. "We bring in entertainment on the weekends. Erin was filling in for another musician in the band who's injured."

Eden raised her eyebrows. "It just seemed like an odd place for a child as young as Liam to be on a Saturday night."

"Normally, I'd agree," Mack said, keeping a reasonable tone, "but the band and the manager intentionally designated it a family-friendly show—most of his performances are. We sat with the same friends Liam's been telling you about for months now." Almost as an afterthought, Mack added, "It turns out Erin is a talented musician."

"Bet that was fun, huh?" Louis had one arm resting on the back of Liam's chair.

Liam nodded, the picture of contentment as he sat at the table, swinging his legs and munching the chips left on his plate. So innocent, Mack thought, and unaware of the tensions simmering below the surface. Odd, too, because Mack sensed something was off as soon as Eden had opened her front door to greet them. Maybe it was the way she'd whisked Liam off to "his room," set up for a boy living there, not paying a visit. *But that is okay.* Mack repeated the words to himself. For seven years, this house, that room, his mom's old bedroom, was Liam's second home. Mack also allowed for the possibility that his jittery, anxious feelings might have clouded his ability to read the room. Not feelings he enjoyed, if for no other reason than he genuinely liked Eden and Louis. He was lost in these thoughts when he heard Eden call his name. "Oh, sorry, my mind wandered off." He looked at her expectantly.

Eden smiled. "No problem. I was saying that I thought Liam might want to unpack and settle into his room now and spend a little time with us before bed."

In other words, Mack, it's time to go away. "Sure. You're right." He got to his feet, ready to make a quick exit.

"Uh, you're going to the hotel now?" Liam asked, his tone curious and a little cautious.

"I am, buddy. Remember I said that you were going to stay here with your grandparents." He glanced at Eden and Louis. "Then I'm coming back tomorrow night, and we'll all have pizza."

"But I don't have a phone," Liam said, his forehead wrinkling. "What if I want to talk to you?"

That question surprised Mack, but fortunately, it also was easily addressed. "Okay, here's what we'll do. Tomorrow morning, I'll call your grandma Eden, and she'll give her phone to you, so I'll get a chance to say hello." He pointed to Louis and then Eden. "But if you ever want to talk to me, just tell your grandparents. They can call me on their phones." This was an arrangement he'd planned to discuss with Eden, anyway.

"Oh, Liam, you'll be so busy doing things with us, you won't think about—" Eden hesitated "—making phone calls." Addressing Mack, she said, "Uh, we thought we'd take him to the mall tomorrow. We'll let him pick something out at the toy store. There's a Ferris wheel. Maybe get him some new clothes for summer. That's okay, isn't it?"

"Sure, of course." He understood. They wanted to be alone with their grandson. Mack never forgot that by taking Liam across the state to a new town, he'd changed Eden and Louis's lives, too.

"I'm working remotely from the hotel, so for me, it will be almost like another day at the office."

Mack moved around the table to Liam's chair. "Time for my goodbye hug, buddy." Liam slipped off the chair and walked with Mack to the front door. Eden and Louis followed and stood behind their grandson. When Mack crouched down, Liam stepped into his open arms.

Eventually, Liam let go of Mack, but he poked his shoulder. "Don't forget tomorrow morning. You're going to call me. Right?"

Mack ruffled Liam's hair. "It's a *promise*." He stood and walked to the SUV. As he turned for one last wave, Eden put her hand on Liam's shoulder and started to steer him away from the door. But when Liam shrugged her off, Eden dropped her hand.

On the way to the hotel, he mulled over Liam's reminder to call. Mack had been a little surprised by that, but if he flipped his thoughts to put himself in his little boy's shoes, he could see the need for clarification about what would happen next.

The Browns hadn't changed even one detail of Liam's room. Mack wondered if the familiarity might trigger some unhappy memories. Maybe even inject a note of confusion about his real home. But like Dr. Harte often reminded him, kids are adaptable, and Liam had quickly settled into his room in the bunkhouse—and bragged about it.

Mack let out a long sigh when he turned onto the street and the house faded from view. *Lighten up.* Liam was only finding his footing. He was away from Mack for the first time in several months. He'd be fine. Still, Liam had looked so small standing in the doorway waving goodbye. It struck Mack that he also had some adjusting to do.

When Mack's call came in, she told him to hold on a second and then hurried out the back door to the big, old-fashioned screened porch. "I can hear you now, Mack. Between the saws and the sanders, we have a lot of machines doing their thing. I've taken to wearing ear plugs some days. How are things going up in Millerton?"

"Waking up alone in a hotel room felt a little odd. But now that I'm talking to you, life feels normal again." Mack paused. "I thought I'd find you at the mansion bright and early. I'm getting ready to get to work online myself. I just got off the phone with Liam."

"And I bet your boy likes knowing you're not so far away. He can always touch base with Dad."

Erin's fondness for Liam came through in the softness of her voice whenever he came up in conversation. "Exactly right. Last night he seemed a little concerned about being able to reach me if he wanted to talk. It means using Eden's or Louis's phone." Mack paused. "But that's okay. It will all work out. I'm going to stop rambling now."

"It must be strange for him to be away from you, Mack, even if the people he's spending time with shamelessly dote on him."

"Trust you to figure that out," Mack teased. "I was confused at first. I mean, they have big plans, starting today with a trip to the toy store."

Erin detected something different in Mack's voice, a tone she hadn't heard before. "Are you wishing you were going along? You sound a little wistful."

"Honestly? Yes. And no. How's that for a definitive answer?" Mack sighed. "This is going to sound kinda silly, but I feel like I'm missing something. A part of me, like my right arm."

"Not silly at all." Erin lowered her voice when she added, "You're his rock now."

"I had an empty feeling when I left him behind last night. I'm not exactly sure why. It's not fear, or anything like that," Mack said. "Eden and Louis love him so much."

But Liam's nights were sometimes quite different from his days, Erin mused. "Are you concerned he might wake up upset? Are you worried his grandparents won't know what to do?"

Mack scoffed. "Mind reader—again. There's a risk. I had an online talk with them last week and gave them a heads-up. I explained why Dr. Harte thinks he's going through this, but..."

"But?" While she waited for Mack to finish his thought, Erin stared across the patchwork of unkempt gardens behind the mansion. In the distance, Quincy and Caroline, the landscape architect, a woman about Erin's age, had their heads together in conversation while they walked on stone paths that separated the garden plots designated for cleanup and planting.

"But nothing, Erin," Mack said, some frustration seeping into his voice. "It's me. I'm overreacting."

"Something else is going on with you, Mack. I can hear it in your voice." Regret set in immediately. Mack probably wouldn't appreciate her calling attention to what were likely his complex emotions.

"I'm a little anxious, that's all. Maybe Liam picked up on that." Mack's voice carried a hint of resignation. "Okay, I might as well admit it. I'm afraid they'll see his grief as a sign that he's not adjusting to being with me." Silence. "And I'm used to being in charge of Liam. For right now, I'm not."

Mack was doing a poor job of convincing himself that all would be well. She was figuring out how to respond when he said, "I know you're at work, and I should get started, too. Part of my plan for the week is to start looking for a permanent place for Liam and me."

"The bunkhouse getting a tad small, is it?" An obvious rhetorical question.

"I hate to admit it. I love the place," Mack replied, "but it's time for me to figure out the long-term plan for Liam, and for me. Don't get me wrong, I'm not going to sell my share of Tall Tale or do anything drastic like that."

Mack was nearly breathless as he said all that in one long breath. It hadn't occurred to Erin that selling the lodge was an idea on the table.

"So, a goal—a dream—is in the works?"

"You're onto me," he said softly. "There's always been a dream in the works. I just haven't talked about it much."

The sound of Mack's voice lulled her into a pleasant, time-out kind of state. But she snapped out of it when Quincy raised his arm, beckoning her to join them. "Hey, Mack, I have to cut this short. Quincy wants to see me out in the garden."

"Go, go," Mack said. "I'll touch base later."

Erin grabbed her jacket and stuck her phone in her pocket. When she joined Quincy and

Caroline, they were in the midst of another optimistic dream.

"This old place is going to be more than a meeting place and a wedding venue," Quincy said. "Caroline also thinks we should renovate the potting shed and other outbuildings. Showpiece gardens, plant sales, a gift shop—all here in the yard."

What Quincy called a *yard* was in Erin's eyes a field.

Caroline grinned at Erin. "I see another renovation project in your future."

"We'll add it to your to-do list," Quincy teased. "I called you out here because I want your opinion, Erin."

Over the next few minutes, Caroline walked Erin through the plan to revive the rose garden and create a wildflower garden using only regional plants. Patios for outdoor parties and live music were part of the vision for Adelaide Creek's showpiece.

Two hours had passed by the time Caroline hurried away for another appointment. Erin was eager to get back to work, too, but Quincy invited her to the Burger Barn for lunch.

"I've got a few things on my mind," he said. "I'd like to run them by you. Can you leave now?"

Since the work crews had assignments for

the day, she was free, so there was no reason not to go.

During the short drive to Burger Barn, Quincy threw out ideas about the ways they could use the mansion's grounds. Her work might expand even more if he wanted her to supervise the rejuvenation of the garden sheds. *Job security*, Erin thought, music to her ears.

When they were seated in the crowded restaurant and had given the waitress their burger order, Quincy rested his forearms on the table. "Okay, Erin, what's up with the missing horses?"

"I wish I knew. No sign of the Burtons' horse, Harris. Or Crosby's. And we don't know if the horse Mack has seen a couple of times now is Harris or one of the others. So far, only two have come back, but the others, at least five, are still out there."

Quincy looked genuinely puzzled, as if this was news to him. That prompted Erin to say, "The owners have reported every incident to the county sheriff, but he doesn't have much to add. There aren't many horse rustlers about, so his experience with them is likely little to none. But what else can the Burtons or Crosby or the other ranchers do but try to get help from the sheriff?"

Staring off into space for a couple of seconds,

Quincy finally answered. "They'll keep their eyes and ears open. Looking out for each other is the way things work around here. Ranchers and locals like Matt and Crosby won't sit back—they jump in to try to help." That was how it was for her and Mack when they chose to watch out the window that special night. They didn't solve the mystery, but other things happened, she realized. For one, Erin's feelings for Mack had shifted. Or maybe she'd only admitted to herself what she'd known all along. "I'll stay on alert right along with everyone else. It hurts to think of these creatures roaming around alone and frightened or worse." She pushed aside the awful images.

"Could be someone's maybe planning to sell them. The sooner we solve this puzzle, the better," Quincy said. Erin acknowledged Quincy's words with a nod. She wasn't ready to surrender to helplessness. Not yet, anyway.

They were well into their burger platters when Quincy spoke up again. "I suppose it's none of my business, but we're family now, right?"

"Ooh… I love it when you point that out."

Quincy narrowed his eyes in scrutiny. "Then indulge this old man. You and Mack seem pretty tight. Are you becoming more than friends?"

Bam…she didn't see that coming. Erin's extra beat or two of silence weren't lost on her boss.

His assumptions were clear on his amused face. Her first response was to blurt that she and Mack were only good friends. But there was that night at his house, their ride, their talks. And of course, that kiss.

"Cat got your tongue, huh?" Quincy chuckled. "I think I have my answer."

Erin didn't have a chance to contradict him, because a text came in. Seeing it was from Grisham, Erin told Quincy she needed to read it. But after she did, she was too excited to speak. Apparently it showed.

"What? Good news?"

"Grisham asked me to join the band permanently. Next gig, Spring Fling." Erin pressed the phone to her chest. This was news she'd been hoping to hear. "The original fiddler decided not to come back. She's moving to Boston for a job."

"As if you needed another reason to stick around these parts." Quincy put out his hand for a high five, and Erin happily slapped his palm from across the table.

She couldn't wait to tell Mack.

CHAPTER ELEVEN

LOUIS'S CALL CAME in after midnight. The big water park day had been fantastic, at least according to Liam and Eden. Since the quality of the day had nothing to do with the nighttime situation, Mack shouldn't have been shocked by Louis's panicky voice. Yet his chest and throat tightened. Liam waking up worried was only one of the possibilities. He threw the covers back, got out of bed, and prepared himself to hear about an accident or a high fever.

His voice shaking, Louis said, "Liam's having one of those…moments you told us about. I guess that isn't the right word, but you know what I mean."

"No, no, that's fine. Is he in his bed?" It occurred to Mack that in this different environment, Liam could have left his room to look for his grandparents. Relief that Liam wasn't ill also helped loosen the muscles in his throat.

He'd take this scenario over any of the scarier ones that crossed his mind.

"Yes, he was in bed, crying. He quieted when Eden sat with him, but then he told her his mom died."

Mack winced. The words, so familiar to Mack, would be stabs in the heart for Eden and Louis. "That's the typical pattern," he said softly.

"Maybe so, Mack. You told us what to say, but now we're a little afraid.

"It's excruciating. He's telling his grandmother that he loves his mom and wants her with him." Louis huffed into the phone. "This wasn't happening in the first couple of weeks after Paula died, when he was with us."

Mack ignored the implied judgment. Instead, he weighed the option of offering to come over and settle Liam down himself. But that would take too long, and he didn't like the idea of his boy spending that much time upset. That left one option. He could only hope Louis and Eden would agree to follow his lead.

"The moments are easier if you can think of them as part of the process he's going through to accept her death."

"We can talk about that later, Mack. But what about now?" Louis asked, his voice cracking. "This minute. How do we get him back to sleep?"

Mack repeated what he'd suggested to them before. "Assure him that his mother knows where he is and that she can always find him." *Thank you, Erin.* "He seems to understand that, or accept it."

Louis and Eden began talking in the background, their voices muffled. He also detected Louis's soft weeping when he came back to the phone to report that they'd spoken to Liam and he was calm, but was still sitting up. "That's okay. You've soothed him," Mack said. "If he's fully awake, I often scoop him up in my arms and put him in my bed with me. Or if he's groggy, it's easier to leave him in his room, but tuck him in with Thunder. Then you can sit with him a few minutes."

"Hang with me on the line, will you, Mack? I'll pass the phone to Eden, and we'll do what you say."

Seconds turned into minutes, with the only background sound their two voices. Then Eden spoke into the phone. "It worked," she said, her voice wobbly. "I talked to him about his mom, hoping he'd drift off, but he was wide-awake by then, not upset or anything, but silent. Louis is carrying him to our bed."

"That's good," Mack said. "Once you put him

down, he'll sleep till morning." Mack reconsidered his words and added, "At least, that's how it's worked so far. It's never been an everyday thing, and there's no way you could have predicted it." Mack heard the words play back in his head, realizing he was talking with Eden like a parent who knew his child.

"She'll always be with him… What can I say? That comforts *me*, Mack." Eden exhaled long and loud. "You know, it may sound a little strange, but sometimes I sense Paula is around. Louis and I miss her so much. I'll put the phone on speaker. Louis wants to say something."

"He's sleeping," Louis said. "Didn't take any time at all. I can see this is better than leaving him on his own too long."

"Right," Mack said, relieved that the pattern was the same with his grandparents as it was with him.

"I was shaken by how deeply he feels this sense of loss," Eden said. "I would have thought enough time had passed for…"

When Eden didn't finish the sentence, Mack responded. "Liam doesn't dwell on these moments. When I told Dr. Harte about them, she said they're part of his grief—but also his healing. I trust her, so I've accepted that explanation."

"I misunderstood," Eden said. "When you

warned us that this could happen, I expected him to be terrified and crying."

"They aren't nightmares, Eden. I'm grateful for that, at least. Otherwise he might be afraid to go to bed."

"Say, Mack, why don't you come here for breakfast?" Louis suggested. "I'm sure Liam would feel more comfortable with you around, and it'd help us out too."

"Sure. I can do that." Tomorrow was their last full day with Liam. "You're taking him to see one of his old friends in the afternoon, aren't you?"

"A playdate," Louis said. "The boys used to get together a lot before...well, before Liam left."

One more night and he and Liam would be on their way home. Mack longed to step inside that old bunkhouse again.

"Better get some sleep, Louis. Believe me, your grandson will be up and raring to go at the same time as any other day. Why don't you call me in the morning when you're ready for me to come by?"

After the call ended, Mack sensed that being together during Liam's trouble had connected the three of them. They were a united front in doing the best thing for Liam. The invitation to join them for breakfast was a sign. Mack was taking it as a vote of confidence.

ERIN CLEANED AND stored her tools to mark the end of another workday, Friday, which for her was the start of a working weekend. That was why quitting a little early didn't matter. The sound of the front door closing and the footsteps on the wooden floor gave her an immediate lift. Other than investing in a fantastic pair of go-with-everything boots, she hadn't indulged in a girlfriends' shopping trip since she'd come to town. Willow, acting in her typical take-charge way, decided Erin needed a change. Now she was picking Erin up for their excursion to Landrum.

"Every time I come inside this place, I'm more and more impressed," Willow said, plunking down on a worn-out leather sofa Erin had dragged from the library to the dining room.

"Don't get too comfortable," Erin warned. "I'm ready to go. C'mon, Neptune, we're taking you home. Who has Naomi?"

"She's with Tom. He's not on call tonight. He tells me they'll be dining on scrambled eggs and cinnamon toast, followed by a round of dramatic readings performed by Daddy."

Erin laughed. No one could read a story quite like Tom. The characters had their own unique voices that rose and fell with the action. He mooed like cows and baaed like sheep, and his body language matched the story's mood. "Well, then, your child is in good hands, so you can relax. What's on your shopping list?"

"I'll know it when I see it," Willow quipped, slapping the arm of the couch. "This trip is just an excuse to hang out with you. Congratulations are in order, I hear."

Erin chuckled. "Which good news are you referring to?"

"Uh, another chance to shine with the band at Spring Fling. You must be so excited." Willow cocked her head. "There's other good news? What did I miss?"

"So much work to do that my job is secure for a good long while. How about that for good news? Thanks to your dad, I can afford to keep Raven and maybe even buy something fabulous for Spring Fling." Erin left it at that. Quincy's second thoughts about the scope of the renovation project were spoken in confidence. For the time being, anyway, his commitment had proved stronger than his concerns.

Willow responded with a slow nod and "Nice going."

Erin wiped imaginary sweat from her brow. "I'm a little nervous about performing. It's still new for me." Erin gave herself a light pinch on the arm. "Hard to believe I'm playing for pay-ing customers."

"Oh, please. You're such a pro." Willow hopped up from the sofa. "We all heard you. Now, let's skedaddle before something gets in our way." Willow grinned. "Speaking of your fan club, how's Mack doing?"

"We texted earlier today. The week has flown by, and the visit is almost over, but so far, so good." Erin was on the verge of mentioning what Liam was going through, but caught herself in time. That was Mack's private business, and he'd chosen to share it with her. Erin picked up her bag and started for the door with Neptune following behind her. She was the last one out for the af-ternoon, so she took care to lock up the mansion.

"Before Liam's mom died, he spent a lot of time with his grandparents," Erin said, "and they showered him with love. He has a room there that's always ready for him."

Willow flashed a pointed look at Erin. It wasn't lost on her, but the reason for it wasn't so clear. She didn't press her, though, and once they were on their way to Landrum, Naomi's first steps and the summer art fair at the lodge were the more pressing issues.

"I wonder why Mack didn't come back to Millerton after he dropped off Liam rather than spending the week working from a hotel," Willow mused as she navigated the SUV into one of the only available parking places on Buffalo Street. Releasing her seat belt, she sent another pointed look Erin's way. "I've been waiting for you to say something, but since you're so closemouthed about this, I'm forced to ask." She raised her eyebrows in expectation. "Is something…uh, *developing*…between you and Mack?"

Erin groaned, and her hands flew to her cheeks. "You sound like your dad. That's what he asked me." She hurried to get out of the vehicle, catching a glimpse of her undeniably apple-red cheeks. This blushing, which was happening with alarming frequency lately, was completely ridiculous yet out of her control. Whenever Mack was introduced into the conversation, her stomach came down with a serious case of flutters and a pleasant buzz zipped along her skin. At least no one could see flutters and buzzing.

Willow let out a hoot as she started down the sidewalk toward a group of shops. "Well, well, well, I apparently hit a nerve."

Erin groaned again. "Okay, I guess you did. But that doesn't mean I know the answer to the question. We're good friends, that's for sure." There was that kiss, though, and the hugs and hand squeezes. No need to talk about that. "But

I'm still not sure how I feel about Mack. Trust can be a tricky thing. It's no secret that if Paula hadn't died, he might never have been part of his son's life."

As if she hadn't heard Erin's answer, Willow asked, "Is it serious? This thing with Mack you're reluctant to acknowledge?"

Erin shrugged. "All I know is that he's easy to be with. We have a great time together. Usually Liam is there. He's pretty easy, too." Erin tried to find the right words for her jumble of feelings. "I'm trying to keep it casual. This isn't something I planned for. Not yet."

"If you say so," Willow teased in a singsong voice. "But tell me, how do you feel when he texts or calls? Are you usually happy?"

Was this a test? Erin fumbled for more words. The answer seemed obvious.

Willow must have thought so. She stopped in front of a shop window and said, "So, what's the problem?"

"I didn't expect to meet someone special now," Erin said, conscious of her plaintive voice. She looked around, trying to distract herself with sights of Landrum, including the Children's Adventure Center down the street. "I planned to establish my life here. Find my way on my own."

"Funny thing about love," Willow said.

"Sometimes it finds you. I never expected that I'd fall in love with a man I'd already known for over a year. Tom and I were on the same volunteer committees. I used to coax your brother onto the dance floor so I'd have a partner."

"Tom told me all about that," Erin said. "Nothing shy about you. Tom said that's why you're so good at your job."

"Maybe so, but I never imagined my baby's pediatrician, the same guy who took my frantic phone calls in the first weeks I had Naomi, would be the love of my life."

Erin smiled. "But unlike me, you'd been looking for a man to settle down with and build a life."

"Isn't that what you're doing, Erin? Building a life." Willow nodded to a chic silky jacket in the window. "Sky-blue. Just my color." She then pointed to a beaded tunic in a deep purple. "And that gem belongs on stage, my friend."

"I'll bet it costs a fortune," Erin said.

"Oh, so what? You deserve it. Let's turn this shopping trip into a celebration," Willow said. "Lots of things seem to be going your way."

Erin laughed at Willow's emphatic tone. It was irresistible. She followed Willow into the store.

THE NEXT AFTERNOON, Mack spent a few hours reviewing first-quarter reports and financial statements for the ranches and the lodge before pushing his chair back from the desk in the hotel room. He usually looked forward to this part of the job. It challenged him and triggered ideas about changes and improvements. But not today. The breaks he'd taken to study real estate listings were much more appealing.

He could find a house in town, great ones, too. Or he could buy one of Quincy's newer homes on Addie Creek. Yet he kept being lured back into a search for a place with a few acres and a stable for horses. He saw a couple of houses that fit most of the items on his wish list and contacted the real estate agent about them. When a commotion outside grabbed his attention, he opened the drapes in front of the sliding doors to the balcony. A couple of dozen crows were gathered in the branches of the trees outside. Amused by how much they had to say to each other, he decided to call it a day and relax with a cold Jadestone beer and let the chattering birds entertain him.

On the way to the room fridge, quick raps on his door took him by surprise. When he opened it, an alarm in his head began ringing. He hadn't expected to see Eden and Louis until the next morning, when he picked Liam up at their house for the trip home.

"Come in, come in." Mack opened the door

wider to let them in. "Can I get you coffee? Tea?" He paused. "Liam is still with his friend?"

"He's having an early dinner at their house," Louis said. "We don't need coffee. We won't be staying long."

"Have a seat," Mack said, pointing to the couch across from the desk. "By the way, I can see how much Liam has enjoyed his time here. He's been telling me lots of stories. I can hear the excitement in his voice." Mack rolled the office chair from the desk to the couch and sat opposite Eden and Louis. He chuckled. "That water park probably is the highlight. He'll tell his friends all about swinging on ropes and swimming through tunnels."

"Yep," Louis said, "it was a great day."

"And last night's episode ended basically the same way they do at home. As you saw for yourself, he was fine when we had our breakfast together this morning," Mack said.

Eden's flat expression didn't change when she nodded. Mack's gut tightened. He was doing all the talking. "Was there something on your mind? I hadn't expected to see you until tomorrow morning."

It gradually dawned on him why they'd stopped by. Perhaps he shouldn't have been taken by surprise, but he was. In a corner of Mack's mind, one he'd struggled to ignore, he entertained the possibility that Eden and Louis hadn't accepted the inevitable. He even understood why.

"This is difficult for us, Mack. We know you've come to love Liam." Eden crossed her arms over her chest. "But we've loved him from the minute he was born. We helped Paula raise him. You didn't."

"And?" Mack rolled his hand toward them, waiting for the words he didn't want to hear. "What?"

"We'd like Liam to stay with us," she said. "We want to be his primary caregivers."

Primary caregivers? A technical term that glossed over what they really wished they could be. Liam's parents. Even though Mack had sensed, but preferred to deny, this was coming, the words brought him to his feet. He dragged his hand down his cheek and around the back of his neck. He forced himself to take a breath. "That's just a fancy term for getting custody of him."

"Please, Mack, hear us out. *Please.*" Louis's pleas made Mack wince.

Fighting against his rising anger, Mack realized that sooner or later, he'd have to listen to their reasoning. Their argument against him. Better now than in a lawyer's office or worse, a courtroom with a judge. Still, he needed to say something to clarify where he stood. "I'm a little taken aback you'd bring this up now when Liam is doing so well. He's had a great week here. And he can have many more. Aren't you glad to know that you'll *always* have these visits?"

"It's not enough, Mack, not nearly enough." Eden shook her head. "Don't close your mind to what could be the best solution for Liam. Stay open and listen to our proposal."

"What choice do I have?" Mack heard the cynicism in his voice. He took a deep breath, the only way he knew to fight off the queasiness that was taking over. *Best solution for Liam...* For Eden and Louis, that would always mean his son would be better off with them. "You want to find a solution? That implies a problem," Mack said, resting his shoulder against the sliding door, "and I don't see one."

"We believe you want the best for Liam," Louis said. "Given that he's lost his mother, he needs all the love and attention he can get. We're retired, Mack. We don't need to run off to our jobs every day." He pointed to Eden. "His grandmother and I can devote *all* our time to him. With us, it's like he has two full-time parents. I'm sure you agree that's ideal?"

"And you've come into his life only because his mother died," Eden added.

Mack carefully considered what he wanted to say. "I've paid for my bad choices. You both know that."

"Uh, as I said, we have an idea to propose here," Louis said. "We're absolutely not trying to cut you out of his life. Far from it."

Mack had thought it curious that Louis was taking the lead on this, when Eden was usually the spokesperson. Then Eden leaned forward and folded her hands across her knees. He sensed a shift was coming.

"We believe it's best for Liam to be with us for the school year," Eden said. "He has friends here, you see."

And he has friends in Adelaide Creek. Mack forced himself not to blurt out counterpoints. Not yet. But it seemed like a preposterous argument.

"As Louis said, we don't have other demands on our time the way you do. We can provide a stable home." Eden hunched her shoulders for emphasis. "We love him, and he knows he's safe and secure with us."

Again, Mack's first impulse was to break in and list his arguments. He was already providing a stable and loving home.

Mack finally started to speak, but noise coming from the balcony diverted his attention. Two crows had landed on the balcony rail. Like a call and response sequence, one crow cawed twice and the other responded in kind. They did it again and one more time.

"What are they doing?" Eden's impatient tone filled the room.

Mack looked beyond the balcony to the trees and the ground below. "There are dozens of crows in the trees lining the parking lot." Mack smiled to himself. In one of Liam's books, crows were messengers and storytellers. Well, he got the message. The break in the conversation shifted something inside of him. His heartbeat slowed as the muscles in his neck and shoulders loosened. "You were saying, Eden?" Mack prompted, his voice low and calm.

Eden frowned as the two birds suddenly flew away and landed on the same branch of a gnarled tree visible in the distance, while the others kept up their chatter. "We don't dislike you, Mack, and we know Liam needs a good relationship with his dad from here on out. That's why we'll agree that Liam should spend his summers with you."

"I see. The school year here and the summers with me? That's what you're proposing?" If he'd negotiated an arrangement with Paula, it likely would have resembled what Eden and Louis were suggesting. It might have been workable, even beneficial. Back then.

Louis nodded enthusiastically. "Right. He's told us he's going to learn to ride horses, and he'd have his summers to do that."

Mack stared across the balcony to the trees where the crows still sat but had gone silent. He gathered his thoughts, knowing that what he said next could mean the difference between this ending amicably or in a big fight. And ultimately, in a courtroom with ugly testimony and the possibility of a breach with Eden and Louis that could never be repaired. The fluttering in his stomach intensified second by second. They'd made their case. It was time to make his.

"You have a wonderful home. It's warm. It's loving. Liam is comfortable there. He was excited about visiting you again." Mack took in a breath. "But it's not *his* home, the place he'll grow up…with me."

Eden and Louis were quiet, gazing at him through eyes that revealed their heartbreak. Then Eden frowned as if puzzled. Had they expected him to agree to their plan? Just like that? Without wasting a second, Mack's thoughts jumped to potential lawyers he could hire. One of his Addie Creek friends could surely give him the name of a good family law attorney. Whatever happened here, he'd contact a lawyer to see what they had to say about his situation. Taking a quick inventory of the people he could go to for help gave him an inkling of peace of mind. Erin couldn't help him on the practical side, but he could confide in her. She always had an understanding ear.

With her arms crossed over her chest, Eden leaned forward in her chair. "Mack? Are you refusing to even consider our idea about what's best for our grandson?"

Max didn't hesitate. "In all honesty, I'm trying to figure out how to respond without having a big blowup here. You—we—have had a good week. We'll have more times like this. Liam loves you. I value that. But his home is with me now. I'm his father."

"It took you long enough to realize that, didn't it?" Eden asked, putting her resentment, her bitterness, on display for the first time. "Years went by and we never saw you. Paula rarely even mentioned your name. You were *nobody.*"

Louis squirmed in his chair. "Eden, no." His sharp tone left no room for doubt that he wanted to stop the direction of the conversation.

Eden lifted her chin defiantly. "I'm only stating the obvious. It was as if Mack didn't even have a child. Then, all of a sudden, he shows up here after Paula died. He never asked us what *we* wanted."

Louis directed his attention to Mack. "Paula

told us that you supported Liam financially. So, money has nothing to do with this conversation," Louis said. "We didn't go into this motivated by recriminations and blame. Paula told us your marriage was as much her mistake as yours. She didn't want us to have a poor opinion of you."

Eden narrowed her eyes. "We never cared about your marriage. We decided anything that brought a precious child into our lives couldn't have been too big a mistake."

Mack made a time-out sign with his hands. "Wait, both of you. Let's get something out in the open now. *I failed Liam.* For years. But I'm not failing him now. He has a good home with me."

"You can't possibly fill the gap left by Paula's death," Eden said. "And you don't have time for him."

Whoa. He wouldn't let that stand. He'd rearranged his life and could prove it. In a courtroom if necessary. "I've made many changes. You're aware I cut my work hours, so unlike many kids in his class, he doesn't need after-school day care. Except for the hours at school, I'm with him all the time." Determined not to be cowed into backing down, he added, "Never once have I tried to justify my past mistakes with Liam. *Not one time.*"

"But can't you see that having *two adults* watching over him, raising him, guiding him, is the best outcome?" The frustration in Eden's voice carried heavy pain.

"No, I don't see it that way," Mack said. "But you don't understand the life he has with me. You don't know his friends, the families that are part of the circle of people he sees regularly."

Silence. Eden's jaw was tight, her mouth fixed in a grim slash. Louis looked more sad than angry.

"I hoped we'd avoided this conversation." Mack went back to the chair and sat, but leaned forward to close the distance between them. "The fact is, I think you're wonderful grand-parents." Mack steepled his fingers in front of his mouth and took a deep breath. "But I've had a second chance with Liam. I've made the most of it. I'm doing everything I can to be a good dad."

Eden's face fell. She couldn't hide the fatigue, and Mack wondered if she'd given up trying. "Oh, Mack, it's not about you being a good or bad dad." She pursed her lips. "To be honest, I was certain Liam would nag at you about coming back here to live with us as soon as you and he left Millerton." Shaking her head, she admitted what she'd hoped for. "During those early online meetups you arranged, we expected him to *beg* us to come and get him."

Louis's eyes opened in alarm. "Obviously, Eden doesn't mean that we planned to ask Liam who he wanted to live with. Not then, not now." Louis held Mack's gaze, communicating now dad to dad.

For the first time since Eden and Louis had arrived, Mack could see the possibility that the conversation could end without immediate threats.

"We should go," Louis said, turning his attention to Eden. "We need to pick up Liam soon."

Eden let out a long, heavy sigh. "We can take you to court, you know. We can make a solid case that we're more fit to raise Liam."

"Hey, let's not get into that now," Louis shot back at Eden before turning to Mack. "This isn't the right time to jump to lawsuits and custody hearings."

Eden kept her gaze on Louis, not Mack. "Maybe so, but that doesn't mean this is over."

To Mack's ears, the door to a future court battle was left open. Eden seemed all too ready to walk in and fight it out. He swallowed back defensive words to keep from repeating himself. Eden and Louis had Paula later in life. Did they not realize that granting custody of a seven-year-old to seventyish grandparents might not be the best outcome, at least in the opinion of a judge? He desperately wanted to avoid that argument, but they had to have thought of it.

Eden cleared her throat. "I do have one more question. Strictly out of curiosity. Is this woman, the one Liam calls the cookie lady, your girlfriend? Will she suddenly become Liam's stepmother one day?"

The question was mildly embarrassing, but mostly it spiked Mack's fear. He couldn't avoid responding. "Nothing like that would ever be sudden." His experience of eloping with Paula ruled that out. "We're friends...close friends. She's part of our social group—mostly couples and their kids who Liam and I hang out with. You've heard him talk about them." He sidestepped the heart of the question, but that seemed the safest path.

Eden finally spoke in a lighter tone when she said, "We've heard a lot about her this week, haven't we, Louis?"

With that, the two stood.

Mack went ahead and opened the door for them. "You've said you don't travel much anymore, but I hope you'll consider coming to Adelaide Creek for visits. You will *always* have a suite at the lodge—at no charge. Anytime, any season." He smiled to lighten the mood, but his voice was hoarse from anxiety, fear. "Hey, I own the place. I can guarantee that."

Louis ignored the suggestion. Instead, he cupped Eden's elbow and started down the hall. "We'll see you at the house in the morning."

That was it? The end of it? Somehow, he didn't believe it. It was all he could do not to send a text to Tom or Jeff to ask for the name of their family attorney so he could contact the person now. He resisted the urge to grab his phone. No cause for panic.

When Mack closed the door behind him, he opened the Jadestone he'd thought about earlier and went to the patio doors. The crows had moved on. Mack had to laugh at himself. He wasn't a superstitious kind of guy. But the crows perched on the balcony railing had distracted him from falling into desperate fear, or worse, anger at Liam's grandparents. Maybe the crows hadn't changed the outcome of the conversation, but those few seconds of distraction had calmed Mack and allowed him to gather his thoughts.

Mack swallowed a mouthful of beer, letting it cool the back of his throat. Erin might have a few thoughts about crows and folklore. She seemed knowledgeable about that sort of thing. He wanted to talk with her anyway, tell her about his conversation with Eden and Louis.

262   FINDING HIS WYOMING SWEETHEART

Without hesitating, he got his phone and made the call. It rang and rang before finally going to voicemail. Disappointing. He left a short, casual message that mentioned combing through real estate listings and saying he was looking forward to being home again.

Eden's question about the so-called cookie lady echoed in his mind. The last thing he'd do right now was cause more upheaval in Liam's life. But the memory of kissing Erin floated into his mind and stayed there. A perfect kiss. Maybe he'd taken her by surprise, but she'd kissed him back. That's what made it perfect.

CHAPTER TWELVE

WILLOW CAME OUT of the dressing room and twirled around in the lemon-yellow pantsuit. "So, what do you think? Seeing your lovely new things, I'm feeling like I need an upgrade, too."

"Hmm…the color sets off your eyes and your hair," Erin said, admiring the way the jacket highlighted Willow's tall, slender frame. "But you'd look elegant in a flour sack." Erin giggled. "I think that expression was already old back when my mom used it."

Willow rolled her eyes but nodded pointedly at the shopping bags in the empty chair next to Erin. "You might claim you don't like to shop, but you don't fool me."

"I splurged," Erin said with a quick shrug. "I don't shop often, so I jump at things that catch my eye—and also fit. Never a guarantee." The tunic Willow had spotted was exquisite, the color of dark amethyst and with a spray of black and purple sparkling beads on the scooped neckline. *A little pizazz*, the sales-woman had said. Erin added black skinny jeans and couldn't resist a pair of dressy boots. And that was only the first shop.

"I can't wait to see you perform at Spring Fling in your new clothes," Willow said. "Everything about you will sparkle."

"I hope so. I've been so focused on my work at the mansion that I sometimes forget about Spring Fling." When her phone rang, she reached into her purse and saw that it was Mack. "It's Mack. I'll let it go to voicemail."

"Take it if you want to," Willow said.

"Nope. I'm spending time with you. We talk regularly anyway. I'll get back to him later." She'd come to expect Mack's daily calls and their friendly exchange of messages, but like now, she often had to wait to get back to him later when she was free. "He and Liam will be driving back tomorrow. He's probably at loose ends in the hotel. I know he's eager to get home."

"Okay, if you say so." Willow's singsong tone made it clear she was teasing.

"That's the second time you've said that today," Erin said. "That mocking you do is making me self-conscious. I'm afraid to say anything about Mack without you sending me one of your all-knowing looks." She made a show of frowning at her friend. "What is it with you and the Mack thing?"

"Showing a little attitude, are you?" Willow lifted her shoulders and raised her hands in the air as if to say, *Isn't it obvious?* "I tease you about it because you and Mack seem right for each other. And before you protest, let's call it a hunch. I've said as much to you before, and nothing has happened to change my mind." Willow softened her tone when she added, "Tom thinks so, too, you know."

"Really?"

"Your brother credits *you* for helping him break down *his* barriers, Erin," Willow said, shifting her stance and crossing her arms over her chest. "You remember how Tom had convinced himself he couldn't be a good dad. The guy who is now the love of my life was denying himself a full life—at least until you came along and talked some sense into him." Willow disappeared into the dressing room.

Of course Erin remembered Tom walking away from Willow, seeing himself as so badly scarred by his past he didn't have what it took to be a good partner. Erin hadn't thought twice about pointing out the flaws in her brother's thinking. When Willow reappeared, she went straight to the counter and paid for her new pantsuit. Erin collected her shopping bags and followed Willow.

After picking up her van at the mansion, Erin hurried home and let Neptune out. It was dark, but the sky was clear enough for a smattering of stars to be visible. When she went inside, she and Neptune flopped on the couch, and she decided it was early enough in the evening to return Mack's call.

"I was hoping you'd get back to me tonight," he said when he picked up the call after the second ring.

She told him about the shopping spree in Landrum and having fun with Willow. "What's up with you? Are you eager to get back home?"

"Very eager. Something happened. I suppose you could say the other shoe dropped." Mack's already deep voice was even deeper.

"Oh? Can you talk about it?"

By the time he finished the abbreviated story of Eden and Louis's proposition, Erin's heart beat a little harder. She had empathy for Liam's grandparents. She had no trouble grasping—even feeling—the magnitude of their loss. But she found herself standing in Mack's shoes. No matter how reassuring he tried to be, she could read between the lines and was gripped by fear for him.

"My brother and Willow had a terrific attorney," she said, "so if the situation develops…"

"No need to finish the sentence," Mack said. "I'm going to line up the legal help as soon as I get back."

"Um…you know, I could…" Tongue-tied, not a familiar state for Erin, she decided not to say anything more. That left her hemming and hawing hanging in the air.

"What, Erin? Tell me."

She sighed, afraid of being misunderstood. "If you're in a situation where you have to fight for custody, I can see why our friendship could be misinterpreted." What was she saying? She had no intention of leaping to conclusions like Willow had. "I mean, I can go away— disappear—more or less. That way you won't have to explain that the cookie lady is no threat to your life with Liam."

"No way," Mack said. "Disappear? That's preposterous, and it wouldn't work, anyway. According to his grandparents, you come up in conversations—*often*. Eden herself asked me about you and our…you know…relationship."

Relationship? Eden had made quite a leap.

"I mean, she asked me about you and your place in my life."

"I'll bet you didn't welcome that kind of probing. What did you say?"

"We're close friends, Erin," Mack said without hesitating. "I left it at that. No need to, you know, elaborate on what might happen in the future."

Erin smiled, thinking of Willow chiming in with *told you so*. But this situation called for something more serious than her friend's teasing. "I'll say it again. If you need me to back out of your life, I will. No questions asked."

"Won't be necessary. Besides, Liam wouldn't like that one bit."

Before she had a chance to respond, Mack was on to the next thing, his trip home. "We're getting an early start, right after breakfast with Eden and Louis. I'll call you when we're back."

Breakfast with Liam's grandparents? She imagined Mack trying to behave as if nothing had changed, but kids had a way of picking up on tension in the air. "Well, then, good luck with Eden and Louis, and travel safe," Erin said before disconnecting the call. She put her head back on the couch. If a legal battle was on the horizon, she was wary again of becoming too close to Mack. She'd had that same thought before and acknowledged that trying to keep her distance hadn't worked. She liked the man, respected him, too. And despite her fears, she'd fallen for him. She cared about Liam, also. It seemed protecting her own heart was no longer the issue. Maybe Mack couldn't see that her presence in his life could be twisted around and made to look bad for him. But Mack was being naive.

A smart, sharp guy, he surely understood his flawed history as a dad was a potential weapon. If not, she'd convince him to face the reality. Her heart might run toward Mack, but that didn't wipe away his past. Or hers.

FOR THE FIRST two hours of the ride across state, Liam was all about telling stories about his week with his grandparents, most of which Mack had already heard over the phone, at least once. The French toast breakfast hadn't been nearly as tense as Mack expected, largely because Liam went back and forth between recounting his adventures of the past week and speculating about what was up at home with the twins and Jillian—and Erin.

"Sounds like you're excited about going back to school," Louis had observed.

"On Monday, the art teacher comes, and on Wednesday, we get to sing with the music teacher." He used his fork to cut off another bite of the buttery French toast Louis had made. Grandpa's specialty, Liam liked to say.

Mack smiled at Louis. "Those are Liam's two favorite days of the week."

Now in the SUV, Liam had gone from reminiscing about the tunnels at the water park to asking when they could go to the Adventure Center. "I want to see the trains."

"We can go after school one day next week." After his talk with Erin, weeks ago now, Mack had given some thought to having Liam's birthday party there. Lunch with the twins and Jillian at a burger and hot dog place across the street from the CAC, followed by a kids' movie the center showed on Saturday afternoons. It could work.

Liam was the best distraction he had from dwelling on Eden and Louis. All night, he'd been wakeful, bogged down in thoughts about his next steps, while assuring himself that Eden and Louis received the message he was sending. As for Erin's offer to go away, he had a one-word response: unacceptable. He wouldn't allow that to happen—she wasn't a harmful influence on him or his custody of Liam. No court in the country could possibly think so. He wasn't taking any chances, though. He'd call an attorney.

After they stopped for fuel and a quick lunch and were on the road again, Liam drifted off to sleep. That freed Mack to think about the real estate listings he'd found online. Eden and Mack wouldn't deter him from getting on with

his life with Liam. Pictures of houses and stables, corrals and trails flitted through his mind,
so it seemed only fitting that he noticed the
simple hand-lettered sign: Acrs & Hse & Brn
4 Sale. Old and worn-out as the sign was, the
arrow pointed toward Barkley, a town smaller
than Adelaide Creek, less than an hour away
now. Mack slowed down and made a right turn
onto the narrow, bumpy road.

When he'd gone a couple of miles, an identi-
cal sign sat in front of a field situated below a
wooded ridge. Curious, he slowed and steered
around a couple of deep ruts visible along the
overgrown driveway. His destination was a wire
and wooden fence ahead, but as he got closer,
he saw the padlock and came to a stop. No real
house in sight. Instead, from the driver's seat,
the view showed only a dilapidated shack and a
barn in the same dismal shape. The collapsing
barn boards were partially hidden by downed
trees and debris from other weathered outbuildings. A deliberate attempt at camouflage, or so
it seemed. No one could legitimately call the
shack a house.

On the other hand, his eye was drawn to the
ridge, where he could see a break in the trees
that indicated a road. Despite the odd look of
the buildings, the expansive fields surrounding
them were appealing. The warming weather

meant they'd soon be covered by prairie grasses and spring flowers.

Liam woke up while Mack was maneuvering the SUV in reverse and avoiding ruts and big holes. "Where are we, Dad? What are we doing?"

"We're having a little unexpected adventure," Mack said. He glanced at Liam through the rearview mirror and pointed to the ridge in the distance. "See all those trees up there? I'm thinking it might be fun to drive a little while to see if I can find a road up there. That way we'll have a view of this old ranch."

"You've never been here before?" Liam asked.

"Nope." Mack smiled and raised his eyebrows as an invitation to join him in anticipation. "First time I've been down this road, so let's do a little exploring. Whaddya say?"

Liam's eyes narrowed. "Are we lost?" Liam posed the question a little suspiciously.

"Lost? Not a chance." Mack chuckled and waved his phone. "We have our handy GPS, and I know the way back to the main road."

"Does that ridge have a name?" Liam asked. "I bet it does. All the ridges around here have names."

"You're probably right, but I don't know what it is, not yet. Maybe we'll find out. Okay, off we go on a bumpy ride." *This could be a colossally bad idea*, Mack thought.

Mack drove another few miles and came to a crossroads, with a sign indicating that Barkley was twelve miles ahead. But the road to the left appeared more promising as a route to the ridge, so that was the direction he chose. The road twisted and wound through woods and sections of rock walls that had been blasted through to create the passage. Along the way, Mack saw other houses, some newish and big, a few older and more like remote cabins. Signs on the turnoffs onto the narrow, usually dirt driveways marked them as private property. But he saw no such signs on the road. The ground flattened on the highest part of the ridge, and Mack spotted an open grassy area between a cluster of mostly old-growth cottonwoods and scrub pines.

"See this, Liam? You asked if the ridge had a name. Here it is." Mack pointed to a molded metal landmark sign for Josiah Barkley Lookout.

"No one's here," Liam said, "but there's a picnic table under those trees."

"We have the place to ourselves. I think it's still too cold for picnics, huh? Let's go have a look." If he was going to get a better look at the acres and those derelict outbuildings, this was the place to do it. He hadn't ruled out building a house himself rather than buying one.

The day had started out cloudy, but the sky had cleared. It was a good day for exploring.

Mack left the SUV and kept his hand on Liam's shoulder as they walked toward the rocky edge of the ridge. As he'd expected, he had a clearer view of the layout below. A relatively isolated cluster of what had once been intact utilitarian buildings. Now Mack could see the full barn. One end led to a makeshift corral. Boards and rocks reinforced an old fence, but the structure wasn't quite high enough to completely hide what was inside. From the top of this ridge, there was no way to miss it.

"Horses," Mack said. He pointed to the animals in and around the buildings. "See, Liam? I'm counting three of them, but there could be more inside the barn."

"One of them looks like Raven," Liam said.

"Close, but this horse has white socks on his lower back legs."

Liam let out a giggle. "Raven does a little dance when Erin comes around. She said visiting Raven was like having a playdate with a really good friend."

"Nice, huh?" Mack said, amused by her description. "When you and I get our horses, they'll be our new friends."

Mack looked for signs of human life, but no smoke was coming from the chimney visible on the shack. A good thing. The whole place looked like one huge bonfire waiting to happen. Tubs of water were in place near the barn. Based on his limited view, the horses were in okay shape. For the moment, anyway. He had no evidence that these were mistreated horses, but the setup screamed makeshift. Once he told Erin about this, he could almost guarantee she'd be curious and want to see the place for herself.

Mack gave Liam's shoulder a quick squeeze. "We ought to get going." He was at once eager to get home and reluctant to leave the horses. "We need to stop at the market and get ourselves some food."

"I'm hungry." Liam reached into his jacket pocket and pulled a single-serving package of trail mix. "Grandpa put this in my pocket before we left. Just in case, he said."

In a pleasant tone, Mack said, "Okay, then, you have your snack while we head out." But another voice wasn't so pleased. In case of what? In case Dad didn't have snacks in the car? Mack caught the accusatory tenor of his thoughts. *Get over it.* Before yesterday's visit from Louis and Eden, that thought would never have crossed his mind. He was not typically a touchy guy. Being at odds with Eden and Louis had left him on edge, defensive, even about snacks in the car.

CHAPTER THIRTEEN

BY THE TIME she heard Mack's story about his detour with Liam to the ridge all the way through, Erin was inclined to say yes to following Mack's hunch to take a trip to the Josiah Barkley Lookout. They'd have sandwiches and a thermos or two of coffee. And moonlight. Irresistible, really. "You may not have heard, but one of Bridget Lancaster's horses is missing now."

"No kidding? When did that happen?" That meant the count was up to eight.

"I got a message from Willow a little while ago, so it was probably last night." Erin groaned in frustration. "This hits close to home for Willow, but I feel bad, too. Last fall, Willow took me out to Bridget's ranch twice, and we rode her horses."

"For the rest of the drive back, I tried to convince myself I was jumping to wild conclusions. But the way those barn boards were arranged into a makeshift corral signaled something was off." Mack paused a couple of seconds. "Even the ratty old For Sale sign makes me think someone abandoned that place and left its buildings to rot away."

Focusing on what Mack's intuition was telling him aroused something in her. He'd stopped at the mansion unannounced to tell her this story when Liam was in school and out of earshot. His suspicions had rubbed off on her, along with anxiety and anticipation. A jumble. But this secret plan Mack had devised troubled her.

"I'm in, Mack. I'll go to the ridge with you. But something is nagging at me. If you think there's even a small chance the horses you saw could be the missing ones, why not tell the owners? If you're right, these horses are close by."

"Legitimate question," Mack said. "But if I say something now and I'm wrong, then I will have led other people on a wild-goose chase. Or I'd have triggered false hope. Or even caused trouble, aroused suspicion of innocent people."

Erin let that sink in. She could have flipped the coin and argued the other side, but Mack had thought it out.

Mack shrugged. "Most have said these are almost always runaway horses that eventually come back on their own—like the two that were gone for only a short time. Let's keep this to ourselves. If nothing comes of it, at least we haven't involved other people." Mack cocked his head and smiled flirtatiously. "What's the worst that can happen? We spend time on the ridge with a starry nighttime view of the mountains."

"Okay then, when do you want to go?" Erin asked, getting up from the garden bench. Break time was over.

"How about tomorrow? I'll ask Jillian to stay with Liam?" Mack folded his arms on the table and leaned toward her. "It's a public lookout, but it isn't likely we'll have company up there. Not this time of year. We'll be able to get up there before dark and keep watch to see what happens."

"Tomorrow it is." Erin glanced at her phone. "I better get back to work. As soon as I leave here, I've got a rehearsal with the band." She smiled at Mack. "Just think, if I can identify Bridget's horse, we would have finally cracked the case."

Mack smiled. "That's what I'm hoping for." They went back inside the mansion and into the dining room. She'd wanted to show Mack her progress. But before she could point out the improvements to the hutch, another visitor arrived. Tom appeared in front of her, carrying two hot drink cups.

"I have a feeling one of those is for you,"

Mack said, lowering his head. For a second Erin thought he might kiss her, but at the last minute, he squeezed her shoulder instead. "Uh, I'll be in touch about our plans." Mack greeted Tom as he hurried away.

"Am I interrupting?" Tom asked. "I come bearing treats, hot chocolate."

Erin couldn't resist the diner's distinctive drink using rich dark chocolate. Tom knew that. Work was delayed yet again. It had been that kind of day. "No problem. I'll come in early tomorrow and make up the time. Have a seat on my visitors' couch. So, big brother, what brings you here?"

"Do I need a reason?" Tom said, raising a brow. He followed her direction and made himself at home on the couch. "I'm headed to the hospital to see a couple of patients. Thought I'd stop in and say hello."

Oh, sure. After her shopping trip with Willow, it didn't take a psychic to figure out what this was really about. "Willow nudged you, didn't she? You came here to probe around in my head. It's about Mack."

"Well, not really about him." Tom pretended to concentrate on his drink, but sputtered a laugh. "Ironic, now that Mack and I passed each other coming and going here. You're in big demand."

Erin liked having a secret, but it meant side-stepping the real reason Mack had come around. She sat at the other end of the couch. "Mack had business in town. He's just back from his trip with Liam."

"I have a confession to make," Tom said. "I did come to probe around in something that probably isn't any of my business. But it's not your head I'm interested in."

"Is that so?" She was right. Willow had a hand in this visit.

"Nope. It's your heart."

Erin groaned. When it came to her brother, it was so hard to hide anything. She took a tentative sip of the hot drink to buy some time before responding. "I suppose I can't talk you out of this conversation."

Tom reached across the cushion and covered her hand with his. "Last year you convinced me to open my heart to Willow. You freed me from a bunch of old beliefs about myself. That because our dad was no prize, I couldn't be a good partner or father. I'd decided I was unfit for love. You helped me get past all that, and—"

"Now you're returning the favor," Erin interrupted before Tom had a chance to finish his thought. Impatience with him rushed in like a wave on an already choppy sea. She hesitated and stared at a dozen chairs ready to be dismantled, repaired and refinished. "I don't know what to say, Tom. The situation with Mack isn't like you and Willow."

Tom gave her hand a squeeze. "But do you really think Mack is the kind of man—today—who would walk away from his son?" Tom hesitated, then continued in a soft voice, "Or you?"

Erin pulled her hand back and wrapped it around the cup of hot chocolate, finding comfort in its warmth. "Oh, please. Why is this even coming up now? And why is Willow so determined to play matchmaker?"

"You didn't answer the question. What kind of man do you think Mack is?"

She stopped herself from blurting that Mack was a good man. She could hear the slightly grudging attitude that lingered about that.

"Since you won't answer, I will. He's a changed man," Tom said, "who loves his son. And Willow—and I, and everyone else around town—can see how Mack feels about you."

She followed up an embarrassed laugh with a long sigh.

"You don't have to say a word," Tom teased. "I think it's obvious the two of you are falling in love."

Erin shook her head, rolled her eyes and huffed out a breath. But she didn't deny it.

* * *

JEFF'S TEXT CAME in on Friday morning. Toffee had disappeared overnight. For Mack, that doubled the urgency of this trip to the ridge. But it also reinforced his confidence that it would pay off one way or another. Erin could identify not only Bridget's horse but Toffee, too. And as bleak as it was to think of Toffee gone, they'd doubled their chances of possibly identifying the animals. He glanced at Erin, who stood next to him on the ridge. It was getting darker, but there was enough light left to see the land—and the makeshift corral—below. "So far, only those two horses are visible." But he saw what looked like vague signs of movement in the barn.

"Yeah, two horses that aren't the least bit familiar to me," Erin said in frustration. "I wonder if those acres are really for sale," Mack mused. "The sign is barely decipherable. The only thing that appears like it could be a recent addition is the padlock." That had occurred to Mack after he'd come back from the ridge the first time. It added to his sense that these horses didn't belong in this run-down place.

Erin gestured to the property below. "It's not going to be light for long. If there really are other horses in the barn, I wish they'd show themselves soon." Glancing up at the sky briefly, she said, "I wonder if I stare long enough at that corral, more horses will magically appear."

"The temperature's dropping now," Mack said. "Why don't we have some hot coffee and watch from inside my car?" They turned toward it, and Erin pointed to a pine tree in the distance. "Look at all those crows."

Sure enough, a dozen or more crows were sitting close together on low branches. Instead of chattering, they were still, quiet. Mack welcomed their presence. For a reason he couldn't explain, he decided they were a sign of good luck. He slipped behind the wheel.

Erin climbed into the passenger seat and retrieved her thermos from her backpack. "My mom used to say that crows always showed up when something was going to change. She called them a good omen." She offered a bright smile before pouring hot coffee into their travel mugs.

Mack chuckled. "I had a feeling you'd have something to say about crows. The missing horses need their luck to change now—tonight."

"Maybe they're right, those crows. Let's hope so." Erin curled one leg under her and faced him. "It's comfortable in here," she said, smiling. "And we can still have a good view of the corral and that shelter." They sat in comfortable silence while they sipped their coffee. Finally, Mack picked up the binoculars and fixated on the shelter, as if the horses inside would be lured to come out by the sheer force of his will. Self-doubt crept in as Mack questioned his scheme. Maybe he should have passed on the information to the owners instead. Let them decide whether to go to law enforcement about this location with its broken-down barn and makeshift corral. With Toffee gone now, Mack was left feeling guilty, as if he was to blame. That didn't make a lot of sense, but nothing about the situation made much sense.

"Any second thoughts?" Erin asked. "Are you thinking this trip could be a case of wishful thinking?"

"I'm not going to lie. Yes, I'm a little worried about this panning out. But I'm definitely glad we're here together." Mack smiled and brushed her cheek with his free hand. "I always enjoy being in your company. This is kind of cozy. Don't you think?" He adjusted the blanket over his legs and hers.

Erin nodded. "It kind of reminds me of camping, which I miss. My cross-country trip with Neptune was fantastic." Her voice had a happy lilt. "We did a lot of camping when I was a kid," Mack said. "My parents took Gayle and me hiking and fishing in state parks. We went to Yellowstone lots of times. My sister and I didn't appreciate it then." Mack shook his head. "I can't believe the way we whined about not having TV."

"Oh, I believe it. Kids miss their phones and video games if there's no internet," Erin said. "We didn't get to do many vacations when I was a kid, but my mom really wanted to see the ocean. When her cancer was in remission, we went to Cape Cod, and she got to walk on those long beaches."

Mack could see the emotion taking over her expression. "I bet that was a great trip."

"It was. We, uh, thought we had more time and would go to New York to see city stuff. Mom wanted to have a look at Coney Island, too." Erin gestured to encompass their surroundings. "She would have *loved* Adelaide Creek. And the lodge and the diner. All of it." As if distracting herself, she reached inside her backpack and brought out a paper bag that held two wrapped roast beef sandwiches. "Let's have our picnic now. I'm feeling optimistic. The people tending the horses are more likely to show up when it gets later and the road is even more deserted."

"Good idea," Mack said, spreading napkins out in the space between them. "We do have some luck on our side. We'll have a three-quarter moon and a clear night, at least." Erin didn't react to his words because she'd suddenly put her sandwich down and picked up the binoculars. Blanket pushed aside, she opened the passenger side door and leaned out. "I see a third horse."

"Toffee?"

His rush of excitement was quickly squashed when she shook her head. "No, and it's not Bridget's horse, either." She cleared her throat and then pointed to the hills off to the left. "We might as well finish our sandwiches. The moon is starting to rise. When it gets higher, we'll be able to see the horses better under the light." Mack might have been discouraged, but time passed as the moon rose in the cloudless sky. He kept his arm around Erin, who leaned comfortably against his shoulder. She raised and lowered her binoculars every minute or so. When Erin pulled her head back, she looked at him directly, her eyes earnest. "If we don't find the horses tonight, Mack," she whispered, "I want to keep looking. I won't give up. The others can decide their own course of action, but let's keep doing what we can to help."

Mack didn't immediately reply, because he didn't know how to phrase what he wanted to say. It involved more than simply agreeing with her. "I knew that's how you'd feel about this.

You put your whole heart into everything you do. It's one of the things I admire most about you."

Erin smiled and placed her hand on Mack's arm. Then she took a deep breath and spoke. "We're not here for the fun of it, but this is so... so *nice*. Spending time with you. Even if it is kind of a stakeout."

Mack chuckled but quickly sobered, conscious of how beautiful she was tucked up next to him. Then he kissed her lips, unexpectedly warm in the cold night air. He began to shift, but she grabbed the fabric of his jacket and held him in place to make the kiss last for another second or two.

"I think it's nice, too," he whispered. Mack took her hand and entwined their fingers. "You know, we can have more nights like this."

Erin smiled shyly, and with a hint of sadness. "But Mack, you have a lot at stake right now. Despite being here with you now, I meant what I said about keeping my distance. I don't want to become a player in a dispute between you and Liam's grandparents."

She was right—up to a point. But he wasn't about to apologize for wanting them to spend more time together. He pulled her close, and then he found her lips, or maybe she found his. Soft kisses, at first, ended with holding each other tight. They stayed like that for probably only minutes, but it felt like a long time. Mack savored every second. Eventually, the moon rose almost directly in front of the ridge. Erin took the binoculars and aimed them below at the barn and corral. "Bingo. Mack, I'm seeing four horses now. Maybe I can recognize the new one." But she sighed heavily. "Oh, no," she muttered under her breath when one horse went back in the barn. "Down to three again."

Mack nodded. And silence filled the car until he couldn't stop himself any longer. It was finally time to say what he was feeling. "Listen, Erin, I don't want any secrets." He shifted his upper body to face her. "This isn't about the moonlight. Or us having an adventure that seems like a fun secret. I'm glad we've been trying to make sense out of these missing horses." Mack was talking fast now. He couldn't seem to slow down. "But I asked you to come with me because I want to be with you. Pretty much anytime, all the time. I'm falling in love with you. It shouldn't be a secret."

Erin's gaze held hope and confusion. "I don't like secrets much, either, but why are you suddenly saying all this now, Mack? And here?"

Mack swallowed. It seemed like it was all or nothing. "I couldn't hold it back any longer. And everyone else has been saying that I... Or we… You had to know how I feel, I hope?" He cocked his head. "Do you like me, too?"

"Well, of course I like you, Mack. Everybody likes you," she quipped, laughing lightly.

"C'mon, Erin, you know what I mean."

Erin let out a nervous laugh. "I'm not used to these kinds of declarations. The one guy I thought was the man I'd have a future with walked away. He and I were not on the same wavelength at all."

None of that mattered, Mack thought. "That's the past. I've told you about my mistakes. Are you afraid of my past? Or the lack of a past with Liam?"

Erin shifted her gaze from him to the corral. "It's not that simple. Especially for you now. You have potential complications."

Mack dug in. He took her hand in his. "Are you going to tell me that you don't see a future for us, Erin? Seriously?"

The howl of gusty wind distracted Mack. Erin stared at their entwined hands, and then she changed her focus back to the corral. She was taking an awfully long time to answer him. He'd messed up. She was right. This wasn't the time or place to talk about the future. He needed to find a way to let her off the hook.

Seconds ticked by. She watched the horses below. But then she turned and looked him in the eye. "I'm saying no such thing. I'd like more nights like this. Just the two of us. And adventures with Liam. Horseback rides on the trails." She took her hand away. "But those things could be dangerous for you and the life you want for Liam. I'm willing to take a huge, giant step back if that is what it takes for you to avoid trouble with Eden and Louis."

Mack scoffed. What she said made so much sense. Short-term. But in that offer to go away, she admitted her feelings for him. "Why are you so quick to walk away, or delay a relationship, if you really have feelings for me?"

Erin jerked her head back. "I can't believe you're asking me that. It's so obvious. I know what Liam means to you. I see it every day. You made a mistake years ago. I don't want to see you pay for it all over again. You'd regret it for the rest of your life."

Mack had a lot he could say in response, but knowing she had feelings for him would be enough for now. "I don't want to borrow trouble, Erin, and I don't know what Eden and Louis intend. I'm seeing an attorney next week." He kissed her again. "Consider that a promise. For the future." He smiled. "Our future."

"Speaking of the future," Erin said, "it must be getting awfully late." She focused again on what was happening below them. "We're back up to four horses, though. The problem is, there really isn't enough light to identify them. I sure don't see Toffee."

"I loathe giving up," Mack said, letting out a low groan of frustration. He joined Erin and raised his own binoculars for a closer look.

"So, how about we stay a *little while* longer?" Erin said.

Mack chuckled. How long was a little while? He didn't ask. "It's a deal."

CHAPTER FOURTEEN

ERIN COULDN'T HAVE said how long they'd been sitting side by side, staring through their binoculars, when the pinpoint of light appeared on the road. "Look, Mack."

"Could be another random car or truck."

"Or not," Erin said. "Headlights. Coming closer. It looks like a van. It's the same shape as mine."

"And it's slowing down." Mack spoke slowly, too.

The couple of other vehicles they'd seen had sped down the road where traffic was sparse. Seconds later, the headlights disappeared. But Erin saw the outline of the van approaching the driveway that led to the padlocked fence. "This is no passing vehicle. And it's white or a light tan or gray." Erin tried to contain the instant judgment that the occupants of the van were horse thieves. "They could be the owners coming in to tend their horses."

"At midnight? Dousing their lights. Suspicious, at least." Mack raised his binoculars. "Someone is coming out of the van from the passenger side and going to the gate."

Erin's binoculars made the guy's every step, every movement clear. He unlocked the gate and pushed it open. She switched her view to the corral. One horse—she only needed to recognize one. That was all. But there were only three outside now. No Toffee or Bridget's Jumper. Erin struggled to fill her lungs while they waited for the next move. "Mack, I can barely breathe. I want an answer. *Now.*"

The van passed through the open gate, rocking side to side on the uneven ground. The driver inched closer to the corral and came to a stop. Two men immediately jumped to the ground from the back of the van.

"So far, four guys, three on the ground," Erin said. "Something about the way they move tells me they're young."

"Yep, they look like teenagers to me," Mack said. "But I can't see what they're doing."

A second later, the beam from headlights illuminated three horses. Erin's heart hammered in her chest. The horses moved awkwardly, bumping into each other at the far end of the makeshift fence. Erin scanned the corral, stopping on one. Shades of gray, light to dark.

White face, white legs. "It's him, it's Jumper. Bridget's horse." It hit like an electric shock. She reeled forward.

"You're certain?" Mack asked.

"Yes, yes, I've ridden that horse, Mack. I'm positive. That's Jumper. He's got a mostly white face and solid white front legs. Unusual markings." She waved her binoculars. "With the lights, I can see the markings through the lens. But I don't see Toffee."

"That doesn't mean she's not there," Mack said, speeding through his words. "She could be in the barn."

Erin closed her eyes to listen for sounds, high-pitched whinnies or neighing. Or human voices. The wind whipped across the ridge, blocking out noise from below.

"They're lugging water jugs, and one guy is rolling hay bales." Mack took his phone out of his pocket. "I'm calling the sheriff. You've got an ID on Jumper. That's enough. I'm not taking any chances."

"I'll call Bridget," Erin said, opening the passenger door and getting out of the car, "but we still only see four horses, counting Bridget's. With Toffee, we should see six, that we know of. Only the two have found their way home. And the one you saw is still out there somewhere. That makes seven."

Mack followed Erin out of the SUV and to the edge of the ridge. "The exact number doesn't matter. We've finally got something solid to pass along." Erin scrolled through her phone until she came to Bridget's number and made the call. "It's ringing," she called to Mack, who'd moved a few feet away. "Still ringing... Come on, Bridget. Pick up, pick up." She looked at Mack, who had turned away and was talking on his phone.

Finally, Bridget answered. "Erin? What's going—"

"We found Jumper. And the others, although we haven't spotted Toffee yet." Erin stopped to breathe. "It's a long story. But Mack's talking to the sheriff right now."

"Where's Jumper? Where are you?" Bridget asked. "How... Are you sure?"

"He's in a corral. I'm at the Barkley Lookout on the ridge. Right this minute, three young guys are rolling hay bales and filling tubs of water. It's Jumper, Bridget. I'm sure of it." Erin filled in a few more details of the story. "I don't know this for certain, but the horses look okay. Like they've had water and food."

"Wow...this is incredible. I know that lookout. It's not far... I'm on my way."

"Wait, Bridget—" But the call was disconnected.

"They're on their way," Mack said, joining her.

Erin stared at the group of horses clustering together in the corral. The headlights illuminated the young guys, who were working fast. Definitely kids in their late teens. "The sheriff doesn't have much time to get here."

Mack agreed.

"I think there's one horse left in the barn," Erin said. "It must be too scared to come out. If we're right about how many horses are missing, the one we can't see has to be Toffee...has to be."

"The second you know for sure, I'll call Jillian, if Bridget hasn't already." Mack reached for his binoculars. "I told the sheriff we'd text him if the thieves take off."

Erin put her hand over her heart, the beats slower now. "We're witnesses, Mack. Thanks to you, we can provide a timeline and more."

"Now I wish I'd called the sheriff when I had my first hunch last week," Mack said. "Maybe they could have caught these guys before Toffee went missing."

"Stop, stop. Your hunch is what's bringing these creatures back to their owners." She watched the three men move around inside the corral. "One kid is checking their thrown-together fence. The driver hasn't moved." She looked over at Mack. He was staring at his phone. "That's not going to get the good guys here any faster," she teased, hoping to lighten the load he was carrying.

Mack lowered his phone and wrapped Erin in a tight hug. "We did this together." Erin stood on tiptoe, put her hands on the sides of Mack's face and gave him a quick kiss.

Even in the dark, his smile lit up his face. Then it disappeared as the low rumble of vehicles approaching could be heard. What looked like a river of light in the distance suddenly disappeared. "They're here," Erin said.

Mack nodded. "An officer told me they'd come in close to the gate, but without lights. They want to keep the situation as calm as possible. I said the thieves look like teenagers."

Erin kept her eyes on the action, conscious of Mack standing beside her, intense energy passing between them. She ran his words through her mind again. "Uh, Mack?"

"Yeah, what is it?"

"In case I don't get a chance to tell you later, I'm falling in love with you, too." Erin smiled to herself. She'd said the words out loud. No regrets.

The sweet, open look on his face told her everything was going to be all right.

IMPATIENT FOR THE end to this mystery, Mack switched the binoculars to a view of the horses, then to the van, and next, the road. Jumper was on the move again, circling the water tubs and then disappearing into the barn.

Next to Mack, Erin stretched her free hand in front of her and opened and closed her fingers several times in quick succession. Then she did the same to the other hand. "I gripped the binoculars so tight, my fingers cramped. It happens with my tools sometimes, too." She groaned. "I wish they'd hurry. Once these guys take off, they might never be caught."

Mack let out a long exhale. "You're right. Two guys are just throwing stuff into the back of the van now." He texted the sheriff: van leaving.

The white van kept its lights on as the three guys climbed inside and the driver pulled ahead to make the turn to exit through the gate nose-first.

"This is it," Mack said as the police car pulled in front of the gate, followed by what were possibly a dozen trucks and cars.

When the van driver completed the turn, he was greeted by flashing red-and-white lights on the approaching cruiser. The van jerked to a stop. Four men spilled out, and two broke into a run toward the woods. Three officers ran from the cruiser, chasing them. The other two teenagers froze in place, but one decided to take off at the last moment. He didn't get far before he tripped and fell to the ground. When he got up, he raised his hands over his head. An officer cuffed him and escorted him to the back of the cruiser. "What a sight." Erin spit out the words. "Caught dead to rights."

A male voice boomed from a bullhorn for the kids who had reached the woods to stop. With the officers closing in, the guys on the run slowed down. Their arms shot above their heads. Erin texted Bridget and Jeff to ask about their location. Seconds later, Bridget sent a message that she and Clint were almost there. "She says other owners will be coming, and Matt is bringing his largest trailer, so they'll be able to transport all the horses back home."

"As soon as we see that last guy in handcuffs, we'll head down," Mack said. "Got it. I'll ID Jumper, and with any luck, Toffee." She threw her arms over her head in triumph. "You did it, Mack. You had a hunch and listened. And the horses are okay."

Except for the one that he'd seen twice now in the woods. "It might have been my hunch, but you believed me. *We* did it." He put his arms around Erin and gave her a quick kiss.

Minutes later, the fourth thief was in cuffs. Matt and Erin drove off the ridge, turned onto the main road and pulled onto the shoulder to stay out of the way. They exited the SUV and walked toward an officer standing next to the closest cruiser.

"We were right," Erin said as she gestured to the four culprits now being put into a transport van. "They're what? Eighteen or nineteen? Twenty tops."

The officer beside the cruiser asked, "You the people who called us about all this?" He pointed behind him.

Erin left Mack's side and moved closer to the fence. She wouldn't be satisfied until she saw Toffee. He couldn't blame her.

Mack gave the officer an abbreviated version of how all that took place. "When my friend identified one of the horses, we figured the rest could be the other missing ones." He nodded toward the transport van where one kid was sitting. "What's the situation?" he asked. "They look young, like teens."

"Dumb kids. We don't know the details yet, but it was a harebrained scheme to break into stables and corrals and steal horses one at a time." The officer scoffed. "Right. Like no one would notice?"

"At least they took care of them," Mack said. "What was the endgame?"

"The grand plan was to transport them across state lines into Idaho. Sell them off as fast as they could." The officer shook his head. "They caved pretty fast once they saw us. And they weren't armed."

"A crime all the same," Mack said, "but I'm glad the horses will go home in good condition."

"Hey, Mack…it's Toffee!" Erin called out, running toward him. "She must have been hiding." The officer pointed with his chin down the road, where a pickup and a horse trailer had come into view. "You called the owners, huh?"

"And here they come." Mack slipped his arm around Erin's shoulders, and she leaned into him. "Those folks will be glad to see their critters alive and well. We'll be talking to the owners later once we've questioned the kids at headquarters."

"Oh, I should tell Jillian," Erin said and stepped away to make the call.

Mack answered a few questions from another officer until Erin returned.

"She's over the moon, of course, but she also said to tell you that Liam is sound asleep with Thunder." She smiled, and he slipped an arm around her shoulders. "It's over, Mack, well, sort of, but we still don't know about that horse you saw in the woods."

Mack agreed. Until he, or someone else, found the horse in the woods, he wouldn't be able to put it behind him. "Maybe that horse escaped the thieves, but he was too frightened to go home."

Erin hugged him, and his heart skipped a beat. "We won't give up, Mack. We won't."

They kept their distance from the corral until all four suspects were on the road to the county sheriff's headquarters in Landrum. Erin hurried to Toffee, the last stolen horse. Her soothing voice brought soft nickering from the horse, and from a couple of the others, too, who stood close together. Mack wondered how much time they'd spent that way, as if there was safety in numbers. Bridget and Clint were the first to arrive with their horse trailer, followed by Jeff and Matt. These horses were finally headed home.

"The bad guys have been found out. The owners are being reunited with their animals," Erin said. "I guess our job is done."

Mack took her hand and gave it a quick kiss. "Time to go, but it sure was a great night, huh?" When they got inside the SUV, Mack looked over at Erin, who was leaning toward him with open arms.

"The best date of my life," she whispered. "For real."

CHAPTER FIFTEEN

Carrying a bakery box in her hands, Erin stepped inside Jeff's reception building, already filled with ranching families, a boisterous group. Now, with all but one horse safely back in their respective homes, the owners were gathered at Jeff's cabins on Sunday afternoon to mark the end of the ordeal. Erin had roused herself from a nap in order to show up for the party, after a quick stop to purchase a three-layer chocolate cake as her contribution. No time to bake cookies.

After she'd picked up her van at Mack's early on Saturday morning, she'd had time for a shower and a change of clothes before heading out again. Catching some sleep wasn't on the schedule.

First stop, the sheriff's department in Landrum, where she'd made her formal statement, met with a detective and later, the district attorney. Mack, with Liam at his side, made the

same rounds, which included answering reporters' questions.

She and Mack ended their Saturday with a
quick meal at the diner. Word had spread, of
course, about the two of them. It wasn't surprising that everyone from the first officer they met
with to the newspaper reporters and the waiter
in the diner wanted to know what had brought
them to the lookout in the first place. The follow-
up comment invariably was, "Kinda cold for a
stakeout, wasn't it?" Without ever intending it,
she and Mack were forever linked with solving
a mystery that had captivated most of the town.

Jillian and Liam spotted her first. "Come see
Toffee and Raven," Jillian said.

"And Dot," Liam added.

"Sure. I'd love to." Erin put the box on a table
near the door and waved to Olivia and Heather
before she went outside with the kids. "Where
are you dads?" she asked.

"Off somewhere talking about something,"
Jillian said with a shrug.

"I bet it's about the horses," Liam said.

"Could be," Jillian said.

Once inside the stable, Erin noted that Toffee wasn't in her usual stall, but in one next to
Dot. "Why did you move her, Jillian?"

"Burroughs and Dad thought it was a good
idea." Jillian made a beeline for her horse and

started her hello pats and hugs. Toffee nickered and nudged, happy to see the girl who loved her so. Liam went to say hello to Dot. "Toffee was a little skittish in the horse trailer on the way home," Jillian said. "She's happy around her two friends. We walked the three of them together earlier."

While Toffee and Dot were getting a little love, Erin gave Raven some and spoke to her in a low voice. "I bet you're happy Toffee is home again where she belongs," Erin said.

"Thanks to you," Jillian said. "That's what Mom and Dad say."

"Hey, Mack gets most of the credit." Erin wouldn't have gone hunting for the horses on her own.

Jillian gave her a skeptical look. "But they said Mack's idea only worked because you could ID Jumper and Toffee."

"Well, it all worked in the end," Erin said, patting Raven. "The silver lining was that the young guys who stole them took pretty good care of them. All Toffee missed was the love you heap on her."

On their return trip to the reception building, Erin spotted Mack and Jeff walking out of the now empty two-story cabin that Olivia and Jillian moved into when they'd first come to Adelaide Creek a year and a half ago. That aroused her curiosity. Maybe Mack thought this was a good place to move with Liam until he was ready to buy his own place. Convenient for Liam's riding lessons, and with a built-in babysitter. Since Erin expected to see more of Mack—and ride together—she could see why he might consider it. But Mack was also serious about looking for a permanent home on a few acres. This small cabin wouldn't match that picture. Whatever the two men were talking about, they were focused. And Mack particularly looked happy. Erin was about to call out to him, but the pair took off behind the reception building. "Are you going to have hot dogs? Liam asked. "There's lots of other stuff, too."

The question jolted her attention back to boy and the party-like atmosphere. "Yes, absolutely." The minute she was inside the crowded room, Erin was surrounded by Bridget and her daughters. "We are over the moon about Jumper," Bridget said. "I'm happy for everyone. Well, except for Crosby. His horse, Sundown, wasn't one of the group."

Erin had heard that from Quincy, but hadn't had time to talk it over with Mack. As she had done with other folks, Erin deflected the credit for the rescue back to Mack. The stakeout had been his idea. Memories of their night on the ridge kept bringing up sweet, warm feelings.

"I saw Mack earlier," said Nan, Bridget's daughter, "but I don't know where he went."

"He's with my dad," Jillian said. "They've been talking a long, long time."

Bridget gave Erin a pointed look. "Let me go with you to the buffet table." She took Erin's elbow before addressing her girls. "Your dad and I will catch up with you when we're ready to leave."

Erin expected Bridget to probe her about her relationship with Mack, something she didn't care to talk about at the moment—except with Mack. Amidst everything else going on, she'd been sorting out her feelings for him. It had been so long since she'd been more than attracted but really drawn to a man. But what came next? "What's up, Bridget?" It was difficult to adopt a casual demeanor, but Erin managed it.

"That's the question I was going to ask you," Bridget said. "Ever since Mack got here today, he and Jeff have had their heads together. First they were in here, then they went to Jeff's office, and now they're outside walking around." Bridget grinned as she raised her hands and wiggled her fingers. "Something's in the air. I figured you might know what it is."

"I have no idea," Erin said, even more curious now. "They're missing their own party, though."

"I'm glad we didn't miss it," Bridget said, taking a couple of steps back, "but I'm going to gather my family. We need to head home. "We've got *all* our horses to feed."

Erin was about to leave the building when Mack's face appeared in the doorway to the back rooms. He beamed when he saw her. "I need to talk to you. I have exciting news."

"Are you and Liam going to move into Jeff's empty cabin? Is that what you and Jeff were talking about?

Mack's exhilaration was replaced by a blank look. "Uh, no." He pointed to the door and took her hand. "Come on. Let's go for a walk. I'll tell you my news outside." He looked like he had more to say, but he stayed quiet.

They went out through the back door and headed toward the stable. "I'm making a big change in my life, but it's just between you and me for now. Jeff and I aren't ready to go public. Not yet. But the two of us are forming a partnership."

"That's amazing, Mack." He looked so happy, Erin threw her arms around him. "I had no idea. Details please."

"We've been talking about it for a couple of weeks, just the two of us, working out some details and clarifying what we each want for the next few years." Mack explained that his investment would help finance Jeff's expansion of cabin rentals and the riding school. "I've thought about it a lot. And this kind of arrangement is the best way for me to give Liam the life I've wanted for him."

"For a boy who wants to be one of the horse kids, it's perfect."

"And there's more. I haven't even gotten to the best part yet. But it means going for a drive."

"Where?"

"That's a surprise," Mack said with a smile. "Do you have time? It's not far from here, or from your place. About five miles or so."

"I'd love to. But I'll follow you. I've got to see to Neptune right after."

Mack asked Jillian if she'd keep an eye on Liam for an hour or so. Happy with the twins and Jillian, Liam waved goodbye without showing any particular concern over his dad leaving. He'd come a long way, that little boy. A few minutes later, Erin followed Mack off the main road and onto a narrow back lane. Mack's mileage calculation was about right, because in another quarter mile, he made a right turn onto a tree-lined driveway. In front of her was a fairly old yellow frame house with a wrap-around porch. It was surrounded by trees on both sides—cottonwood, oak and ponderosa pine. She climbed out of her van and followed Mack up the stairs, which were in better shape than the front door and window frames. But Erin could see beyond that. Especially when she turned around and took in the unobstructed view of the ridge and the mountain peaks behind it. "This is it, isn't it, Mack? The right place for you and Liam."

"Yes," Mack whispered, his eyes soft with emotion.

"It's got everything," Erin said. "It's obviously big enough, and this view is breathtaking. And if you and Jeff are partners, you don't need a barn or a stable for your horses."

"I haven't told Liam yet, but I bought Dot for him. I'll officially give her to him for his birthday." Mack smiled. "Wait until you see the inside. Now, granted, it's been neglected, but the basics are sound." When he opened the door, Mack pointed to the brick fireplace. "That's the first of many gems in this house."

Erin scanned the spacious kitchen, dining area and living room, all part of a pleasing flow of open space. She walked toward the kitchen, remarking on the faded oak window frames. "So many windows, and they're nice and big." Simple, elegant wooden frames with clean lines. "Maybe the wood needs some work, but I think I can help you out with that."

"I saw the listing when I was in Millerton, and I had a look as soon as I got back. I told the real estate agent I'd let her know, and as soon as I saw it, I was certain we'll be happy here." Looking directly at her, his eyes were full of expectancy. "I hope I was right. I made an offer this morning, and I got a text before I arrived at the lodge. It was accepted."

"Oh, I'm sure you're right about this, Mack. Liam will love it." Erin was close to tearing up. It was so much more than a big house. It was a warm place surrounded by beauty. She saw it as an expression of Mack's love for his child.

"Not only Liam and me." Mack held out his arms to encompass the room. "This is for *us*."

His words jolted every cell. Us? He included her. Already? "What do you mean?"

He jerked his head back and frowned. Then he whispered, "Erin, what does falling in love usually mean?"

"Oh, I don't know. Date. Spend more time together. Explore the trails on horseback. Share dinners at the lodge. Have fun with Liam at Spring Fling." *Share some kisses. Rest my head against your chest... More kisses.*

Mack's face brightened a little. "Good to hear. But when we get married, this way we'll already have a perfect house." He grinned. "You'll be even closer to Raven. And to your brother."

Erin's heart pounded. He had it all planned out. Lightheaded, Erin didn't have a response, not one that matched his rose-colored glasses attitude. If she had the energy to speak up, she'd challenge him with three words: *Eden and Louis*.

"I'm sorry, Mack. I really need to go." She kept her voice light as she backed away from him. "You know, I'm still sleep-deprived. We can talk about all this later."

"Uh, okay," he said, obviously puzzled. He raised his hand in a half-hearted wave. "Lots to talk about. Good things, Erin."

She said goodbye to Liam, thinking she agreed with only half that statement.

"EVERYTHING IS ABOUT Spring Fling, Mack," Willow said. "Your first. Adelaide Creek's biggest, baddest event."

"Can't wait," Mack said, trying to maintain a cheerful facade as he scanned Willow's schedule for his hours in the booth to promote Tall Tale. Willow intentionally positioned them in a large space next to the health network that Tom and Olivia were a part of. The lodge was featuring its health club, raffling off memberships and offering five-minute chair massages. Willow had gone all-out.

"Erin's first time at this festival, too. And since Grisham's Strummers are performing, both of you are part of it." Willow planted her hands on her hips and smiled as if she had a secret. "We're all set. Nice work. See you on Friday, first shift."

On the way out, Mack made a quick stop at the deli to pick up two blueberry muffins. Liam had decided blueberry muffins were one of his top five favorite foods, pizza always being the first in his heart. Burgers were a close second, with blueberry muffins locked in a tie with blueberry pancakes for third. The memory of Erin so easily bantering with Liam about his favorite meals and treats seemed a long time ago now.

Ten days had passed since he and Erin had solved the mystery of the missing horses. The new business deal was complete, with other professional changes in the works. The school year was ending, but by the time it started again, he and Liam would be settled into their new house, and Liam would have a summer of riding lessons behind him. And Erin? She was on his mind all the time, but most of his calls to her had gone to voicemail. His other attempts to reach out were met with the same two excuses, work and band rehearsals.

Mack thought back on what he'd said that had caused Erin to distance herself from him. It wasn't when he'd confided about his new role in the riding school and the Stanhope cabins. She'd been excited for him. The cold shoulder occurred when he'd brought her to the new house. When he'd talked about it becoming her home, too. One day. He'd misjudged that moment badly. By the time he got to the pick-up line at Liam's school, he had rehashed it in his mind over and over again. It never got any better. "Everyone is talking about riding on the Ferris wheel at the festival. Can we do that?" Liam asked when they were underway.

"Of course. That's part of our Spring Fling game plan."

"Remember, Dad, I'm too old for the carousel."

"I heard you the first time, Liam, and that was days ago. No carousel." Mack smiled at Liam in the rearview mirror. The Burton twins had convinced Liam that kids who rode real horses were way too old for the carousel.

Liam's excitement about Spring Fling was another sign that Mack's hopes for what Adelaide Creek would do for Liam, and him, had proved possible, there for the taking. Another phase of Mack's dream had been put into motion when he had his talk with Andy.

They set up an online meeting, and it came as no surprise that his mentor and business partner had gone from surprise to relief when Mack told him he wanted to get out of the holiday ranch business. Not only was Andy happy to buy him out, he'd been expecting it. As icing on the cake, Andy accepted Mack's offer to buy Andy's share of Tall Tale. The best part of the meeting was clearing the air and agreeing they could alter their partnership and stay friends.

Through all Mack's planning and preparation for the upcoming changes, Erin remained the unanswered question.

As Mack rounded the curve onto the driveway and the quarter-mile trip to the bunkhouse, Liam brought him back to the detail at hand. "Did you buy muffins for our snack?"

Mack chuckled and held up the deli bag. "Guess what kind."

"Better be blueberry," Liam said, mocking a serious warning tone. Then he giggled at his own antics.

Music to his ears, the sound of Liam's giggles.

DAYLIGHT WAS COMING through the blinds and forming stripes on Erin's blanket. Barely awake and not quite alert when her phone buzzed, she rolled over, grabbed the phone and saw the text was from Mack.

My place...in backyard...come see

Erin jumped out of bed. She had a good feeling about this invitation. "C'mon, Neptune." She opened the door and let the dog out, then shook food into his bowl in the kitchen. A little voice was trying to put a lid on her excitement, but she shushed it. The mystery of the missing horses was their thing, hers and Mack's. Erin would never refuse the chance to see that one last horse up close.

Dressed in jeans and a sweater, ready to go, Erin grabbed a giant blueberry granola bar to eat on the way. Halfway out the door, she pivoted around and put two more bars in her backpack for Liam. And Mack.

A truck she recognized as Crosby's was parked in front of the bunkhouse. Instead of going inside, Erin clipped a leash on Neptune and kept the lead short as she walked through the grass to the back. There he was, more dark tan than brown with a reddish-brown mane and tail and white markings down his chest. He had an almost perfect rectangle of white, no longer than four or five inches, on his face. A beauty, but thin, too thin. Crosby stood next to him. They'd put him on a long lead rope and secured the line on the porch railing. Crosby's doing, Erin assumed.

Mack approached and said hello. She pointed to Sundown. "How did you keep him around long enough for Crosby to get here?"

Before Mack had a chance to answer, Crosby said, "Poor horse was tired and hungry. He lost some weight, but he did okay considering how long he was out there alone."

Erin asked permission to approach Sundown, and Crosby quickly agreed. She spoke softly to the horse, and he snorted softly in return. "Did you miss everyone?" Erin asked, laughing to herself. It wasn't quite baby talk, but she recognized the singsong tone she used with Naomi— and sometimes Raven.

She scanned the area around her. "Where's Liam?"

"Eating cereal and getting dressed," Mack said. "School starts two hours later this morning. Some kind of teachers' meeting. We don't have to rush off."

Crosby grinned. "Might as well tell her, Mack. 'Cause I gotta be on my way. I'm meeting up with Quincy first thing."

"Tell me what?"

"We made a deal," Mack said, pointing to Crosby and then to himself. "I'm buying Sundown. Jeff will be here with the horse trailer in an hour or so. He'll take him to the stable. That's where this guy will live from now on."

"Oh, Mack, he'll be in great company at Jeff's. This is fantastic." He was getting what he wanted. "I'll be able to visit him every time I go to see Raven."

"I know," Mack whispered.

"Why are you giving him up?" Erin asked Crosby.

Crosby cleared his throat. "My kids are getting older and don't have as much time to ride. My youngest is leaving for basic training in a couple of weeks." Crosby's tone was wistful, and he lifted his shoulders in a quick shrug. "Things change. My wife and I will keep the dogs and cats, but probably sell the other horses, too."

Erin couldn't find the words that fit the mood Crosby created.

Mack did better, though. "Well, Sundown will get a lot of attention and be well cared for at Jeff's. Sundown will be seeing a lot of me and my boy."

"My horse, Raven, also boards there, Crosby, so I'll be around Sundown," Erin added.

"Appreciate that," Crosby said. "I need to be on my way. Can't keep Quincy waiting." He cast a lopsided smile Erin's way. "Now, can we?" He took long, quick strides to his company van.

"No, no. That's why I'm right behind you, Crosby." Erin reached into her backpack and took out the bars. "Here—I brought these in case you and Liam needed a quick breakfast, what with everything going on."

Mack had to take the bars she thrust at him or let them drop to the ground. "Wait...wait. You're leaving? But we need to talk."

"I have to get to work."

Erin started for her van. She might have made a quick exit, too. But Liam had other ideas when he flew out the door and rushed to her side. "Did you see our horse?"

"I did." She sent him a warm smile. "Isn't he beautiful?"

His eyes were huge, his expression earnest. "My dad is going to ride him, and I'll ride Dot." He crouched down to send Neptune to a state of bliss when he rubbed her ears.

"Dot is such a sweet horse. She's already such good friends with Raven and Toffee."

When Mack joined them, his blue eyes were full of concern. "Are you really going to leave now? We have so much to talk about."

Not in front of Liam, we don't. She gave him a pointed look and gave Liam a couple of quick sidelong glances. "Another time. Don't you re-

member what I told you? I'd disappear. Not
hang around…" She called for Neptune to follow and waved to Liam. She avoided Mack's
eye and headed down the long drive to the road.

When she got to the mansion, she read a text
Mack had sent a couple of minutes before:

disappear?? we need to talk… Y are you running away?

Without thinking it through, she texted back:

you pushed me away…we need time…not the
eloping kind

CHAPTER SIXTEEN

"WHAT'S HAPPENED BETWEEN you and Erin?" Willow posed the question when the traffic at the Tall Tale booth was winding down for the opening afternoon of the festival. "You two were getting so close. Now I never see you together, and you haven't mentioned her once today."

"I'm not sure, exactly. I messed up, but I don't know how to explain what's going on." His first Spring Fling was underway, and during a break from his shift in the Tall Tale booth, he and Liam had eaten their fill of hot dogs and split a funnel cake. The air was filled with the mixed scents of popcorn and pizza, burgers and tacos. Now Liam was with the twins at the Burton ranch for his first sleepover. "Maybe now isn't the time to go into it?" Just then, several older couples stopped at the booth to ask what they might find enjoyable to do at the lodge. The three couples moved along to the next booth, and Willow started gathering the brochures and packing them in the boxes stored under the table. "We'll close up in a few minutes, and we can head to the food tent for dinner. Tomorrow is another day. Expect even bigger crowds on Saturday."

Mack went through the motions of the evening. He joined Tom and Willow and other friends for a barbecue dinner and avoided the subject of Erin. It was hard not to think about her, though. She'd been right to be concerned about a custody battle, but mostly wrong that he'd ever push her into something she wasn't ready for. Elope? He would never do that again. He had gotten ahead of himself, but that was because he loved her. Sure, he wanted to marry her and be a family—one day.

When Mack met with the family attorney, he'd told her everything, starting with marrying Paula, knowing that as the story unfolded, he was presenting the ammunition the Browns could use against him in a custody fight. But he could counter with a rundown of his efforts with Liam. He could point to a friendly, kind, curious little kid who would soon celebrate his eighth birthday with his new friends at his party at the Children's Adventure Center.

Mack was determined to fix what he had broken. His heart, not to mention Liam's, couldn't take not having Erin in their lives. His time spent with her had meant the world to him. About to text her, he saw one from Louis show up on his phone. A simple enough message: pls call. No mention of Mack's invitation to visit over the Fourth of July. Mack left his rib dinner at the table and searched for a quiet spot until he found one by the craft booths that had shut down for the night. He made the call.

Louis answered and dove in. "Before we talk about other things, Mack, how's Liam doing? Any more problems during the night?"

"It's been weeks since he's woken up worried about his mom," Mack said. "According to Dr. Harte, it's encouraging. He talks about her and remembers her, but in a positive way. I'm grateful for that, and the doc's help and… for Erin's." Mack paused. "The pediatrician, Dr. Tom, thinks the same. That it was part of his grieving." Mack then changed the subject. "Have you thought about a visit? I'll reserve a suite today."

"We'll take you up on that," Louis said, "but after the holiday, if that's okay."

"Of course. It's entirely up to you. Anytime is fine."

"Here's the reason we called," Louis said. "Uh, Eden and I have something we want to say to you." He spoke the last words in one quick breath.

Mack's heart, already beating faster, pounded harder. "I'm listening, Louis… Eden."

"Louis and I are never going to get over losing Paula." Eden stopped, as if to gather her courage to continue. Mack could relate. This was a challenge he hadn't wanted or expected. Finally, she said, "But we're hoping that Liam can still thrive. Without his mom, it won't be a typical childhood, but he will always know he's deeply loved. We've been talking it over. And we consulted with our attorney."

Mack closed his eyes, bracing himself, but also responding to the sadness in Eden's voice.

"We've concluded—admitted to ourselves—that as much as we adore him, we don't have all that's needed to raise a boy as young as Liam, not when he has a dad willing and able," Louis said. "And all we want is for you to keep your promise that we'll always be in Liam's life. We've let go of the idea of taking custody of him."

Mack couldn't ignore the pressure behind his eyes. He hadn't cried in years, but what it had cost these two people to come to this decision wasn't lost on him. His chest ached. He could barely speak. And when he did, he reiterated his promise to them. "Liam needs all the love you shower on him. You're the link to his mother. I don't want him to forget Paula. She was a great mom. Liam is a testament to that."

"We believe you, Mack, we do." Eden sighed. "One more thing. It wouldn't be unusual, maybe even expected, that Liam will have a stepmom one day. And if that turns out to be Liam's cookie lady, so be it." Her tone was light, but Mack knew that had been a hard thing to say.

"So, we'll call you next week, Mack, and let you know when we'd like to come," Louis said, all business now.

"You will always be welcome here." Mack took a deep breath. "Your call means a lot to me. I can't even…"

"We know. Bye for now." Louis ended the call.

Mack needed a minute to grasp what had happened. When he looked up, he spotted a row of crows lined up on a tree on the far side of the festival field. There must have been a dozen of them. Maybe it was silly to think they were some sort of sign, but Mack didn't care. He was happy to see them.

ERIN STAYED AWAY from Spring Fling to avoid Willow and Tom—and Mack. Instead, she'd taken Neptune to the mansion with her for moral support, and immersed herself in her efforts to fix a mistake—her mistake. She'd misjudged the damage to a swath of oak on one of the built-in pieces, and in trying to fix it, she'd been overzealous with the sander. She'd created a scar in the wood that would be difficult to hide. She could give up on it and use wood filler. Who would notice? But that would be the easy way out. It wasn't her way. Or so she liked to think. But that was exactly what she'd done by walking away from Mack—refusing to listen to him. The more she sanded the roughness around the edges of the jagged scar in the oak, the more she was reminded of Mack. He'd made a mistake, a big one. And he could have taken the easy way out and left Liam with Eden and Louis. But he hadn't. He'd gotten past his fears, and she'd seen the results in the child she'd come to love. Her heart ached missing Mack every day, but she was stubborn, insisting she was right. Now she realized she was the one standing in the way. How foolish. Like she'd never made a mistake? She's the one who had to make things right between them. If it wasn't too late.

Tonight. When the frenzy of the festival was over, she'd find Mack and ask him to forgive her. Erin got to her feet and rushed to put away her tools. "Come on, Neptune, time to go." All the way home, and while she got ready to meet her bandmates, Erin sorted out what she wanted Mack to know about her feelings.

More than that, she would tell him her vision of the life they'd share when the time was right for him and for Liam. Later, at the music tent, she caught Grisham's contagious excitement about, as he put it, "wowing the huge audience that showed up to hear them." Their best performance ever, that was what he wanted. Feeling confident in her sparkly amethyst tunic cinched with a black velvet belt, she followed Grisham's lead onto the stage. Showtime had come at last.

As he'd done at the lodge, Grisham opened the set with a lively instrumental. Good. After a minute or two of warmup on her fiddle, her jitters disappeared, and she got in the game, putting everything she had into her fiddle solo. For this night, every other concern would fall away, and she'd play her heart out. And from the singalong tune "City of New Orleans" to her solo Scottish folk ballad, she let her spirit soar.

Grisham moved from bluegrass to country and Western to a few popular songs everyone knew. About halfway through the set, she spotted Mack standing alone along the side of the tent. From that point on, she was singing for him. Grisham had asked her if she'd close out the first set with the old Bob Dylan favorite "Make You Feel My Love." As she sang the first verse with only the muted sound of the guitars and bass backing her, Erin deliberately sang it for Mack and hoped he got the message.

When the set was over, she kept her gaze on him. Only when the applause died down did she put her fiddle aside and go to meet him. She wouldn't wait another minute. But he'd moved, and now she lost sight of him. She started for the stairs, and there he was at the bottom, holding his hand out to her. She took the few steps down and walked straight into his open arms.

"I'm sorry, Mack. I'm sorry that I ran away."

"We have so much to talk about," Max said softly as he kissed her on both cheeks and took her hand. He grabbed a bottle of water, opened it and handed it to her on their way outside. "You must need this."

"We don't have much time, Mack, but—"

Mack interrupted her with a kiss. "We can talk for days and years, Erin. I just need to say that you were right. I was making all the plans, jumping in, not asking what you want. Rushing you." Mack stepped back and put up both hands in surrender. "I promise I will never ask you to elope."

Erin laughed. "I was afraid. For you, for Liam. But of course I want a future with you." She reached for his hand. "Will you forgive me?"

"You didn't really need to ask." He smiled,

and she knew right then that she'd love this man forever. "I talked with Eden and Louis. It's over. They aren't taking me to court."

Choking up at times, Mack told her about the call with his in-laws. She saw his compassion, but also his resolve to keep Liam close to them. "I'll be honored to meet them when the time comes, Mack. Count on it."

"We'll take our time," Mack said. "I love you more than I can say, but we'll make sure Liam is okay. And then I will properly propose." Mack smiled sadly. "I also promised his grandparents that I'll keep his memories of Paula alive."

"I wouldn't want it any other way," Erin said. "The memories of my mother are precious to me. Even as young as Liam is, he will always remember his mom."

At the sound of her name, Erin spun around. Grisham held out his palm. The start of the second set was minutes away. "Are you staying, Mack, or do you have to get Liam?"

"Oh, I'm staying. Liam was eager for his first sleepover with the twins, but tomorrow night he'll be with me." He leaned over and whispered, "I can't wait to hear you sing again."

"I'm singing only for you tonight, Mack." She reached up to put her hands on his cheeks and stood on tiptoe for one last kiss. "Love you, Mack. Think of all the fun and wonderful things we'll do this summer—and the next and the one after that."

"Starting right now," Mack said, "and with a song."

Erin hurried into the tent and up the stairs to the stage. She picked up her fiddle and sighed from happiness. Every note she played would be for Mack, and Liam, and come from her full heart.

* * * * *

For more great romances in this miniseries from acclaimed author Virginia McCullough, visit www.Harlequin.com today!

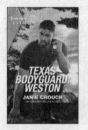